White Lies

White Lies

A Novel

JEREMY BATES

Oceanview Publishing
Longboat Key, Florida

ISBN: 978-1-60809-043-3 (cl.)
ISBN: 978-1-60809-048-8 (pa.)

Published in the United States of America by Oceanview Publishing
Longboat Key, Florida
—— www.oceanviewpub.com

2 4 6 8 10 9 7 5 3 1

PRINTED IN THE UNITED STATES OF AMERICA

For my mother and father

Acknowledgments

First and foremost special thanks to my incredible editor Patricia Gussin for her excellent insight and for keeping the entire process upbeat and fun. Hats off to all the other amazing people at Oceanview Publishing, including Bob Gussin, Frank Troncale, David Ivester, Susan Hayes, and George Foster. On a personal note, cheers to my wonderful and loving parents, Gerry and Linda, and my ever-supportive fiancée, Alison. If I haven't mentioned anyone I should have, I apologize. I had to save room for my siblings, Nicholas and Sophy, who took no part in the production of this novel whatsoever.

A lie never lives to be old.
—Sophocles

The least initial deviation from the truth is multiplied later a thousandfold.
—Aristotle

White Lies

Chapter 1

The storm began when she was driving north on U.S. Highway 2, almost four thousand feet above sea level. The low-lying clouds, black and bloated, abruptly split open, as if slit by a surgeon's scalpel, letting loose a torrent of slanting rain. Flashes of white lightning and rumbles of thunder quickly followed. *Wonderful,* Katrina Burton thought, feeling as though a peeved-off God had just turned the hose on her. The road was already dangerous enough with all of its zigs and zags. Adding rain was about as helpful as polishing the ice on a slippery slope. She flicked the wipers on high, shooing away the water sloshing down the windshield. She turned up the radio so she could hear the song playing above the tat-tat-tat-tat on the roof. "Bad Moon Rising" by CCR. She liked classic rock, especially late sixties, early seventies stuff, so she got into it, singing the words she knew while humming the ones she didn't. Eventually she lost her mojo and gave it up altogether. There was only so long you could act the fool, even when you were by yourself, in a car, with not another soul around for miles.

She rubbed her eyes. They were getting sore from staring at the road for the past two hours, which continued to unfurl ahead of her like a long black carpet with no end. It was a tiny two-lane thing, winding up through the forested slopes of the Cascade Mountain Range in northern Washington. The pot of gold at the end was the town of Leavenworth, where she'd been offered a job teaching high school English. She didn't know yet whether she was more excited or nervous about starting this new chapter of her life. Probably right in the middle, which was about where she should be.

Her buddy sitting on the passenger seat beside her burped—
at least she thought it was a burp. He made some strange noises
sometimes. She glanced at the boxer: six years old, fawn coat,
white socks on his feet, black rings around his eyes, like a rock star
who'd gone a little nuts with the eyeliner. He was snoring softly, the
sound muffled because his snout was tucked beneath his forepaws.
He was adorable—a big, fat adorable piece of caramel. He let her
sing, she let him snore. A match made in heaven. "Not nice
weather, hey Bandit?" she said in that silly singsong way people do
when speaking with animals, children, and anyone who's topped
the big eight-oh. He cracked open an eye and gave her a half-
baked look. *You talkin' to me, sister?* it seemed to say. She scratched
him between the cropped ears. "It was a rhetorical question, bud.
Go back to sleep." He yawned and did just that. No snoring this
time. Not yet, at least.

The Honda's high beams flashed on a reflective yellow road
sign that indicated an upcoming sharp turn. Katrina eased her
foot off the accelerator. The last thing she wanted or needed right
then was to slip off the slick road. She was in the middle of
nowhere, God's country, and God was apparently not in the best
of moods. He might decide to toss a lightning bolt her way for
kicks. Moreover, her cell phone's battery was dead. She'd known
that before leaving Seattle, but she'd had enough things on her
mind and hadn't bothered charging it. Lazy, yes, but she couldn't
do anything about it now. So if she did go slip sliding and found
herself grill over trunk in a ditch, AAA would not be an option.
She would have to stay put until another car came along, which
might not be for a considerable amount of time. She'd seen only
two vehicles pass her in the opposite direction during the past half
hour. A small sedan and a tractor trailer loaded with what she'd
thought was raw lumber.

The bend appeared. Banking left, Katrina tapped the brakes,
slowing to less than ten miles an hour. Halfway around it, she was
surprised to see the dark smudge of a person shuffling along the
narrow shoulder. The person's back was to her, but judging by the

height and build, it appeared to be a man. Her approach was masked by the storm because he seemed oblivious to the fact she was creeping up behind him until the headlights threw his elongated shadow ahead of him, as if it had been spooked out of his body. He spun around. His arms were folded across his chest, to ward off the chill of the rain. He stuck a thumb in the air, using his other hand to shield his eyes from the rain and light. His red T-shirt and jeans were drenched. His dark hair was plastered to his skull, framing a boyish face.

Katrina drove past without slowing. Cruel? Maybe. Smart? Absolutely. No way was she picking up a stranger. She was a single white female, and it was a dark and stormy night. She'd seen the movies. But as her eyes lifted to the rearview mirror, and she caught the man—boy?—staring after her, something inside her crumpled. She began to reconsider. What was he doing way out here at this time of night in the midst of a thunderstorm? Surely not soliciting a potential victim. So was he lost then? Or worse, had he been in an accident?

"Dammit," she said, torn. "What do you think, Bandit? Give him a lift?"

Bandit raised his sleepy head and barked once, loud and sharp. It was either a yes or a plea to let him sleep in peace. She took it as a yes and eased the car to the shoulder of the road. Wet gravel crunched under the tires as she rolled to a stop. She glanced in the rearview mirror again and saw the boy hurrying toward his ride. Her reservation vanished. She was helping someone. She felt the way she did when she tossed a homeless guy a couple bucks: warm and fuzzy inside. Bandit knew something was up. He leapt to his feet, his blunt muzzle jointing wide in what could be interpreted as a doggy smile. Apparently he thought they were getting out to stretch their legs. He loved two things in life more than anything else. Going for a walk around the block, and roadside rest areas—especially ones populated with unsuspecting children ripe for harassing.

"Not now, buddy," she told him. "Get in the back." She patted the top of one of the suitcases stacked on the backseat. Bandit gave her a pleading say-it-ain't-so look. She was having none of it. "Go on, go."

He made a snort and a disapproving "woo woo," the same noise he would make if his Kibbles 'n Bits weren't fixed quickly enough. Spoiled dog. She was going to have to start enforcing a little more tough love around the house. Head hanging low, Bandit clambered reluctantly between the seats, turned in a tight circle, and settled down on the suitcase. If dogs could sulk, he'd be sulking. Katrina punched off the radio—just the DJ doing his spiel—and waited. Rain drummed on the roof of the car. The windshield wipers thumped back and forth, back and forth, almost mesmerizing. The passenger door opened, letting in a burst of wet alpine air. The boy climbed in. The green glow from the cluster of dashboard instrument gauges illuminated his features clearly for the first time, and Katrina was surprised and slightly alarmed to discover he appeared older than she'd initially believed, perhaps early twenties. He was also bigger than she'd guessed. Six feet give or take an inch, though thin and bony. His knees touched the glove compartment. She didn't know what that meant exactly, his size, only that it didn't make her feel as confident as she had moments before when she was feeling warm and fuzzy. She was about to tell him he could slide the seat back but decided she didn't want him to get comfortable. She wouldn't be taking him far. Leavenworth was only thirty minutes away, at most.

He closed the door with a bang that seemed to shake the car. Katrina could hear an echo of her mother's voice from years past: *Don't slam the door, Trina!* He ran his hands through his hair, brushing it back from his face.

"What were you doing out there in this storm?" she asked him, trying for nonchalance.

"Car broke down," he said bluntly. "How the hell do you turn up the heat? I'm goddamn freezing."

Katrina was slightly taken by the rough language. Still, she pointed to the temperature gauge, which the hitchhiker cranked to the maximum. A roar of warm, stale air blew through the vents.

"What was wrong with your car?" she pressed. She didn't care. She was just trying to break the ice—and ease her nerves a bit.

"Flat."

"No spare?"

"Nope."

He tilted his head back against the headrest and closed his eyes. Going to sleep? she wondered. A little rude, but fine. He wasn't exactly proving to be the best of company. But had she really expected him to be Prince Charming? A guy trudging down the highway at a little past midnight on a Friday night? *No, she'd expected a polite young man who'd be appreciative she'd picked him up.* Then again, according to him, his car *had* broken down, and he'd been in the storm long enough to get soaked to the skin—so he had the right to be a little cranky, didn't he? She knew she would be.

She put the car in drive and angled back onto the highway.

The boy-man burped. She frowned. She didn't care that he'd burped. It was a natural bodily reflex. Bandit did it all the time— only Bandit's burps didn't smell like Scotch. *Smart, Kat, smart. Pick up a six-foot-something drunk stranger.* She shook her head. She was milking melodrama, and she knew it. The possibility he might be drunk concerned her a little, but it certainly didn't fill her with fear. Everyone got drunk now and then. Hell, she did it a little more than she probably should. So what? It didn't turn you into an axe murderer. Didn't mean you started carrying a hunting knife tucked up your sleeve. Besides, she had Big Bad Bandit with her. He might not be a killer attack dog. Actually, he wasn't even big and bad—more like loyal and loving. But he was still a good sixty pounds, all muscle—he only *looked* like a fat piece of caramel— and he could be quite intimidating if he wanted to be.

A number of miles passed. More black and winding road. More rain. More silence. Gradually Katrina's thoughts turned from the hitchhiker to the bungalow she was renting in Leavenworth. She already had the keys. There were three of them attached to a Niagara Falls keychain: front door, side door, and a smaller bronze one, the purpose of which she wasn't sure. Mailbox? Milkbox? Secret cellar laboratory? The real estate agent had given the set to her two weeks before, when they'd met in a Starbucks to sign the two-year lease. The bungalow was only semifurnished. Fridge, stove, washing machine, not much else. There wasn't even a bed. But the owners—an old couple who had fled to Sacramento to be close to their children and grandchildren—had left behind a futon, which was what Katrina would use her first few nights until the movers brought the rest of her belongings and furniture later this week. Not that she was complaining. Any excuse to do some shopping was a good excuse. She was looking forward to puttering around town this weekend, picking up some plants, pillows, art, and whatever else she saw that would make her home more, well, homey.

Far off in the distance lightning flashed, backlighting the bowels of the storm clouds. It was an awesome sight, awesome power. It put you in your place, a tiny thing of flesh and blood and bone. Rightly humbled, Katrina's thoughts returned to the hitchhiker, and she realized she'd never asked where he was heading to. His decidedly unimpressive first impression had blanked the question from her mind. She glanced at him, to ask him where to, and was both startled and embarrassed to find his eyes now open, staring at her legs. *Creepy Christ.* She self-consciously tugged down the hem of her skirt, which had risen a few inches up her thighs during the long trip. Certainly not high enough to scream skank, but enough to garner disapproving glances during Sunday Mass in church—and approving glances from hitchhikers who slammed doors and burped Scotch.

"What's your name?" he asked her.

Katrina hesitated.

"I'm just making conversation."

"Katrina," she said.

"I'm Zach."

"I never asked you, Zach. How far are you going?"

"Depends. How far are *you* going?"

It was a logical question, but suddenly Katrina wasn't sure she wanted to tell him.

Oh, come on, Kat, she thought chidingly. *So what if he's in his twen-*

ties. And so what if he's had a few drinks. You've been through the argument. It doesn't mean he's looking for a blonde trophy to hang above the fireplace.

No, maybe not, a different voice shot back. *But if he's been drinking, he shouldn't have been driving, should he have? And think back a bit. Do you remember seeing any cars broken down along the side of the road? Because you would have noticed one, wouldn't you have? You're not exactly driving down I-5 in L.A.*

She did not remember seeing any broken-down cars. A chill whisked through her. Maybe she *had* been a bit too premature in picking up a stranger. But what was she supposed to do about that now? It was too late to tell him, "Sorry, pal, I made a mistake, you're rather weird so please get out. Thanks very much. No hard feelings, right?"

"How far you going?" Zach repeated. She could feel his eyes on her.

"Just up to the next turnoff," she told him, surprising herself with the lie.

"Lake Wenatchee?"

Sure, she thought. Why not? "Yes," she said.

He nodded. It was the most effort he'd put into the conversation thus far. "Nice area. You live there?"

"Renting."

"By yourself?"

She hesitated again. She didn't like the direction this was heading.

"Just a question," he said.

"I have Bandit with me."

At the sound of his name, Bandit let out a happy bark. The man jumped. He cranked his head around on his neck and flinched when he saw Bandit on all fours, grinning at him. The boxer barked a second time, louder than the first. *Good boy.*

"Will you tell that goddamn thing to shut up?"

"Quiet, boy," she said, telling herself she would fix his kibbles on time for the rest of the week. For the rest of the *month.*

"Big dog," the man muttered, facing forward again.

Under more regular circumstances, Katrina would have said, "He's harmless." But now she said, "He's very protective."

"So what do you and bowwow do out there on the lake, Kat? Must get kinda boring, huh?"

Her jaw tightened. There was something about the way he said "Kat" that gave her the creeps. It seemed almost—lecherous. What she imagined a man in a rusty, beat-up Oldsmobile might sound like as he offered candy to a guileless child. A golf ball-size nugget of dread formed in the center of her chest.

"I'd prefer it if you didn't call me that," she said.

"Kat? Why not?"

"I'd just prefer it."

"Whatever." Anger? She didn't know. Snide, definitely. "So," he went on, "it must get pretty lonely out there by yourself? You get much company?"

"Listen, Zach," she said, mustering forth her teacher's voice. "I don't think these questions are appropriate."

"Why not?"

"I don't know you."

Silence. Tense and long. Katrina wondered how the boy-turned-man-turned-creep was going to react to that candid statement. Like one of her students, who would swallow his or her pride to avoid detention? Or like a bad drunk who'd lash out at whomever, whenever, just because he couldn't help himself? She didn't know. She was having a hard time getting a read on the guy. He was rude and obnoxious, even somewhat intimidating. But there was something else about him, just a feeling she was getting, that it was all an act. A bit of tough guy bravado. Puffing out the chest, sucking in the gut kind of thing.

In the end, the hitchhiker did not bite or snap back. He dropped the matter, for which she was very grateful. She focused on the road once more, keeping her eyes peeled for the sign that would announce the turnoff to this Lake Wenatchee, where she was apparently renting a cabin or something along those lines. All the while she was acutely aware of the man beside her. She knew she wasn't out of this yet. She wouldn't be until he was out of the car and disappearing in the rearview mirror. Suddenly she thought of Shawn, and she wished he was there with her. Shawn had been the founder and CEO of a Pacific Coast regional transport company. He'd also been her fiancé. He'd been average height and slight of build, certainly not physically intimidating, but he'd carried himself with the confidence that came with knowing when you spoke, you were listened to. The confidence was one of the things she'd liked best about him. It made her feel safe in his company. She never had men whistling or honking at her, like she did when she walked down a busy street alone. Shawn, however, had passed away over a year ago, at the age of thirty-seven. His death still hit her hard every time she thought about it, especially in the dead of night, when she was alone in the dark in bed, either having been awakened from one of her reoccurring nightmares, or simply unable to sleep.

The Honda rattled, as if it had just been peppered with machine-gun fire. Startled, Katrina yanked the wheel to the left, steering the car clear of the shoulder.

"What the hell was that?" The man sat bolt upright.

"Sorry. I must have drifted."

"How do you guys get your licenses?"

"Excuse me?"

"Women drivers."

Katrina said nothing but added sexist to her passenger's less than stellar résumé. The guy was turning out to be one in a million. From the corner of her eye, she saw him checking her out again. This time he was much less discreet. His eyes crawled over her body like a cluster of little spiders, eating away her clothes until there was nothing left to cover her and everything left to see. She tried to ignore him. Gripped the steering wheel more tightly. Too tightly. She forced herself to relax, though her heartbeat continued to race the rapid swoosh-swoosh of the windshield wipers.

Where was the damn turnoff?

The golf ball inside her had swelled to the size of a tennis ball. Katrina considered stopping and demanding the unpleasant young man get out. She didn't, and the reason she didn't frightened her. What if he wouldn't get out? She certainly couldn't over-power him. She would have to either remain on the shoulder of the highway in stubborn defiance, stranded in the middle of nowhere, or keep driving, a hostage in her own car. It was crazy. How the hell had things gone this far? No—how had she let them? She wanted to rewind time so she could drive by the hitchhiker without stopping. Maybe toot the horn in passing. But she couldn't turn back time, of course, so she followed the only option afforded to her: stared straight ahead and pretended everything was all peaches and cream. Pretended the man beside her had a prim British accent, a Windsor knot around his neck, and a wife named Grace and a puppy named Crumpet.

The headlights cut two circular swaths of light out of the black-ness, barely illuminating the ghostly trunks of the trees that crowded both sides of the road, creating the effect of traveling down a long, dark tunnel.

"You know, Kat," the man said, still eyeing her. "You remind me of someone I know. Kandy. That's her name. Kandy with a K, like yours."

Just then, off to the right, a green road sign appeared, an-nouncing the turnoff to State Route 207 and Lake Wenatchee State Park. Katrina felt almost weak with relief.

Thank God!

She cleared her throat. "Sorry for such a short ride," she said, trying not to sound too pleased about the abrupt end to her per-sonal slice of *The Twilight Zone*, "but this is as far as I can take you." She pulled over to the shoulder a third of a mile farther ahead and flipped on the emergency lights. She could leave him here without feeling guilty. She'd dabbled in a good deed, and though it didn't work out, it was the thought that counts, right? Besides, the rain had dwindled to a light sprinkle. At the very least, she'd given him shelter from the storm for the past ten minutes.

He didn't get out. She looked at him, waiting. He just sat there. What did he want? A kiss? *More* than a kiss? She shoved those chill-ing thoughts aside.

"Listen, Zach—"

"Just give me a minute to dry off."

Oh no you don't, buster. Don't even try it. "I really have to get going."

"You like hockey? I like the Red Wings."

"No, I don't watch it—"

"What's your place like?"

"Sorry?"

"Your place. On the lake."

"Listen, Zach. It's late and I've been driving all night. Now please get out."

"Is it actually on the lake? Or back in the trees?"

Katrina began to panic. Why was he stalling like this? Was he lonely? Wanting company, someone to talk to? *Wanting more than a kiss?* God, could that be true? Could he possibly be so daft to think they were going to tear off each other's clothes and steam up the windows? No, she didn't believe that. Then again, maybe she was on the wrong track completely. Maybe he wasn't thinking about tearing off each other's clothes, just tearing off *her* clothes.

Headlights appeared in the rearview mirror, two small pin-pricks, which quickly grew larger, brighter, chasing the shadows to their nests in the foot wells and beneath the seats. In the rare light Katrina risked a glance at the hitchhiker and found him not only staring at her, but staring at her with glazed eyes. Glazed, drunken, lusty eyes. She swallowed. The dread that had started off as a golf ball now filled her entire chest, making it difficult to breathe.

The car zipped past, sinking them into darkness once more. Katrina felt like a castaway who'd just watched a rescue plane fly by overhead. *Goodbye, good luck, you're on your own.*

"There'll be another along soon," she said, though she didn't believe that. "You can get another ride."

"You want to get a drink? Something will probably be open in Coles Corner."

So he's from around here, she thought inconsequentially.

"No, thank you," she said.

The hitchhiker named Zach turned in his seat so his body became square to hers. In that moment he seemed to grow larger.

Either that, or the car had suddenly become much smaller. Katrina had the mad urge to shy away from him, but the seat belt held her firmly in place. Trapped. Sweet Jesus, she was trapped. In her own car. *And she had brought this all upon herself.* That thought burned itself upon her brain like a brand into a cattle's flank. All she'd had to do was keep driving. Why did she stop? Why did she have to be the hero? A fleeting thought, her epitaph: *Katrina Burton. She asked for it.* It was then she realized she had never felt true terror before, because for the first time in her life she experienced the wild, frenzied buzz that accompanied imminent mortal danger. This is what you read about in the news, she thought. Unsuspecting woman picks up hitchhiker who overpowers her, drags her into the woods, rapes and murders her. Was that what happened to Kandy with a K?

"*Get out now,*" Katrina said in the strongest voice she could spit out.

The man flinched. "Hey. What's your problem?"

"Get out!"

"Calm down," he said, and reached for her.

She smacked his hand away. "Don't you dare touch me!"

Bandit leapt to his feet and began growling.

"Listen," the man protested, his head swiveling from Katrina to Bandit and back to Katrina. "I wasn't going to do anything. Christ."

"Get out, right now," she told him in a low, threatening tone she scarcely recognized. "Or I swear to God, I'll get that dog to take a good mouthful out of you."

"I wasn't going to touch you."

His words had a ring of truth to them, but by then Katrina couldn't have cared if they'd been carved in stone and found in a burning bush.

"Get out!"

He winced. Hesitated. Shoved open the door and got out. Katrina stamped the gas pedal and tore away. The door remained open until acceleration swung it shut.

"My God," she whispered to herself.

The heat continued to blast full power from the vents. She

clicked it off. Bandit stuck his black nose between the seats and whined softly.

"It's okay, buddy," she told him, as much to calm herself as to calm him. She patted the passenger seat for him to join her. "It's okay. Come on."

He hopped into the front seat where he remained standing at attention, his jaw set in a resolute under bite, his chest stuck out, his muscular front legs stiff and straight. The ultimate guard dog. What would she have done without him?

As Katrina left the hitchhiker farther and farther behind, and her cocktail of adrenaline and fear began to subside, she questioned whether she had, indeed, overreacted. But that was a moot point, she told herself. The only thing that mattered was that it was all over.

By the time she reached a sign reading LEAVENWORTH, POP 2074, her mind had turned to her new future there, and she tried not to give the unsettling episode with the hitchhiker another thought.

Chapter 2

"What can you tell me about this one?" Katrina asked, gently touching the leaves of a three-foot-tall strawberry plant.

"Oh, yes," the bent, elderly woman said from beneath a wide-brimmed straw hat. They were walking side by side in the green-house out back of a nursery located in the heart of downtown Leavenworth. Dotted throughout the jungle of temperate and tropical plants were a good handful of fountains, sandstone stat-ues, and garden gnomes for sale. The air was rich with the peaty smell of soil and the sweet fragrance of flowers. "We have several types of alpines. This is the white variety. Highly recommended since it doesn't attract the birds."

"How do the berries taste?"

"The flavor is very intense. They need to be eaten soon after they're picked, as they deteriorate rapidly when they sit around. They don't freeze well either, but, my, do they make great pre-serves!"

Katrina was more of a jam person herself but, hey, she was al-ways up for something different. She'd packed up her entire house and moved to a tiny village in the mountains after all. That thought still unleashed a whisper of uneasiness inside her. She hoped she hadn't been premature in deciding to come out here. She didn't think she had the energy or fortitude to start over yet again. Her nesting instincts were calling out to be heard more and more every day. "Okay," she said. "I'll take this one also then."

"Excellent! Now do you have a van, or a compact car? Because I can wrap your plants to fit—"

"Actually, I walked here today. If it's all right, I'll collect every-thing tomorrow."

They returned inside and Katrina paid for her purchases. She scooped out several little fridge magnets from a bowl on the counter. One read SAVE OUR EARTH, PLANT A TREE. Another: PLANT A LITTLE HAPPINESS. The third: I ♥ MY MOM. She added the first two to the bill; she returned the third to the bowl with a lump in her throat. A mother hen minus the chicks, that's what she was. It was slightly tragic.

She scribbled her signature on the Amex receipt and was just about to leave the shop when she froze. Outside on the other side of the glass door was *him*—the hitchhiker. His hands were jammed into the pockets of his loose jeans, his head down, his hair blow-ing in the wind. Katrina had only gotten a brief glimpse of his face before he'd passed by, but she knew she was not mistaken. She couldn't decide whether she wanted to chase him down and de-mand to know why he was stalking her, or run out the back door. In the end she merely stood there, second-guessing her initial sus-picion. Stalking her? No, she wasn't thinking straight. It was just a coincidence. Had to be. Because even if he'd been crazy enough to spend the night tracking her down for whatever sick or venge-ful reason, how had he done it? She'd told him she lived on Lake Wenatchee, not in Leavenworth. She'd never mentioned Leaven-worth. She was sure of that. And it wasn't like someone could have told him a Katrina had just moved into town. She didn't know a soul in Leavenworth, and not a soul knew her. Unless—unless he'd contacted someone at the high school? No. Ridiculous. She'd only told him her first name. Certainly she hadn't told him she was a teacher. She was being paranoid.

But what was he doing here then?

There was only one answer. He lived here. Not in Peshastin or Dryden or some other nearby town. Right here in Leavenworth. Hell, maybe they were neighbors. She could invite him over for strawberry jam, and they could reenact their showdown on the highway for kicks.

Talk about starting out on the wrong foot.

"Dear?" the elderly woman said. "Is everything all right?"

Katrina nodded and left the shop. She glanced down the street, the way the hitchhiker had gone. A mother pushing a baby carriage. A rotund middle-aged man painting the sign outside his shop. No hitchhiker. She headed off in the opposite direction. The September sky was a bright azure blue, scrubbed clean from the thunderstorm the night before. The wind was sharp and crisp, carrying with it the hint of autumn. In the distance, behind the gingerbread-style storefronts, the snowcapped peaks of the Northern Cascade Mountains towered majestically. She turned off Front Street the first chance she got. Her earlier rationale aside, she couldn't shake the feeling Zach the hitchhiker was following her, ducking behind a mailbox or garbage can each time she looked back over her shoulder.

The bungalow she was renting on Wheeler Street was a quaint redbrick with white shutters and matching trim. It was set far back from the road and just visible through the branches of two massive Douglas firs and a ponderosa pine. The grass in the yard was shin high. The flower garden was dead. The ivy crawling up the front wall only reluctantly gave way to a large bay window. If she left it how it was, it would make a perfect haunted house for Halloween next month. However, becoming the town witch was not in the playbook, and with a little work—including the addition of the plants and flowers she'd purchased today—it would clean up nicely.

The reason she'd chosen this place, as opposed to something a little more up-market, was the space and privacy it offered. She'd spent most of her life living in tightly packed city neighborhoods. So when the real estate agent had mentioned a single-bedroom, single-bath bungalow on a four-acre lot, she'd driven down the following day for an in-person inspection, quickly snatching it up. Her little slice of nature, she'd thought then, and now.

Katrina followed the stone pavers to the front porch, unlocked the door, and stepped inside the foyer, closing the door again behind her. As an afterthought, she peeked through the beveled glass in the door. The street was empty in both directions as far as she could see.

She slid the deadbolt solidly into place.

Unpacking.

That's how Katrina spent the remainder of the afternoon. Unpacking and making the house as comfortable as possible with the few belongings she'd managed to cram into the Honda. She placed her favorite African wood carvings around the living room and plugged her stereo system into a wall socket—leaving the stereo sitting on the floor, as there was no table to set it on. As she looked around at all the beige walls and empty floor space, she realized she was going to have to go on an even more extensive shopping spree than she'd originally planned. She greeted the prospect with a spark of excitement. Unlike many other small towns, whose main streets were lined with mom-and-pop diners and barbershops advertising ten-dollar haircuts, Leavenworth's Front Street was a string of pearls boasting fashionable clothing shops, specialty cheese and wine boutiques, and chic galleries. Not to mention its exotic foreign vibe, thanks to the authentic European architecture and store names such as Das Meisterstruck and Haus Lichtenstein.

After the Depression some eighty years ago, the Great Northern Railway Company had rerouted its railroad and the sawmill had subsequently closed, destroying the lumber industry and leaving Leavenworth little more than a ghost town. Thirty years onward, however, entrepreneuring—or desperate—community leaders concocted a plan to remodel their ailing hamlet into the form of a Bavarian village, complete with traditional festivals such as the Autumn Leaf Festival and the Christmas Lighting Ceremony. Consequently, Leavenworth was now a medieval-themed village that attracted over a million tourists a year. All that was missing were chubby men with dodgy facial hair dressed in lederhosen. And as far as Katrina was concerned, it was a refreshing contrast from the pollution and noise and general big cityness of Seattle. She did hope it had a good coffee shop though.

By five o'clock she was getting ravenous. Who would have

thought unpacking could work up such an appetite? She decided to open the last two boxes in front of her, then make something to eat for dinner, maybe the salmon she'd picked up today from Headwater Inn Grocery. Salmon with ginger sauce and steamed jasmine rice. Sounded good to her. She cut the masking tape that sealed the first box and extracted some paperbacks she hadn't read yet, a folder that contained recent credit card receipts, more books, and a thick pile of cards bound by an elastic band. The sympathy cards she'd received after Shawn's funeral. She'd donated all of Shawn's personal belongings of value to the Salvation Army, then disposed of anything else related to him except those items of sentimental worth. These she'd given to his parents. But she hadn't been able to let go of the cards. She needed to move on with her life, yes, understood. However, she also needed to keep at least one reminder of the man to whom she'd been engaged to marry. To erase him categorically was not therapy. It was cruelty—to the memory of the person and fiancé he'd been.

The second box contained her MacBook, a black nylon case that held her CD collection—Chopin, Mozart, Tchaikovsky, and the gang, as well as some acid jazz and early rock—a bunch of wires the purpose of which she wasn't exactly sure, and her digital camera, a high-tech toy that had gotten very little use lately. Tucked down at the very bottom of the box were a number of framed photographs. She lifted them out. The top one was of her as a child: blue eyes bugging out of her heart-shaped face, blonde hair tied back in pigtails. She stared at the photo with the rusty, aged feeling you got when you reminisced. Her life seemed to flash before her eyes, her ups and downs, her moments of joy and sorrow, and out of the jumble of images emerged one long-forgotten memory, a show-and-tell session back in elementary school. A boy in her class named Greg—Greg something, something Greek—had shown a Japanese anime magazine his father had brought back from a business trip to Tokyo. Katrina's classmates had all seemed to think the girls in the comic-book pictures bore a striking resemblance to her, and for the rest of the year everybody teased her by calling her "Japrina." She remembered only pretending to be insulted, because she secretly enjoyed being compared to the beautiful anime girls with their bright eyes and colorful hair. She told Shawn the story on one of their first dates, and he surprised her over dinner a few days later with a Sailor Moon doll. Later that same evening, tipsy from a bottle of wine, they both agreed that some twenty-odd years down the road the likeness was still apparent.

She had thrown the doll out with the rest of his gifts to her.

Therapy that time, not cruelty.

The remaining pictures were of her close friends. Martha McGee, a happy Mrs. Cleaver with two young boys. Pamela Doherty, a New York City publishing manager who was currently on maternity leave and whose baby shower Katrina would be attending in the near future. And her best friend, Bianca Silverstein, a marketing executive for a big Seattle-based advertising company. Bianca was single but had a nine-year-old girl from a previous marriage to her high school sweetheart. Katrina felt that nesting urge once more, stronger than ever.

The last picture, larger than the rest and in a heavy silver frame, was of her parents, their arms around one another, happy, loving, the whole nine yards. Like Shawn, they had left her much too early. Unlike Shawn, they had not died peacefully but in an explosion of metal and glass. It happened two weeks before Christmas in 2002. Katrina had been working on her teacher certification degree at the University of Washington. She had been summoned from the lecture hall to the dean's office, where the dean had explained that her parents had been driving along State Route 99 just outside of Everett that morning when they'd hit a Shiras moose. The collision killed them instantly. Katrina had never before or again experienced such a ruthless emotion as the one that had clubbed her that morning, not even when Shawn died, because she'd at least had time to prepare for his sad fate. The dean wouldn't go into any more detail, but she later learned her parents' sedan took out the adult bull's legs, hurtling the seven-and-a-half-foot tall beast straight through the windshield. The impact crushed her mother's rib cage and vital organs, as well as broke her neck and back. A tine from the velvet antlers pierced her father's chest, going straight through his heart and pinning him to the seat.

Katrina switched off the memory, banishing it for now, something she had become very good at over the years. She tried to bring up some pleasant ones of her parents, but she couldn't focus on any for longer than a few seconds before they wavered and broke up, like mirages. Unfortunately, they seemed to be getting more and more vague and insubstantial with the passing of time. She feared one day they may disappear forever. It wasn't fair, she'd always thought, at how the bad ones remained vivid while the good ones faded away.

Bandit, ever attuned to her rollicking emotions, padded over from where he'd been lying next to the fireplace. He flopped down beside her. She scratched his head, grateful for his company.

The shrill ring of the telephone made her jump.

For a moment Katrina remained seated cross-legged on the floor, trying to make sense of what she'd just heard. She knew it was a phone—the old-fashioned clanging of a rotary phone, not the musical jib of her cell—only she hadn't installed a landline.

She stood, knowing she would have to answer it, even though she knew it couldn't possibly be for her. Curiosity demanded it. A third ring. As she narrowed in on the source of the noise, she decided the call must be for the old couple from whom she rented, now sunning themselves in Sacramento. They'd simply forgotten to cancel their service and an uninformed friend was trying to reach them. Maybe a friend counting down the days in an old-age home who didn't know Monday from Friday. Or maybe it was nothing but a wrong number.

Five rings. Six.

Finally she found the phone, a maroon thing sitting on a dusty shelf near the back door. The cord was stapled into the wall before it terminated in the jack located in the footing that ran along the floor. She snatched up the receiver and said hello.

There was no response.

"Hello?" she repeated.

No reply.

The obnoxious disconnect tone buzzed in her ear. Whoever it had been had hung up. She replaced the receiver on the cradle.

Don't overreact, she told herself. *You simply missed the call. After all, it had rung—what? Six? Seven times? And don't even start thinking about the hitchhiker. He's not stalking you. He didn't see you today. Even if he did, how the hell would he get this number?*

She was right, of course. But knowing that didn't ease her nerves.

Shaking her head, Katrina went to the kitchen to make something to eat but found she was no longer very hungry. She eyed a bottle of Australian Pinot Noir on the counter top. It was a 2001 reserve from Panorama Vineyard in Tasmania. Supposedly expensive, a gift from a close friend after Shawn had passed. She'd been saving it for—she didn't know. For something special, at any rate.

Oh, what the hell, she decided. It should probably be in a cellar anyway.

She opened the wooden box it came in, lifted the bottle from the cushioned velvet, and filled a burgundy glass halfway to the rim. She returned to the living room, where she curled up with Bandit in the armchair and turned on the small TV that, along with the armchair and futon, had been one of the few furnishings left behind. She watched an episode of a syndicated sitcom, then flicked to *Dateline*, which was featuring a story about an allegedly dangerous fugitive on the run who was suspected to be in the Seattle area.

Katrina only saw the first few minutes before her eyelids became heavy from the wine and she drifted off into a deep, dreamless sleep.

Chapter 3

Tuesday morning. The first official day of school.

Katrina arrived early to get settled in and to meet some of her coworkers. Walking from her car to the main office, she passed a few senior boys huddled in a circle, smoking cigarettes. They eyed her but didn't say anything. Probably wondering who the hell she was. Her students—the younger ones at least—liked to tell her she was too young and pretty to be a teacher, which always both embarrassed and pleased her. She got more looks inside, from early-bird kids already sitting at their desks, looking out their classroom doors when they heard her heels ringing on the tiles. No one was at the office yet, so she made her way to the English Department. She had a so-so idea of the school layout from when she'd visited for her interview. Skype would have saved her the two-hour-plus trip, but apparently the principal was a little behind the times when it came to technology. Only one teacher was in the staffroom, a mustachioed twenty-one-year veteran named Steve who showed her how to use the very basic coffee machine, then gave her a lowdown on the troublesome students.

At quarter past seven the teacher's room began to fill up. A secretary stopped by and asked Katrina to come with her to the vice principal's office. Yes, boss. The VP's name was Diane Schnell. She was a tall, no-nonsense woman whose hair was pulled into a severe bun that tolerated absolutely no errant hairs. The kind of woman that terrified kids; the kind of woman that made a perfect VP. Katrina had met her during the interview in June.

"Ah, good morning, Katrina," Diane Schnell said, waving Katrina inside her small and cluttered office. She'd been standing behind her desk, looking out the window. One wall was taken up with a bookcase full of textbooks and three-ring binders. On the other walls hung several crudely done acrylic paintings by kindergarten students—at least Katrina hoped for the sake of the school's Art Department they were done by kinder tots. "I trust you had a good summer. Have you found everything you need this morning?"

"Yes, the other teachers have been very helpful. Thank you."

"Wonderful, wonderful," she said, though it was the type of "wonderful" that really meant "Enough chitchat." Katrina remained standing just inside the door; she hadn't been offered a seat. "I have a bit of news for you. We have a new superintendent this year. He oversees a few schools in Chelan County. He's young, you know." She said this last bit in such a way it became clear she did not think young people should hold positions of importance on the school board. What sixty-something Diane Schnell thought as of young, Katrina could only guess. "Anyway, he's come up with a few ideas he thinks, well, I don't really know what he thinks. What concerns you is that, as a new teacher, you will be observing a few of your colleague's classes this morning. To get a feel for how we do things around here. That means you and I will be sitting in on the first two periods. Since you're teaching freshmen, and they're in an assembly until ten o'clock, the scheduling will all work out fine. Do you have any problems with this?"

Katrina was about to protest. She had nearly eight years of teaching experience under her belt. But she held her tongue. She knew better than to make a fuss on the first day of anything. Especially to someone like Diane Schnell, who likely kept a list of her enemies in a notebook and who wore Poison by Christian Dior simply because it was labeled "poison." Besides, as she'd learned firsthand countless times before, teaching was full of this kind of idiotic bureaucracy. It was always easiest to simply take it all in stride. So she nodded, said something silly like "even teachers need to be taught," then followed Diane to the classroom of a Mrs. Horton. They took empty seats at the back.

Mrs. Horton, a history teacher, resembled a chubby swan with her almost nonexistent chin and long neck. She accepted Diane's

request to observe her lesson graciously, but Katrina could tell
their unannounced arrival had flustered the woman—and with
good reason. As it turned out, she didn't have much planned for
the first day back after summer vacation besides a general outline
of the material the class was to cover over the first semester.

Regardless, Diane took about a half page of notes. While the
VP was scribbling away, Mrs. Horton caught Katrina's eye and
shook her head, as if to say, "Get used to it." Indeed, Katrina began
to wonder what Diane's real motivations were for these impromptu
visits: to give Katrina a feel for how other teachers ran their class-
rooms, or to give herself a Machiavellian excuse to appraise her
staff, some of whom had probably been at this school for years and
to whom a formal evaluation on the first day of class would be
nothing but an outright insult.

The bell rang at twenty past eight. Katrina and Diane were up
and off, on their way to find their next victim. With barely a knock,
the VP breezed into the second-period classroom they would be
observing, stated their purpose, and proceeded to make introductions.

Katrina was speechless.

The teacher, a tall, young man dressed in jeans and a Detroit
Red Wings hockey jersey, was staring at her with equal amazement.

It was the hitchhiker.

Katrina was sure Diane had noticed the uncomfortable intro-
duction. But perhaps not wanting to ask any questions with twenty
sets of eyes trained on them, she simply indicated for Katrina to
follow her to the back of the classroom, where they both took a
seat. Katrina sat there in a daze. She kept expecting someone to
jump up and tell her it was all a joke. That didn't happen, as she
knew it wouldn't, and slowly the reality began to sink in. She was
in some serious hot water. Not because she had done anything
wrong. She hadn't. Only because there was now going to be some
explaining that needed to be done—some very awkward explaining.

Mr. Marshall—or Zach, as he'd called himself the previous
evening (*Zach's back, baby*, she thought stupidly)—seemed to have

recovered from his shock at seeing her and began reading off the
roll call. Lindsey? Here. Jacob? Here. John? Here. Frantic woman
who kicked me out of her car? Here. More than once, when he
was matching a student's face with his or her name, he caught Katrina's eye, hesitated briefly, then moved on. Katrina knew Diane,
sharp as she seemed to be, was likely not missing any of these
furtive glances, and she felt increasingly tense. What could she possible say? The truth? That she'd picked up a hitchhiker who'd
turned out to be a drunken creep and who'd kept checking her
out in such a way she was certain he was going to—

To what? Rape her?

No, she'd seen the look in his eyes when she'd yelled at him.
He was a fool and a sleaze, yes. But a rapist? No. Nevertheless, he
had harassed her. Goddamn right he had. And that was something
that was going to have to be discussed.

Katrina recalled a long-forgotten incident from her first year at
Washington State, when she'd been living on campus in the student residences. Every dorm room had been equipped with computerized locks that required a keycard to open them. Each floor
supervisor had a master keycard in case of an emergency in which
access to the room became necessary, or in case a student returned
from the bars smashed without his or her key. One night the supervisor who oversaw the second floor of the east wing, Charlie
Reaver—aka "Chubby" or "Reefers" because he was overweight
and smoked a lot of pot—used his keycard to gain entry to the
room of a pretty, bookish girl named Suzy Limmick. To do what?
Who knew for sure? Maybe he thought a big fat guy surprising a
girl sleeping in her bra and panties would be romantic. Suzy apparently didn't think so. She freaked. It was a big scene. Shouting.
Accusations. People sticking their heads out of their dorm rooms
to see what all the fuss was about. Others who came back late from
the bar hanging out around Suzy's door, everyone trying to figure
out what had happened, gossiping, speculating. The next day Suzy
told anyone who would listen to her version of events. Eventually
the university performed a formal inquest into the matter. Chubby
explained he'd simply gotten the rooms mixed up, as he'd wanted

to get into a friend's room to borrow a video game. He was cleared of any fault. Nobody Katrina knew believed the flimsy excuse, but because Charlie was a lot more popular than Suzy, *she* was the one who became ostracized. Similarly, Katrina knew if word of her and Zach's late night encounter spread throughout the school, it would quickly become grossly exaggerated, fantasy would circulate as fact, and most of her coworkers would likely sympathize with Zach, someone they knew.

And that was simply unacceptable. She would not become a Suzy Limmick.

As a consequence, it seemed she only had one option. Somehow she would have to get Zach alone and convince him to keep a lid on what happened. Which shouldn't be too hard. He was the Charlie Reaver here. He was the one who should want this kept quiet the most.

With that settled, Katrina returned her attention to the classroom proceedings. Zach had finished checking the attendance and was now sitting on the corner of his desk, relaxed, looking almost like a real teacher, minus the requisite clashing dress shirt and tie. He was asking students what they knew about philosophy. Blank faces. No hands in the air. "Let's start with the word itself then," he said. "*Sophia* is Greek for 'wisdom.' *Philein* means 'to love.' So what have we got?" He pointed to a sleepy-eyed student in the front row. "Martin?"

"Uh—wisdom love?"

"If you're a caveman, maybe. Most people put the verb before the object. Madeleine?"

"The love of wisdom."

"Hello! Now we're talking. You taking notes, Martin? Pick up your pen."

Mr. Zach Marshall went on to outline the specific philosophers the class would be covering this semester, which included Nietzsche and Jean-Paul Sartre, both of whom reasoned freedom and identity were constituted by the decisions and choices people made. "We are what we do," Zach expounded, pausing for dramatic effect. "Not what we say we are." Katrina had a sinking sensation that last point was some sort of sly existential jab at her. Nevertheless, Zach continued blithely along, and she had to give credit where credit was due. He knew his stuff and had the students listening with more attention than those she'd observed during the last period. Diane, too, seemed to be taking fewer notes.

All the while Katrina tried to form some evaluation of the odd, young Zach Marshall—or boy-man, as she continued to think of him as—who'd entered her life in such a bizarre and unexpected fashion. She'd been right when she'd guessed his age to be somewhere in the early twenties. In fact, it looked as though he didn't shave, or if he did, no more than once a week. His hair was dark brown and shaggy, his face gaunt and pale, which accentuated the brilliance of his unusual green eyes. Like chips of jade on bone china, she thought. In sum, it was an exotic look, and if she hadn't known better, she would have had a hard time deciding whether he was a code-writing computer geek or a speed-balling rock star. Get rid of the hockey jersey and she'd probably lean toward the latter. Maybe a young Rod Stewart or Ronnie Wood. Then again, maybe not.

The bell finally rang. Talk about a long fifty minutes. She felt as if she'd been sitting there for hours. The students clambered to their feet and made a general exodus toward the door. Zach busied himself sorting the papers on his desk, doing a poor job of trying to appear nonplussed.

Diane went to the front of the classroom. Katrina followed.

"Do you two know each other?" the VP asked after the last of the students had left. It wasn't a question, but it wasn't a statement either. Somewhere in between.

"No," Katrina said quickly before Zach could say anything to the contrary.

Diane's calculating eyes kept calculating. "It's just that both of you seemed, well, as if you'd seen each other before."

Silence, brief but intense. The hesitant silence that precedes a lie. Katrina's mind reeled for an excuse. Zach beat her to it. "Ah!" he said. "I believe I did see you, Miss Burton. In town this weekend. You were shopping at—"

"Victorian Simplicity," she improvised, naming the first shop that popped into her head.

Diane looked at Zach quizzically. "What were you doing in there?"

Katrina realized her mistake. Victorian Simplicity specialized in women's fashion and collectables along the lines of dishes, dolls, and tea sets. *Stupid, stupid.*

But Zach recovered smoothly enough. "It's my mother's birthday next week," he said. "I was getting her a present. Ended up with—what are those things called? Right. A mortar and pestle."

Katrina wasn't sure whether Diane believed their tale or not, but she didn't press them further. Instead, she told Zach he had given an interesting lesson, nodded for Katrina to join her, then exited the classroom. Katrina didn't have to be told twice. She followed the VP out, leaving Zach staring after them, expressionless.

Chapter 4

Katrina was eating lunch at her desk, browsing a quirky online news story exploring whether Jesus, had he been alive today, would believe in evolution, when a teacher stuck her head in the door and introduced herself as Monica Roberts. She was young and energetic and had big, curious eyes, as if she was seeing everything for the first time. Katrina liked her instantly.

"So you're the new teacher everyone is talking about, huh?" Monica said. "Guess you really are as pretty as they said." Katrina felt heat rise in her cheeks. "You know, you're more than welcome to join us in the faculty lounge."

"I would have," Katrina said, "had I known where it was."

"It's right by the library. I'll show you tomorrow. Actually, I have to run. Cafeteria duty. Ugh. But I wanted to stop by to tell you about tonight. Did Hawk Eyes mention anything?" When Katrina only frowned, Monica added, "Right. You wouldn't know, would you? Hawk Eyes. That's what we call her, Diane, the VP. Haven't you noticed? Black eyes, sharp nose, and everything?"

"What was she supposed to tell me?"

"She wasn't supposed to tell you anything. I just thought she might've. Then again, we didn't invite her, not formally, but she knows about it. We do it every year. Wait—I'm sorry. I'm babbling. People say I babble. I'm trying to get better." She gave her mouth a rest, maybe to organize what was going to come out next. "Back to School Night. That's what we're doing tonight. Nothing special. A bunch of us just go down to the pub and have some drinks. You know, long summer, get back together, catch up. It's fun. You should come. Get to know everyone. So? What do you think? Wanna come?"

Katrina wasn't really a pub person—she didn't like the dark and sometimes dingy atmospheres, the greasy food, the general rowdiness—but she thought it would be a step in the right direction of losing the stigma of the new teacher. "Sure," she said. "Just tell me where and when."

"It's called Ducks & Drakes. On Front Street. And come as soon as you can get your butt out of here."

Monica smiled, showing big white teeth to go with her big curious eyes. Still cute though. She reminded Katrina of a Care Bear, maybe Cheer Bear. That, or a person whose face got used on the cover of Hallmark birthday cards.

After she left, Katrina didn't return her attention to the Jesus story. A new and unsettling thought had struck her. What if Zach Marshall was there tonight?

No matter, she told herself. That would save her the trouble of seeking him out. Because the sooner they could get their stories sorted, the better.

Ducks & Drakes was loud and standing-room-only busy. It had old-time British pub charm, and Katrina felt a little like Andy Capp as she stood inside the entrance, looking past the mash of people for the other teachers. It was one big room with what appeared to be a roped-off lounge near the back. Sports were playing on the four TV sets and music blared from speakers. Behind the bar, which had about a dozen beers on tap, was a blackboard with a "This Day in History" list, as well as the names of a couple celebrities whose birthdays were today. Katrina looked around and spotted everyone on the back patio, which offered a spectacular view of the mountains and the churning Wenatchee River, which she'd read was famous for its white-water rafting. Fourteen teachers—eight male, six female—were crowded around two tables that had been pushed together. Three half-full pitchers of beer sat on the tables, alongside two baskets of fries and a tower of nachos swimming in the works. Someone had ordered a hamburger because on one white plate was a leftover crescent of bun, a broken bit of patty, and untouched garnish.

A few quick introductions were made with people Katrina had not yet met—these were much more jovial than any had been at school, which was likely due to the flowing beer—then the geography teacher Vincent topped an empty mug. He handed it to her, saying, "It's called Whistling Pig, dear, and a damn fine red ale at that!"

Conversation whirled around her, competing with the chatter of the people surrounding their table, who were either taking in the view or smoking cigarettes. Katrina was listening but not really listening. Mostly she was wondering where Zach was. She hadn't seen him anywhere inside, and he wasn't at the table. Had he decided not to come? Because of her? She was just about to resign herself to that fact when she heard someone mention his name in passing, laughing afterward, as if Zach had been the butt of a joke. She kept listening as the teacher—a youngish fellow named Graham who had a spongy red afro, droopy mustache, and crazy muttonchops—finished his story: "So he went to the bar and came back, right? We were sitting down in the lounge, playing Double Dragon on the Nintendo they have hooked up in there, and I'm kicking ass, and Zach's doing all right, then all of a sudden the fucker bends forward and spews all over the machine!" Laughter around the table. "Seriously, it was disgusting. He was too fucking blitzed to clean it up. The waitress was livid! I think they actually banned him from here for a while."

"Well, the ban is apparently over," Monica said. "I saw him over by the pool tables."

"Playing by himself?" Graham said. "What a frog."

Katrina excused herself and went back inside the pub. The pool tables were up by the front, near an air hockey table. She made her way toward them, and there he was, Zach, not playing pool but throwing darts. He saw her approach but didn't smile or wave or react in any way. Not that she'd expected him to. In place of his Detroit Red Wings jersey was a fine-knit wool sweater. His hair, although still shaggy and Rod Stewartish, had a bit more texture to it, as if he had used some pomade. When she stopped in front of him, she could smell a spicy lavender cologne. Seeing him now, dressed up and in a mundane bar environment, she could hardly believe he had ever made her fear for her safety. The other night already felt like a dream, something that happened but didn't really happen.

"Hello, Zach," she said. "I hoped we could have a word in private."

He shrugged without looking at her and threw a dart. "Go for it."

She frowned. *Go for it?* Where was the embarrassment? The apology? Because as much as she may have overreacted on the highway, *he* had been the one who had harassed *her*.

"Isn't there anything you wanted to say?" she pressed.

"Nope." He refilled his mug from a pitcher of beer he was apparently drinking all by himself. His words weren't slurred, and his eyes were clear and alert, but she had a suspicion he was drunk again. "Can't think of anything."

She was in no mood for games and cut straight to the chase. "Why didn't you get out of my car when I asked you to?"

Their eyes met for an instant before he threw another dart. But it had been long enough for her to see he was fiercely embarrassed. Was it remorse? About time.

"Well?" She realized she'd crossed her arms across her chest. Her right fingers were tapping her left bicep impatiently.

"How the hell do I know?" he said. "I was pissed."

"That's not good enough for me, Zach. You scared the daylights out of me."

"Yeah?" The final dart. Triple fifteen. "Why? What did I do?"

"You don't remember?"

"I told you. I was pissed."

Could that be true? Could he really have been that drunk he didn't remember what happened? At least the details of what happened? She remembered his glassy eyes when he'd turned toward her. Maybe, she thought. Zach went to the board to collect his darts. Two teachers slightly older than herself, though she couldn't remember their names, made their way to a nearby pool table and racked the balls.

"Listen, Zach," she said as soon as he returned, deciding to be the bigger person and end this right then. "I want you to forget about it. Forget everything that happened. As far as I'm concerned, we never met before this morning. Deal?"

He gave her his full attention for the first time, and she was surprised to see that anger now burned in his eyes. "Just like that, huh?" he said, scowling, and she was getting a glimpse of the Zach from the other night. "You kick me out of your car, for no good reason, in the middle of a goddamn storm, and you expect me to pretend that nothing ever happened?"

"I told you, you scared—"

"What did I do?"

Katrina glanced toward the teachers at the pool table. The one with the goatee and glasses was bent low over the felt, taking aim with the cue, while the other one—beer belly, ruddy nose, chipper disposition—had his head tipped back, draining a beer. She couldn't tell whether they were listening to her and Zach's conversation or not. Probably were. "You—" she began a little more softly. "It wasn't what you did. It was—I can't explain it."

"Isn't that convenient."

"Don't get sarcastic with me."

"Where did you go after you dropped me off? You never turned off for Lake Wenatchee."

Christ, she thought. Another glance at the teachers playing pool. All cool, it seemed. Back to Zach. She considered telling him the truth. That she came straight to Leavenworth. But she reconsidered. In his present state, drunk and worked up, the truth didn't seem to be the best option. It would only light a fire under him and incense him further. And she didn't want to see an incensed Zach. Not here, not now. He was too unpredictable. She had to placate him before their conversation drew any more attention than it might already have. "I drove to the next turnoff," she said. *Count 'em up, Kat*, she thought. *That's lie number—what?* She didn't know. She'd already lost count.

"And you doubled back?" He barked a laugh. "You think I'm an idiot?"

The duo playing pool was joined by a third person, an old fellow with an outrageously loud Hawaiian shirt. Katrina thought he'd said he was a chemistry teacher.

"Keep your voice down," she warned Zach, "or I'm leaving."

The bluff didn't work. He went on just as loudly as before, "You expect me to believe you live on Lake Wenatchee? That you make a two-hour-plus round trip commute to work every day?"

Monica, Katrina noticed, had just stepped inside the main room. She looked around, spotted Katrina, waved, and started over.

"Listen, Zach," she said harshly, aware she was now very much on the defensive. How that happened, she had no idea, but she had no time to waste thinking about it. "If it really matters, I'm renting two places. One on the lake. One in town, on Wheeler Street. You satisfied?"

His eyes narrowed suspiciously. "Why would you need two places?"

"The cabin's a getaway."

"You must be getting paid a helluva lot more than I am."

Monica had stopped to speak with their waitress, likely ordering more drinks, buying Katrina valuable seconds. She swallowed. She needed to nip this thing in the butt. Right now. "My parents were killed in a car accident," she said in a voice that was almost a whisper. "They were well off. The point is, I don't teach because I have to, I do it because I want to. Okay?" She stared at Zach, feeling awful. The part about being well off was true. Nevertheless, it was one thing to lie about where she lived because she had been in fear of her safety. It was another thing altogether to keep feeding that lie with more lies, as she was doing now, especially incorporating her parents' death into the whole mess. But he had her against the ropes, and she could see no other option.

Zach snorted, as if to express his disbelief. He pushed his way past her just as Monica arrived.

"I guess I didn't have to come rescue you after all," she said, watching Zach go. "He's a good guy. But you heard Graham ear-lier. He tends to drink too much. Like, way too much. Some people say he's an alcoholic. I don't know if it's true. But it's what some people say. I don't think I've ever seen him sober outside of school."

Katrina shook her head. She was amazed by the dichotomy of Zach's character. This morning he'd given a stellar lecture on phi-losophy. Now he was half trashed and carrying on like a first-class asshole. She couldn't help but think of Dr. Jekyll and Mr. Hyde.

"Come on," Monica said, taking her arm. "Let's go back to the table. You're missing the fun."

They returned to the rowdy group of teachers just as the waiter brought two more pitchers of beer. Katrina sipped hers, ate a cou-ple fries, and tried to enjoy herself. She failed spectacularly. Twice she glanced down the table at Zach and saw him chatting with a fe-male teacher. About what? About her? About the encounter on the highway? Was he telling the truth or the Chubby Reefers ver-sion? *So the new teacher, Katrina, picks me up and we get talking, and she invites me back to her cabin on the lake. But I say slow down, woman, and she's furious and swings to the shoulder and kicks me out, in the middle of a goddamn storm. Can you believe that?* Katrina clenched her jaw. Should she go break them up? But how? Monica, she realized, was still speaking to her, telling her about some of the art galleries around town, asking her if she wanted to visit one this weekend. Sure, she said. Why not? The replies were robotic, her mouth on autopilot. Her mind was still parked down at the end of the table.

What were they talking about?

Katrina got up and went to the bathroom, mostly to walk off the nervous energy zipping around inside her like a bad caffeine high. She stared at herself in the mirror. Told herself she was over-reacting. So what if Zach told everyone what happened between them. So what. It was just an embarrassing misunderstanding. It wasn't the end of the world. Let him talk. She didn't care.

Only she did.

As soon as she returned to the table, Zach stood up, looking tall and gangly. He tapped his glass with a fork until he held everyone's attention. "I know tonight was meant to celebrate seeing everyone again after the summer vacations," he said with a crooked smile, and the butterflies in Katrina's stomach started beating their wings. "But I don't think it would hurt for it to double as a welcoming party for our newest teacher, Miss Katrina Burton." Everyone clapped. Someone even whistled. "So," he added, raising his mug and sloshing a little beer over the lip, "here's to Katrina!"

Katrina looked at Zach guardedly, the way you look at carnival barkers promising you an easy win at one of their midway games. Because was that it? That's all he wanted to say? God, she hoped so. She reluctantly stood as the table toasted her. "Thank you for putting me on the spot, Zach," she said to a few chuckles. "As you all know, this is my first day at Cascade High School. But from what I've seen of it so far, it looks like a wonderful place to work, filled with wonderful people. Unfortunately, I haven't had a chance to really get to know anyone here yet, but I look forward to doing so in the future. As a matter of fact, once I get my house together, why don't you all come by one night for dinner or something along those lines?"

This was met by a cheer and a jumbled consensus that it was a fine idea.

"Why not have it at your place on the lake?" Zach asked. His voice seemed to slice through everyone else's like a very sharp knife.

The talking stopped. Katrina's heart felt as if it had halted midbeat. She glowered at him.

"What's this?" someone asked.

"She has a cabin on Lake Wenatchee," Zach said.

Katrina wanted to smack him. He'd set her up from the very start.

"Really?" said Bob the math teacher. He was a bear of a man with a short, neatly trimmed beard and the booming voice of a tenor. "I think I can handle that!"

Suddenly everyone started talking at once, asking questions, making plans. Katrina was amazed at the speed it was all happening. She felt like she was watching a tornado coming straight for her house: she knew there was nothing she could do to stop it, only pray it would change course. So how could she make the current party talk change course? Come clean and confess? Tell everyone she'd only told Zach she had a cabin on the lake because he'd frightened the bejeezus out of her and she'd wanted him out of her car? Given everyone's inebriated state, they might have laughed it off. At worst she might become a Suzy Limmick, an ostracized tattletale. After all, it seemed Zach was not held in especially high regard by anyone present. Unfortunately, this wasn't the path she chose to take.

"Actually," she said, "this weekend's no good."

"Why not?" Zach asked, clearly amused.

"Because—" She could feel everyone's eyes on her, expectant. A second inched by, followed by another, as equally distended and painful. Then some brain cells kicked in. "Because I don't have any furniture."

"So what?" Zach said. "Does anyone care if there's nowhere to sit?"

The collective insisted they didn't.

Katrina wished she'd been able to think of something better to say, but any longer deliberation would have appeared to everyone to be exactly what it was: an excuse.

"So it's all good?" Zach said.

"How far is it?" Monica asked.

"Half hour," Zach told her. "You know that."

"I mean door to door."

"Almost an hour," Katrina improvised hopefully.

"I'm not driving," someone said.

"Me either."

"I ain't if I'm drinking."

"Cabs?"

"Expensive."

Just as Katrina's hopes were rising, Zach said, "What about a bus? We can charter one. No, even better—we can get Lance to drive one of the school buses. If everyone chips in five bucks, that should cover it."

The excitement was renewed. Katrina opened her mouth to object but couldn't think of anything to say. Monica, who must have noticed her distress, said, "Listen, hooligans. Nobody's been invited yet."

Thank you, Monica.

"What?" Zach said to Katrina, that knowing glint still in his eyes. "You don't want us to come?"

"Sure. Of course. To my house. When it's ready."

"What's wrong with your cabin?"

Her mind was racing. What could she possibly say? Nothing. She was at a dead end with her lies, and she'd taken it too far to come clean with the truth. Not that she would give Zach the satisfaction of seeing her cave. She looked at him. He was smugly awaiting her response. Fury built inside her. All this was his fault. He was like a big dark cloud hanging over her that refused to go away. God, she'd never detested someone as much as she detested him right then. He was actually getting off on this.

"So?" Zach pressed.

Her protests were getting her nowhere. The more fuss she put up now, the more difficult it would be to tell a credible excuse later in the week, when she'd had time to think of a proper one. So she shrugged, which everyone took as an invitation.

It was a circus. It was a nightmare.

For the remainder of the evening, Katrina put on a show of having a good time, though she was having anything but. She felt like an absolute phony. Which she was. No doubt about it. And that's what bothered her the most. The fakeness of it all. She never lied. She was an honest person. The kind who would bring a wallet to the local police station if she found one on the sidewalk.

During the drive back to the bungalow, Katrina went over everything that had happened, and she began to realize just how close-knit the community was she had joined. At Garfield High, where she had taught in Seattle, most of her colleagues never saw each other outside of work, choosing to hang out with their non-work friends—friends who would not bring their days home with them. Would not kill the night complaining about problem students or heavy workloads or curriculum changes. But in Leavenworth, with a population of a little over two thousand, the buffet table was slim pickings and you couldn't be so choosy. If Gary the baker was having a party, you went to Gary the baker's party. Why not? What else was going on? There certainly were no expensive clubs or restaurants. No see-and-be-seen social scenes. People, it seemed, were just people, all up for a good time, whatever and wherever that may be.

Such as a party at a cabin in the woods that didn't exist.

How had things spiraled so far out of control?

Doesn't matter, Katrina told herself decisively. It was done. Now she had to fix it. She began thinking of excuses to get out of the mess she'd gotten herself into, but by the time she parked her car in her driveway, she hadn't been able to think of a single one.

Chapter 5

Zach cracked open his eyes. Darkness. Had he overslept? Was he late for work? No. The room was ink black. No morning sunlight slanting through the basement hopper windows. He turned his head toward the clock. It was 10:03 p.m.

He rubbed the sleep from his eyes and sat up. The entire room tilted crazily. Christ. He noticed he was still fully dressed, jacket and shoes included. His first thought: he'd drunk too much again. Second thought: where the hell had he been? He remembered. Ducks & Drakes. The teacher thing. He'd stayed until—when? Didn't know. But it had just been getting dark when he'd wandered up his driveway. Which meant he'd only been asleep for a couple hours or so.

He stumbled to the bathroom and flicked on the light, which was way too bright for his liking. Then he took the longest goddamn leak of his life. He shook, tucked, zipped, and felt a heave in his stomach. He doubled over and vomited into the toilet bowl, which he hadn't had time to flush yet. He vomited again and again until his throat stung with gastric acid and his eyes watered with tears. A deep breath. Some relief. But he didn't get off the floor. There was still more that wanted to come out.

Zach had a fear of public spaces. He had first begun to dread them while he was a freshman in high school, and to this day he tried to avoid them, especially crowds. They made him feel exposed and anxious. At the age of thirteen he'd experienced his first panic attack while at a festival at Peace Park in Seattle. When the attacks began to occur more and more often, he did some research and concluded the culprit to be agoraphobia—a fear of open places. Actually, it was a little more complex than that. More like a fear of places from which escape would be difficult in case of a panic attack. In a sense, people like him were afraid of their own fear. A retarded disease if he'd ever heard of one. Up there with performance anxiety, or werewolf syndrome. But that's what he had, what he had to live with.

Nevertheless, in January of his senior year everything changed. His parents had gone east to Spokane for the weekend to visit friends, and Zach had invited his buddy Marcus Elliot over for a sleepover. They broke into the liquor cabinet and took sips from all the bottles of spirits, getting smashed in the process. Marcus suggested they go cause some shit around the neighborhood. Zach's standard reaction would be to decline, but this time, numbed by the booze, he found the prospect of leaving his imagined safe place didn't bother him in the slightest. Booze was the ticket, he realized. His magic pass. It changed his life, for good and bad. The good: he could go out at night and socialize, as long as he was juiced up. The bad: he became a bit of an alcoholic in the process.

Up it came, the beer and the fries and whatever else was in his stomach, a burning projectile. Zach dry heaved until there was nothing left but fumes. But it was good for him. More relief. He felt less nauseous. Less blah. He went to the kitchen and rinsed out his mouth with a glass of water. Gave the cupboards above the counter a perfunctory glance. Nothing. At least nothing easy to prepare. He wasn't really hungry, but he wanted something to line his stomach. Needed something if he didn't want to be a walking zombie all day tomorrow. The Country Store Mini Mart would still be open. Even better, the McDonald's across the street from it.

Zach carried his Trek mountain bike up the basement stairs and hopped on it. He started down Birch Street, thinking about Big Macs and McNuggets and cheeseburgers. The night was cool, the bluish-black sky filled with stars. Not for the first time he wished there was a strip joint in Leavenworth. There wasn't. The closest was the Rainbow Roadhouse, a bar-cum-strip club outside of town. That's where he'd spent Friday night. Where he'd met

Kandy, a new dancer with nice hips and long legs and hair that smelled of watermelons. He'd paid her for a dance, then asked her out. She told him some bullshit about not dating customers. He called her a whore and spent the rest of the money in his pocket—his taxi money—on dances with other girls, to spite her. All in all it had been a shitty evening. Being caught in a downpour on the way home had made it even shittier.

And then Katrina Burton had picked him up.

Lying bitch.

The details of Ducks & Drakes might be a blur, but he could recall enough to know he didn't believe her cockamamie story about having two places, one on the lake and one in town. It was just as bad as Kandy's lie about not dating customers. Did everyone think he was a fucking idiot? Well, he got back at Kandy, sort of, and he got back at Katrina too. He smiled, replaying the toast he'd made. But surprisingly, she didn't buckle. Which meant she was either incredibly stubborn, or she was telling the truth. Where was it she'd said she lived? he wondered. Wheeler Street? Well, maybe he would do some detective work and swing on by. Because if she could afford a cabin on Lake Wenatchee, she would more than likely have something pretty grand here in Leavenworth. Simple deductive logic.

He made a quick U-turn—Wheeler was over on the west side of town, pretty much as far away as you could get from McDonald's, which was on the east side, near the school—and reached the street some five minutes later. Each property was fairly isolated from the next. Most windows were dark, except for one or two in which the bright flicker from a TV set seeped out from behind closed curtains. Zach pedaled the entire length of the road until it ended at someone's farm. He didn't spot Katrina's black Honda Civic, and he became more suspicious than ever. Had she lied about where she lived in town as well? He couldn't think of any reason why she would. Unless she was a genuine pathological liar. That would make his day, hell yeah. *Hey Bob, you hear the latest on the new teacher? Yeah, a pathological liar. Crazy. If she says she's not, she's lying. Ha!*

He started back down the street. Halfway along he finally spotted her car. He'd missed it on the first pass because it was at the end of a long driveway, partly hidden by the branches of a large pine. The house was a modest-size bungalow. He couldn't tell for certain, because it was draped in shadows, but it didn't appear to be in the best of conditions.

Not a hole in the ground, he concluded. But definitely nothing special.

He was contemplating what this meant when a light flicked on in the front room. A moment later Katrina passed before the front bay window, wearing something blue. Before Zach knew it, he was off his bike and moving up the driveway to get a closer look. He stopped behind the Honda. He could see inside clearly now. Some boxes were stacked against one wall, but aside from that the room appeared to be mostly unfurnished. He could also see the start of a hallway. Doors opened off of it, but because of his angled line of sight, he couldn't see into any of those rooms.

Katrina appeared again.

He had a much better view of her from the closer range. She was walking back and forth, her head down, as if she was looking for something. The blue thing she was wearing was a terrycloth bathrobe, sashed tightly at the waist. The throat was open, revealing the crest of her cleavage. She bent over, out of sight for a moment, stood, went to the hallway, flicked off the lights.

For a moment Zach didn't move as he wondered what he was doing—or was about to do. The words "trespassing" and "peeping" and "stalking" all ran through his head, but he was pumped up on something, and he dismissed them just as quickly. Then he was dashing across the lawn, passing beneath the bay window. He turned the corner. The shadows were deep and black, offering him more cover. He crept forward, one hand trailing along the ivy-swathed wall. He felt frightened and electrified at the same time. His footfalls were silent on the soft grass. He came to the back of the bungalow and peered around the corner. Yellow light shone through a small window twenty feet away. He was about to start forward when the light went out, plunging the house into darkness.

That slapped Zach's senses back into his head. He blinked, feeling like a sleepwalker who'd just come awake to find himself standing in his neighbor's kitchen. His heart was pounding and he was sweating. *What the hell had come over him?* He'd never done anything like this before. He was filled with surprise and disgust. Disgust he was a fucking pervert. And shame. *Jesus Christ, Zach.* He quickly backtracked the way he'd come, invisible eyes on him, watching, judging. He climbed on his bike and rode home. Screw McDonald's. He was feeling edgy and vulnerable and wrong. Like he might just have a panic attack right then and there.

He pedaled fast.

Chapter 6

Katrina woke up at six a.m., fresh and eager to start the day. That ignorant bliss only lasted a few moments until she remembered the events of the previous evening. She wilted. Zach. Goddamn Zach the hitchhiker. She recalled him announcing to the other teachers she had a cabin on the lake, the excited chatter about the party that followed, and her own reaction—standing idly by with what was no doubt a doe-in-the-headlights look stamped on her face, as if she was star struck by the idea. *Party? My place? Bring it!* And underlying those memories, as silent and dangerous as a crocodile slinking beneath the surface of the watering hole, was the faint yet unshakeable feeling she'd crossed a line when she'd vaguely agreed to host the party from which there was no turning back.

But there was nothing to do about that but get up and on with her day. She showered, ate an apple, then drove to Cascade High School. No who-the-hell-are-you? looks today. Most of the students had likely seen her around the hallways yesterday. Even if they hadn't, students talk, and she would have been the subject. As she approached the English Department, she had a prickling feeling she was going to walk in to all the teachers gossiping about her party, asking for directions, what they should bring, spreading the word until soon the whole school would know about it. That didn't happen. In fact, no one mentioned anything from Ducks & Drakes at all. At noon in the faculty lounge—a Spartan place dominated by Formica tables and chairs—she was sure Monica or Big Bob or even Helen, the art teacher, a chatterbox without a lid, was going to light a conversation that would ignite a discussion. No one did, preferring other topics such as the Mariners and the pitcher who won the Cy Young Award last year and whether the cafeteria food was healthy or not. Today it was a slice of lasagna and a roll, lean green beans, canned fruit, and veggies and dip. Big Bob said these lunches were the healthiest thing he ate all week; a couple of the female teachers tsk-tsked him. Regardless, it seemed what happened outside of school, stayed outside of school. Katrina was fine with that. Just fine indeed. And by the last bell of the day at two, she'd decided she'd worked herself up into a fuss about nothing.

She was in the parking lot, about to hop in her car, thinking about stopping by the little Italian place she'd seen the other day on Front Street and bringing home a pizza for later, when Zach strolled by, pushing a bicycle. "How are you feeling today, Zach?" she said, simply to say something.

"I don't get hangovers," he replied, appearing annoyed, as if he'd been asked that question a number of times today already. A gust of wind tussled his mop of brown hair. He swept it back away from his eyes, the way some of her students did, and she was reminded again of just how young he was. Tall, brash, annoying. But just a kid. He continued past her.

"Whoa, hold on there, mister," she said. Kid or not, he wasn't getting away with the stunt he'd pulled that easily. If she kept letting him push her around, he was only going to start pushing harder, like a playground bully. "Do you want to explain what you were trying to accomplish last night by telling everyone about my cabin?"

He gave her a look she couldn't read. "What are you talking about?"

"You know what I mean."

"Actually, I don't." He turned away, scratched his nose, turned back. "Oh—by the way, I talked to some of the other guys today. Everything's still set for the weekend. Still good to go. I'm going to see about renting the bus."

Katrina stiffened, as if the temperature had just plummeted twenty degrees. She knew she'd heard him right. She just couldn't believe what she was hearing. "What do you mean, 'still on?'" she demanded.

"The party."

"This is exactly what I mean! God, Zach. Why are you so intent on meddling in my affairs?"

"Hey," he said, holding up his hands, appearing contrite even though she knew he was about as contrite as a snake caught sucking back a mouse. "If you didn't want to have a party, you shouldn't have agreed to it."

"I never confirmed anything."

"Sure you did."

"No, Zach, I didn't." *No, Zach, you little shit, I didn't,* had been on the tip of her tongue, but she held back. She would not allow herself to sink to his level. "If you remember correctly, *you* made the suggestion I have a party. *You* invited everyone."

"You agreed."

"I didn't say I would for sure. In fact, I don't believe I said anything."

"You shrugged. Same thing."

"No, it's not, you lit—" Her voice was ice. Cool and hard and dangerous. "It's not. It's a very big difference."

He turned away again, like he was having a tough time holding her stare. Good. Another scratch of the nose. But when he looked back, there was amusement in his eyes. Hesitant amusement, even uncomfortable amusement, but amusement nonetheless. Like someone who knew he was in the wrong, but also knew there was nothing you could do about it. "So why didn't you just say no?" he said.

"Because you put me on the spot."

"Whatever."

"You don't want us to come?" she said, mimicking him the best she could. She was getting pulled into his childish world after all, but she couldn't put on the brakes.

"You're a grown woman," he replied. "You can make up your own mind." He shrugged. "Anyway, this really isn't a big deal."

"Yes it is," she said, clipping her words.

"Why?" A kind of cunning flickered in his eyes, replacing the amusement.

He knows what he's doing, she thought. *He knows exactly what he's doing. Trying to get me to cough up the truth.*

Well, he could try until the cows came home. She was more resolved than ever to see this through.

"Listen, Zach," she said, her voice Sunday pleasant again. "I'm going to take care of everything. Just stay out of it, okay?"

"Is that all, Miss Burton?"

She didn't like his condescending tone. She didn't like anything about him. "Good night, Zach."

He started away and mumbled something that sounded an awful lot like "bitch."

"Excuse me?" she demanded, but by now he had mounted his bike and was pedaling off.

Katrina got in the Honda. Yanked the door closed too hard. She turned onto Chumstick Highway, making a hard right, trying not to squeal the tires. They still squealed. She was enraged. Just when she thought she'd gotten out of the mess she'd gotten herself into, thought her life was going to settle back down into a regular routine, Zach comes whistling by the very next day to stir the pot.

What was his problem anyway?

But she knew, of course. He was a genuine brat. Aside from that, he was still extremely ticked off—and probably more than a little embarrassed, as he should be—about what happened Friday night on the highway, and this was his way of getting back at her. She sighed, angry and confused. Because now she was back to square one. Instead of having the ugly situation fade away on its own, as she'd naïvely allowed herself to believe, one of those things people get excited about when they're drunk but never speak of again, she would once more be forced into thinking up an excuse. And ironically, to set herself free from the sticky web of lies in which she was becoming increasingly ensnared, she would have to tell yet another.

She vowed it would be the last.

• • •

Zach grinned wickedly as he rode his bike home. He had never actually brought the party up with anyone today. It had been a ruse to see how Katrina would react, to smoke her out, so to speak. And although she had yet to buckle and confess, there was now no longer any doubt about it. She *had* lied. Not only to him, but to everyone who'd been at the pub. This certainty lifted his spirits tremendously.

Katrina pushed open the door to the small hardware shop. An electric chime announced her entrance, though nobody called out to greet her. She took three steps inside, then stopped. In places like this—men places—she always felt uncomfortable, out of her element. Like she was allowed to be there but wasn't supposed to be there. Even the smell of paint, metal, and wood seemed suddenly alien. It was the same feeling, she supposed, men had when they accompanied their girlfriends or wives into Victoria's Secret.

She glanced tentatively around, wondering where the nails would be located. Unlike in a supermarket, the aisles were not labeled. To the left of her was a pair of pumpkin-orange Black & Decker lawn mowers, their prices slashed, likely to move them before the snow started falling. In front of her were several pyramidal arrangements of paint cans. She stepped around the display and peered down the first aisle she came to. The eight-foot-tall shelves were lined with power tools and hand tools and other such equipment that looked like kitchen utensils on steroids. *Garlic press? Sorry, but why don't you try my deadhead mallet. Don't forget the safety goggles!* The next aisle was crammed with coils of wire and small plastic bins, each brimming with nuts, screws, nails, and a number of other gizmos.

She bent down in front of the nails, thinking she had done quite well, finding what she needed in less than two minutes. She was trying to figure out what size nails would be best when someone asked her if she needed a hand.

Katrina looked up and was surprised to see a tall, broad-shouldered man smiling down at her. She stood, smiling back at him. He was handsome in an almost exotic sense of the word. In place of a neatly trimmed haircut and clean-shaven face was raven-black hair pulled into a loose ponytail and about two days of dark stubble. He looked partly Caucasian, but his black eyes and high cheekbones and strong chin reflected his Native American heritage. He was wearing a short-sleeve button-down cotton shirt that revealed thick forearms covered with green-and-black sleeve tattoos. Physically, he was the antithesis of the pretty-boy, suit-and-tie power-broker look—Shawn's look, really. But Katrina found she was instantly attracted to him. His presence exuded a strength and attraction to a degree she'd rarely experienced.

"I need some nails," she told him. It came out a little rusty and she cleared her throat. "To hang some pictures."

"You're new to town?"

"Yes, I am."

"Thought so," he said, nodding. "I've only been here a short time myself. But I would have remembered seeing you around, someone as pretty as yourself, no question there." He winked. It wasn't sleazy; combined with his smile, it was charming.

Katrina's mind went blank. Horrified, she tried to think of something to say.

"Drywall?" he said.

"Sorry?"

"The walls you're hanging your pictures on. Are they drywall?"

"Yes, they are. I think."

"I know just the thing then." He led her a couple aisles over and pulled a small package off one of the racks. Through the clear plastic she could see a bunch of bronze-plated thingamijigs that looked like large fish hooks. He handed it to her. "Much better than nails," he explained. "You don't need to hit a wall stud. You don't even need any tools. Just stick one of these puppies into the drywall and give it a twist. They transfer the weight from the hole to the wall and can hold up to fifty pounds."

She examined the package. What could she say to impress him? "Monkey Hooks?" she said, reading the label.

"The best."

"All right. I trust your judgment."

He handed her another pack. "On the house."

"Oh, no. I couldn't possibly." She began digging through her handbag for her wallet.

"Call it a welcoming gift."

She hoped she wasn't blushing. "I'm Katrina," she said, holding out her hand.

He shook. Strong yet gentle. "Jack Reeves."

Outside, the evening sun was setting, splattering the sky with a dazzling blend of amethyst purple and ruby red. A breeze carried the fresh, green scent of pine needles. Katrina started west, admiring the Victorian Tudors with false half-timbering lining the street, the scalloped trim on the pointed rooflines, the folk-art cutouts on the balconies, the wall frescoes. Window boxes and barrels were everywhere, overflowing with colorful flowers that perfumed the air. She passed shops filled with nutcrackers, dolls, beer steins, music boxes, toys, and other collectables. Take away the touristy aspect, and she could almost believe she was walking through a living, breathing German village from centuries past. Maybe something out of an old Brothers Grimm fairytale. She was happy, content. It was the best she'd felt in a long time. And she knew why too.

Jack Reeves.

She'd always believed when, or if, she met another man, the first after Shawn, it would begin as a friendship, progress slowly, and eventually grow into something that was meaningful and complex. She'd never imagined it would occur with a burst of magnetism and desire—

Now, now, Kat, she thought, chiding herself, and feeling extremely embarrassed at having to do that. *You're acting like a lovestruck schoolgirl. Like this was love at first sight.* Which was ridiculous. He gave her two packs of hooks. That was all. He didn't ask for her number. Didn't invite her to dinner. Hell, she didn't even know if he was available or not.

There was no ring on his finger.

She stopped in her tracks, surprised with herself for noticing that fact. She looked back the way she'd come. She could still see the cast-iron lantern that hung above the door to the hardware shop. The lightbulb inside it was on, burning a soft yellow. No one entered or exited the shop—no one, in fact, was on this section of street—and Katrina was caught by the bizarre fantasy she had imagined the entire encounter. But that was only natural, she figured. It still felt dreamy, uncanny even, her entire psychology—a psychology she'd built brick by brick so it would protect her, protect her from being hurt, devastated, ever again—could be so quickly and dramatically knocked down. But that's exactly what happened. Knocked down and flipped on its head.

And in the space of minutes.

"Who are you, Jack Reeves?" she said quietly to herself.

Once home Katrina slipped a *Queen's Greatest Hits* CD into the Sony stereo system sitting on the floor, then started hanging some pictures she'd brought with her from Seattle. The hooks Jack recommended were incredible. Poke, twist, voilà. Sturdy too. She could probably hang a small flat-screen TV on a couple of them.

She was in the middle of leveling an oil painting by a funky contemporary artist she'd picked up at one of the galleries she used to visit when her cell phone rang. It was the first call she'd received since the unnamed someone rang the landline the other day and hung up. She turned down the volume on "Another One Bites the Dust" and snatched up her phone. She checked the display. It was her younger sister, Crystal.

"Chris!" Katrina said.

"Is that Queen?" Her voice was slightly sarcastic and impersonal, like a late-night radio DJ's. Katrina thought this every time they spoke, and she decided they needed to spend more time together. Your sister shouldn't sound like a stranger to you.

"Good old rock opera."

"What are you doing? Having a party?"

Katrina turned the stereo off completely. "Yeah. Eighties theme. You should see my hair."

"How was the move?"

"No problems. How's college?"

"Different. Still getting used to the craziness."

"And your classes?"

"It's only the third day, but I think they're going to be all right. Except maybe this classical civilization course. It's at nine in the morning and the assistant teacher is apparently a real prick."

"Can't you take it at a later time?"

"Doesn't fit my schedule. Anyway, enough about school. Just called to see how you'd feel about some company this weekend? You know. Big old house. Strange town. Must be a little creepy up there in the mountains by yourself?"

"You got one out of two," Katrina said. "It is a strange town. But it's a tiny one-bedroom house. I'm actually sleeping on a futon on the floor. But I'm fine. No need to worry about me."

"I'm not worrying. Just thought it would be good to hang out. Besides, I don't mind taking a weekend off to get away. Frosh is crazy so far. A lot of fun, but, well, like I said before. Pretty wild. Over the next couple weeks all the girls are rushing sororities. Not my thing, really."

Katrina knew what her sister meant. While in her first year at Washington State, she'd allowed herself to be rushed by Gamma Phi Delta, more out of curiosity than anything else. It was fun at the time. But would she do it if she was nineteen again? Probably not. It wasn't the initiation. That wasn't half as bad as the movies and urban legends made it out to be. What nagged at her were the girls—or sisters—themselves. They had been shallow, two-dimensional, like cardboard cutouts of real people. Congratulating you for making the cut, then slandering you behind your back. Promising to be friends for life, then plotting to steal your boyfriend. Caring more about appearances than substance, more about how you looked than what you said. This was all a broad generalization, of course, because some of the girls were very nice and sincere and smart. But her overall impression had been of a mini-Hollywood. Fake tans. Fake boobs. Fake smiles. No substance. She quit after two months.

She wondered if this was what Crystal was experiencing, thus the reason she wanted to get away. "Well," Katrina said, "if you don't mind sleeping on the floor, be my guest."

"Saturday then? There's this floor crawl thing in my residence. A bunch of rooms are selected, each has a theme. Vodka in the Russian room. Tequila in Mexico. Get it? I don't really want to go, and if I stay here, I'll pretty much be forced to."

"Sure. Hopefully, my furniture will be here by then." She paused, remembering it was this weekend her supposed cabin party was set to rock the woods. But that was okay, she thought. Perfect, actually. She could tell everybody her sister was coming up for a visit and she would be spending the weekend showing her around. "Chris, this is important," she said, "make sure you give me some warning if you're going to cancel."

"You have a big date or something?"

"Just tell me you'll let me know in advance if you're canceling."

"Will do. How are the men in Leavenworth? Should I bring my heels?"

Katrina thought first of Zach, then of Jack. "They're an interesting bunch," she said.

There was a ruckus in the background. Crystal said, "All right, Kat. Gotta run. I'll call you Friday or Saturday to tell you when I'll be at the bus station."

They said their goodbyes and hung up. Katrina's homemaking vibe was broken, so she left the chore of hanging pictures until tomorrow and went to the kitchen to pour herself a glass of the expensive Pinot Noir, which was still three-quarters full. She grabbed the romance novel she was reading—a steamy thing about a sex-starved blacksmith and a sex-starved noblewoman—and ran the water for a bath. Unlike the rest of the bungalow, the bathroom had been recently renovated. During the first and only meeting she'd had with the owners, they'd told her they'd removed the partition wall separating the main area from the laundry to open up the small space. The washer and dryer were now in the basement, which was cluttered with a generation or two of forgotten belongings, some of which may be rare and valuable such as the *New York*

Times newspaper she'd seen on top of a stack of dusty, moldy boxes. It was the Sunday, July 20, 1969 edition, the headline proclaiming: "MEN WALK ON MOON: Astronauts Land On A Plain: Collect Rocks, Plant Flag."

The present arrangement made it slightly inconvenient for Katrina to wash her clothes, but she thought the tradeoff was worth it. According to an adage she lived by: a small living room was cozy, a small bedroom was practical, but a small bathroom was a nightmare.

Katrina added to the steaming bathwater two teaspoons of a vanilla-and-lime scented oil she'd purchased on Front Street the other day, lit a few candles, and undressed, tossing her clothes in the hamper in the corner. She slipped into the tub, sighing as the heat seeped into her muscles, all the way to her bones. Very nice. Exactly what she needed. These past two days had been a bit of a mini-rollercoaster, and now that the ride was winding down, it was time to relax. She took a sip of the rich, silky wine, closed her eyes, and thought about Crystal. She was concerned for her little sister.

After their parents had died, and Crystal, then eight, had moved in with their father's sister and her husband, Crystal began retreating into herself, becoming more introverted, spending most of her free time by herself rather than with friends. This self-imposed ostracism lasted for much of high school until her senior year when, finally, she began to act more how a seventeen-year-old should act. And much to Katrina's relief, she went to her prom. Her date had been a goofy-looking fellow in a cheap tux and a splattering of acne, but she'd gone, and that's all that mattered.

That summer, between high school and university, she got a job at a seasonal resort, working in the dining room as a waitress with a number of others her age. The resort was on Bainbridge Island, thirty minutes by ferry from Seattle, which meant she had to stay at the staff lodgings. A doctor couldn't have ordered better therapy, as she was in constant communication with the other staff and guests. By the end of the summer, it seemed as though she'd come out of her shell for good.

Still, her suggestion she pay Katrina a visit, only days after she started at the university, was not a good sign. Katrina wasn't going to delude herself into believing Crystal simply wanted them to spend some quality time together. They'd just seen each other last week when Katrina had driven her to Seattle University and helped her move into her dorm room. No, it seemed her sister was having problems adjusting once again.

Deciding to have a good talk with Crystal this weekend, Katrina set the matter aside and took another sip of the wine. She caught a glimpse of herself in the mirror: hair tied into a messy bun atop her head, a warm flush to her cheeks. Not bad for thirty-two. But she was in a world where young was better than old and she wasn't getting any younger. During the six years she and Shawn were together, she had never really given her age much thought. But now, single, she was all too aware of the invisible expiry date she couldn't necessarily see, but men definitely could. Hypocrites, the bunch of them, she thought. Why did they not have expiry dates as well? They used to, when they became impotent. But now with Viagra—well, look at Hugh Hefner.

She set the wine aside, ruminating on that. Her eyes eventually drifted up to the black rectangle hovering in the wall above and beyond her, where the window was situated. As far as bathrooms went, it was fairly large, fitted with a regular pane of glass rather than glass brick or some other such design that offered more privacy. She knew she would have to get a curtain for it at some point, but she didn't feel there was any rush, considering she had no immediate neighbors.

She picked up her novel, mindless of her wet fingers, and began to read.

The phantom moon floated in the black-water sky, a cosmic eye that seemed to be watching Zach as he took the skullcap out of his pocket and tugged it down over his head so it covered his ears and hid his eyebrows. He pressed himself tighter against Katrina's Honda Civic. His heart was knocking against his rib cage, and he became aware of the fact he was not so much frightened as he was excited. His eyes never left the brightly lit front bay window.

He could scarcely believe he was here again, doing what he was

about to do. Maybe it was how gamblers felt when they found
themselves at the blackjack table the night after losing their daughter's graduation savings, or heroin addicts chasing the dragon the
first day out of rehab. He knew he should turn around right then,
call it quits while he was ahead—which in this case meant not in
jail—but he couldn't. He couldn't get the memories of the previous night out of his head. They had consumed him all day. The
erotic thrill he'd experienced, the knife-sharp adrenaline rush,
the satisfying knowledge he was getting a one-up on Katrina, a
twisted kind of power trip. And then all of a sudden—he didn't
know when it happened, just that at some point it *did* happen—
he was no longer reminiscing but planning.

For tonight.

Right now.

Nevertheless, as the minutes slugged by, and Katrina had yet to
appear in the window, Zach became increasingly anxious. He was
going to miss her again. *Do it then. Go. Now.*

He pushed away from the car and darted across the front lawn,
beneath the heavy branches that blotted out much of the sky. He
slowed when he reached the wall he'd skirted the night before. A
light was on in one of the windows. He crept silently forward and
stopped when he was adjacent to it. He was unable to bring himself to look inside.

What if Katrina saw him?

No—that wasn't possible. Who sat at their window, staring out
into the night? Maybe crazies in the state insane asylum who were
doped up on medication and who rocked back and forth in their
rockers. But he imagined Katrina had better things to do. Besides,
even if she did randomly glance out, the glare from the lights inside would only allow her to catch her own reflection.

Zach peered inside.

Two nylon suitcases stacked against an unadorned wall. A jug
of Brita filtered water on the hardwood floor, next to an empty
glass. Clothes in a messy heap in one corner. The only sign it wasn't
home to a squatter was a neatly made futon mattress doused with
an assortment of colorful pillows.

Living room—strike. Bedroom—strike. So where was she? In the kitchen baking cookies? He hoped the hell not. He moved on and reached the far corner of the bungalow. Looked around it. There were two more lighted windows along the back wall. The closest was the north-facing bedroom window. The other was the one he'd approached seconds too late the night before.

This time he didn't hesitate. He hurried forward and peered in.

It was the bathroom.

Several candles were burning, creating soft pools of yellow light. Shadows jittered as if frightened by the very flames that had created them. Directly in Zach's line of sight was the bathtub. Katrina was in it. She was submerged up to her neck in bubbles, reading a book, her head resting on the lip opposite the faucets. Naked as Eve. Zach stared. He didn't know for how long. Only that at some point he began to have an unsettling feeling, a shifting in his gut that sent breezy shockwaves up the back of his neck. Something was wrong. It took him another few moments to realize what it was. He was actually staring into the bathroom mirror. That meant the tub—and Katrina—were right on the other side of the wall, less than two feet away.

Katrina reached over the side of the tub and exchanged the book for a glass of red wine. The water frothed, momentarily revealing her right breast. It was round and full. The nipple was a light shade of pink. Zach felt himself getting aroused. He pressed closer to the wall, his eyes widening. He could hear his breathing; it had become a little quicker, a little dryer. Katrina finished what wine was left and dangled the empty glass in front of her by the stem, as if she was contemplating something. Then, with a suddenness Zach wasn't at all prepared for, she stood up, a cascade of water running down her upper back. He was so surprised he stumbled backward a step.

Something cracked under his foot. It sounded as loud as a gunshot in a funeral home.

Katrina's face appeared in the window. A curious expression.

When she saw him, her eyebrows shot up. Her eyes became saucers. Her mouth dropped open and she screamed.

Zach fled. Maybe he'd screamed too, but he didn't think so. He bolted along the back of the house, around the corner, toward the street. Blood was thumping so hard behind his temples he wasn't aware of any other sound, only a constant drone, as if he'd been slammed by a large wave and pinned beneath the ocean.

What the hell had he stepped on? How had she seen him through the glare?

Candles, he realized. There *wasn't* any glare.

Had she recognized him?

He was halfway across the lawn when he heard a dog bark. He didn't break stride but glanced in the direction from which the bark had come. On the sidewalk, near where the mouth of Katrina's driveway met the road, a man walking a black-and-white dog was standing perfectly still, staring at him. Zach couldn't imagine what he must be thinking as he watched someone dressed like a shadow running from a house as if a legion of demons was licking at his heels.

The dog snapped the leash taut. Started barking more furiously.

"Stop!" the man shouted.

Zach didn't. If anything, he ran faster. He snatched his bike from where he'd left it leaning against one of the big trees in the front yard, hopped on, and pedaled furiously. He heard footsteps giving chase. More barking, closer. He pedaled faster, half expecting the dog to attach itself to his leg at any moment. That didn't happen. The footsteps and barking diminished. He'd left his pursuers far behind. He tore off the skullcap and stuffed it in his pocket. Wind rushed past his face, turning the tiny beads of sweat on his brow icy cool. He sped down Birch Street and shortly thereafter reached his place, a stucco-and-timber two-story Victorian with a pointed roof and an overhanging roofline. He went to the side door, carried his bike down the stairs, and dumped it in the corner—all the while his vivid imagination was glibly exploring the ways in which forensic guys in crime scene suits could prove what he'd done tonight. Hair, fabric, blood. The skullcap would have kept his hair on his head, and he didn't cut himself. His clothes? He stripped off his shirt, pants, and shoes, and dumped them all in a green plastic garbage bag, which he shoved into the cupboard beneath the kitchen sink. First thing tomorrow he would dispose of the evidence in a proper fashion. Next he took a shower, not so much to wash away any dirt he might have acquired as to mark a return to normalcy. By the time he'd toweled off and dressed again, he felt calmer, more in control.

In the kitchen, he put the kettle on for a cup of instant coffee. While he waited for the water to boil, he told himself he was over-reacting. A CSI team wasn't going to comb over Katrina's house. This was Leavenworth, not Miami. And it wasn't like he'd killed anyone. He'd just looked in a goddamn window. But it wasn't as simple as that, and he knew it. He was a fucking Peeping Tom. That might not be as bad as being a rapist, or a pedophile, but the stigma would be almost as ugly. Like those guys who used cameras to look up women's skirts. Pathetic. Sick. Sleazy. Desperate. He'd lose his job, that was for sure. He was a teacher. Teachers, like politicians, weren't allowed to do any wrong. Especially not a wrong like this. Not in the eyes of protective parents, anyhow. In fact, he'd be lucky if he wasn't chased from town by an angry mob of moms and dads wielding pitchforks and burning torches. Would he make the local papers? Surely. He could imagine the headlines: "Local Teacher Caught Peeping on Coworker" or "Nightcrawler Busted!"

A whistling. The water was ready. Zach grabbed a mug with a picture of the Eiffel Tower on it from the cupboard, added a spoonful of Nescafé coffee crystals, then poured in the steaming water. He sat down with the mug at the table and replayed every-thing that had happened, trying to remember Katrina's exact re-action. A curious expression, like she'd expected to see a raccoon, or maybe a deer. Her eyes widening when she saw a man in black instead. Then the scream. He didn't think she'd cried out a second time, but he couldn't he sure. The memories right before he'd been caught were already starting to form into one indistinguishable haze. More important, however, was whether or not there had been any hint of recognition in her eyes.

He didn't know. It had all happened too fast. He shook his head.

How the fuck had he let himself get caught up in this?

Katrina. It was her fault. Not directly, of course. She didn't put up pink lights in that front bay window of hers, dress in heels and a corset and not much else, and tap the glass to solicit passing neighbors. But she did kick him out of her car, which got him pissed enough to start a vendetta against her, which led him to check out her house.

No, he couldn't blame her. *Man up, Zach*, he thought. *This is your doing, yours alone.* Yes it was, and somehow he would have to get himself out of it. He began going over his story in case Katrina had, in fact, recognized him. He'd come home from work, had dinner, had a Scotch and soda. This was all true—though he wouldn't tell the cops just how strong the highball had been, or how many he'd had, for that matter. Then he'd—what? Stayed in and watched television? Sure. Why not? Simple was best.

Zach sat in silence, staring into his black coffee, waiting for a knock at the door.

Chapter 7

Someone was banging on Katrina's front door.

She was in the bathroom, a statue standing in the tub, like a naked woman who'd been petrified after glimpsing Medusa's face. Although fear had frozen her body, her thoughts were liquid fire, racing through her head. Who the hell was knocking? Couldn't be her neighbors. They were so far away they wouldn't have heard a gunshot, let alone a scream. The intruder? Crazy. Why would he be banging on her door? Did he want to talk? Explain what he was doing? *Excuse me, ma'am, I was just getting a few cheap thrills. Didn't mean to alarm you. Didn't mean to get caught either. So how about we just put this embarrassing little misunderstanding behind us? Whaddya say?* Was there time to call the police? Yes—the police. She had to call the police. Right away. That broke her paralysis, got her moving. She stepped out of the tub and yanked on her robe.

The pounding at the front door became louder, more insistent.

Where was her phone? In the kitchen?

She gripped the bathroom doorknob, but hesitated. Bandit was barking—he'd been barking the entire time, she realized, though she'd only just tuned into it now—but she thought there was another dog barking as well. She listened. She was right. Two dogs. Burglar, rapist, murderer—or whatever category the godforsaken bastard fell under—he surely wouldn't have brought a dog with him. Curiosity replaced her fear. She opened the door and almost got bowled over backward by Bandit, who leapt up on his hind legs, his forepaws pressed against her thighs. She shook him off impatiently and went to the foyer.

"Who is it?" she called. Her voice wasn't as confident as she would have liked it.

There was a moment of silence in which she half expected a gravelly voice to say, "I'm going to huff, and puff, and blow your house down!" But the voice that spoke up was mild and polite, if not somewhat concerned. "Quiet, boy. Shh." To her, "You don't know me, miss. My name's John Winthorpe. I was out walking my dog when I saw someone running out of your yard. I wanted to make sure everything was okay."

Katrina slid the safety chain in place, unfastened the deadbolt, then opened the door a wedge. The man on the doorstep was dressed in gray jogging pants and a gray sweatshirt. Middle-aged and spectacled. Katrina had only gotten a glimpse of the man in her bathroom window, which had amounted to little more than his eyes and the bridge of his nose, but she nonetheless knew this was not the same man. The dog, a black-and-white border collie, snorted. Bandit went nuts.

"Just a second," she said. She closed the door, unclasped the chain, then swung the door a little wider. She grabbed Bandit by the collar and told him to behave. He whimpered but went quiet. "Did you get a description of this person?" she asked.

"Height and build, sure. And a brief glimpse of his face. Are you okay? You look shaken."

"I saw the man too." She found it more difficult to articulate what had happened than she would have thought. "He was watching me through the bathroom window."

"Good God! Have you called the police?"

"I was about to. I . . . I just need a minute."

"Of course." John Winthorpe patted his dog. "Listen, if you want, Molson here and me will wait out front. Keep watch until the police arrive."

"Thank you. But I think I'll be fine."

"You sure? They might want to question me as well."

That was true, she thought. After all, he'd apparently gotten a better description of the intruder than she had. "Well, if you don't mind waiting around."

"Of course not. What are neighbors for? We'll be right out here. Just holler if you need us."

Katrina opened the door wider and stepped back. "Why don't you come in? I'll put on some tea. I don't know about you, but I could use it. Molson's welcome too."

As if to show his gratitude, the border collie stepped forward and sniffed her feet as she led them inside. Bandit began whining again, pleading to be let go. She released his collar so he could get acquainted with his new friend. The two canines immediately began playing Ring Around the Rosie.

"Either you've previously lived in a monastery," John said, glancing around the barren living room, "or you're still waiting on your furniture."

"Please, have a seat. I only have one. But it's comfortable."

"Can't be vigilant sitting down, can I?"

Katrina retrieved her cell phone from the bedroom and dialed 9-1-1, feeling apprehensive as she did so. She'd only called emergency services once before, when she was ten or eleven, on a dare. She'd hung up as soon as the dispatcher picked up. The dispatcher called back, but Katrina didn't answer, navïely believing that would be the end of it. It wasn't. A police cruiser pulled up to her house ten minutes later. The two big cops at the door gave her a verbal dressing down, telling her it was a very serious offence, what she did, and she could possibly go to jail. She promised she'd never do it again, and she hadn't. Until now—until she really needed their help. She told the dispatcher what happened. The woman asked her a number of questions. What was her location? What was her callback number? Was there a crime involved? Had she seen the suspect? Finally she was informed an officer would be by shortly to take a statement. Katrina hung up.

"Someone coming?" John asked.

"Yes, right now."

Less than five minutes later a black and white pulled into her driveway, reminding Katrina once more of that dare all those years ago. It was a powerful image, a police car. It was the archetype of authority. It seemed to promise order would reassert itself. Wrongs would be righted. Criminals would be punished. *Peeping Toms would be caught.* Katrina had the front door open before the cop had climbed the front steps. She invited him inside and offered him a cup of the jasmine tea she had brewed. He declined. She went on to tell him what happened. At his request she showed him the bathroom. The air was redolent with the bath oil. The candles were still burning. She flicked on the overhead light and blew out the flames.

While the cop—Officer Murray, he'd introduced himself as—examined the bathtub and window, Katrina took the opportunity to study him. He was downright small, maybe one hundred and forty pounds with his clothes on. He stood at around five foot five—including the extra inch his shiny black boots gave him. The standard equipment that made the typical barrel-chested cops so intimidating, such as a duty belt and gun, almost seemed to weigh this particular fellow down. The image was embellished by his apparent need to continually hitch his belt higher, a jerky, stop-motion action. A balding crown covered by a desperate comb over, buckteeth, too-large uniform, and the sense he was standing as straight as possible to gain an inch made him appear a caricature of authority. His attitude, however, was anything but comical. His eyes were intense, his tone clipped and to the point. It was clear he took his job very seriously. "So you say you were in the bathtub when you heard some noise"—he consulted his battered notebook in which he had been scribbling notes—"and when you turned around you saw some perp watching you?"

"Yes," she said.

He crouched down beside the bathtub and craned his neck to see up toward the window. "But from this angle, wouldn't it have been tough to see out?"

"I was standing."

"But you were having a bath, isn't that right?"

"I was getting out."

"That's when you heard the noise?"

"I think he might have stepped on a plastic flower pot. I saw a few out back the other day. Should we check?"

"Not necessary," Officer Murray said dismissively, jotting more notes in his notebook. He addressed John Winthorpe, who'd followed them into the bathroom. "You say he was tall and lanky? Anything else?"

"He was wearing a black pullover and black slacks."

The cop nodded and raised his chin, failing to look bigger than he actually was. "I'd put out an APB, but I'm afraid it wouldn't do any good. I'm the only one on the beat tonight."

"You're kidding?" Katrina said.

"Small town, ma'am."

"So you're not going to do anything?"

"Given neither of you got a good look at the perp, there's not much I can do."

"What about footprints? He must have left footprints. You can get plastic molds, right?"

"This isn't a murder scene, Ms. Burton. From what you've told me, all we have here is some pervert looking through your window. I understand how that might bother you, but these kooks are usually harmless."

"This has happened before? Recently?"

"No, ma'am. Real Peeping Toms are rare."

"Maybe that's because they don't get caught," she said cynically. She knew she should be grateful to the cop, but she couldn't help it. He was pretty much telling her all options were off the table.

"I'm thinking," Officer Murray said, not rising to the bait, "what you have here is just some guy getting his kicks. Probably no more dangerous than those guys who cop a feel in a crowded place." He stuck his notebook in his belt with a solid shove, as if to signal the matter was settled. *Justice served. Don't call me, I'll call you.* He took the peaked cap that had been tucked under his arm and replaced it on his head.

"That's supposed to be comforting?" To Katrina's reasoning, it was about as comforting as saying, "Don't worry. He doesn't rape woman. No, no, he just harasses them. Gives them a good scare. He's harmless."

"Better than a real crazy outside your window, Ms. Burton."

"But that's the point! What if he *is* crazy? How do you know he's not? What if he has a psychological disorder? What if this kind of voyeurism is an addiction to him? What if he comes back? What if he decides a quick look isn't enough?"

"I doubt it," Officer Murray said matter-of-factly.

Katrina clenched her jaw. Why couldn't the dispatcher have sent her a real cop? Not half a man with half-baked thoughts on law and order? "So what happens?" she asked, not bothering to hide her frustration.

"I'll cruise around the neighborhood. See if I spot anyone who matches the description you and Mr. Winthorpe gave me. Who knows? Maybe I'll get lucky."

"And if he doesn't happen to be walking aimlessly around?" she demanded.

Officer Murray gave his belt a hefty tug. "Like I told you. There's not much else I can do. Without a good description, he could swap clothes and be any tall fellow out there."

"What about a stakeout?" John suggested. "Like Ms. Burton said, if he comes back—"

"We don't have the manpower for that."

"But what if he does come back?" Katrina pressed. They were going in circles, but she couldn't steer the cop straight.

Officer Murray shrugged. "Try to get a better description of him."

"Sure," Katrina said. "Maybe I'll just set up a canvas and paints."

John grinned. Officer Murray, seemingly impervious to sarcasm, simply asked if she had a gun.

"Of course not," she replied.

"I suggest if you don't feel safe, Ms. Burton, you go out and buy yourself one." He tipped a nod to them both—*all in a good day's work, ma'am,* it seemed to say—then returned to the living room. He paused at the front door to hike up his belt once more. He nodded at the front bay window. "I also suggest you get some blinds."

He left. John and Katrina remained where they were, in silence, listening to his booted footsteps descend the front steps. The slam of the cruiser door—which Katrina no longer thought of as the archetype of authority. The grumble of the engine, fading, fading.

"That didn't go too well, did it?" John said, breaking the protracted silence.

She sighed. "I suppose I was a little rough on him. He was just doing his job."

"I think you handled yourself quite admirably. You've been through a lot. God knows how my wife, Carol, would have reacted had she caught some man peering through her bathroom window." John chuckled. "Yee-gad! That would be something. Likely she would want to move to a new state." He shook his head, still contemplating that. He added, "Just lock up carefully tonight. And I wouldn't be too frightened, if I were you. Officer Murray was right about one thing. These guys are cowards. They're after a cheap thrill, that's all. You'll likely never see him again. Not if he knows that you know he might be out there. Which he does now. Nevertheless, you might want to look into getting a handgun, even if it remains in a shoebox in your closet. You know, just in case."

Suddenly Katrina felt extremely tired, deflated, like a balloon that had just lost a good bit of its air. All this seemed too much. The scare Zach had given her out on the highway. The possibility a good number of her colleagues were planning for a party at a cabin she didn't own. The fact there was a Peeping Tom lurking around the neighborhood. If she was the superstitious type, she would have believed the gods had put a curse on her so she would attract bad luck wherever she went.

"I take Molson for a walk every evening around this time," John went on. "If it means anything, I'll keep an eye out for anybody who resembles this creep."

"That's very kind of you. But you don't have to."

"I insist. Give this old man some excitement."

Katrina thanked John for his concern and showed him and Molson out. She returned to the kitchen, dumped her tea she'd barely touched down the drain, and systematically checked to make sure all the bungalow's windows were locked. To be on the safe side, she stripped the sheets off the bed and pinned them over the two bedroom windows, using the Monkey Hooks she'd gotten earlier.

She wondered what Jack Reeves would say if he knew this was how she was using the hooks he'd recommended. It seemed as if she'd met him days ago, not hours. She tried to remember their exact conversation. She couldn't recall any specific details, only a broad rainbow of emotions. Instant attraction when she looked up and saw him standing there, tall, dark, and handsome. Delight when he winked at her. Embarrassment when her mind hit a patch of fog and she couldn't think of anything to say. Regret when she had to leave the store, wondering if she would see him again.

It amazed her she could feel any of these romantic emotions at all, let alone for a relative stranger. Shouldn't she be in mourning? How long was long enough? It had already been nearly two years. A hellish, lonely two years. How many nights had she remained awake in bed, unable to sleep? How many hours had she spent staring into the mirror, examining the wrinkles that creased the skin around her eyes and along her brow, wrinkles that had never been there before? Sometimes during those moments she'd felt as though she'd been looking at the face of a stranger. She'd been not only devastated but lost, drifting aimlessly on an unseen current. It had terrified her to know she might never again find that person she used to be. So she'd made a choice. Close her eyes and float off into the vast expanse of obscurity that threatened to swallow her, or begin paddling in some direction, any direction, and hope she'd hit land. She paddled. She started looking for new teaching jobs around the state—not in Seattle, she had to get out of Seattle if she wanted to start fresh. It had been good therapy. Day by day she began to regain her appetite for simple pleasures. She no longer cried herself to sleep or slept for several hours during the day.

So it *had* been long enough, she thought. She'd put in her

penance, served her time. Wasn't the next logical step to find someone else? Not someone to replace Shawn. Someone to fill the emptiness he'd left inside her.

It was dangerous, she knew, to be thinking of Jack Reeves in this way, as a kind of savior figure. She knew nothing about him. He could turn out to be a jerk, or a player. He might not have a wife, but he could very well have a girlfriend. Why wouldn't he? He was charismatic and handsome. Still, she didn't care about any of that, she realized. She'd already made the decision. She was going to give herself over to, if not Jack, the idea of Jack—a new man, a new start.

Katrina changed into her pajamas—she didn't usually wear them, but she didn't usually have a peeper sneaking around the neighborhood—turned off the lights, then lay down on the futon. The night settled over her, soft and quiet, like a second blanket. But she was unable to fall asleep right away. Not after everything that had happened. Staring into the dark, she began composing a list in her head of what else she might need from the hardware store tomorrow afternoon.

Chapter 8

"Zach?" Katrina said, poking her head into his classroom. "I want to talk to you. It's about yesterday."

Zach was seated behind his desk, a Styrofoam cup of instant noodles in front of him, a pair of chopsticks poking out of it like antennae. He was dressed unexpectedly respectable in a jacket and tie, which was definitely a step up from his hockey jersey. He still looked like a kid, someone too young to be a high school teacher, but he was getting there. A bizarre thought popped into her head: one day he was going to make a very fetching man. She pushed that image away quickly, embarrassed to be thinking such a thing.

He turned to her. An expression that seemed to hover somewhere between suspicion and fear splashed across his face, only to evaporate the next moment. She wondered what that meant.

"I wanted to apologize," she said, keeping her voice neutral. Not pleasant, not angry. Just business as usual. The voice you used on the phone when trying to sort out a questionable bill. He deserved nothing more. "I have a bit of a temper. Sometimes it gets the best of me."

Zach's features thawed. He seemed to visibly relax. "Well, thanks, I guess. Anything else you wanted to discuss?"

"Actually, there is," she said. "It's about the party. I talked to my sister last night. She's coming up to visit me this weekend. I'm going to be showing her around. There's simply no time for me to have people to the cabin. And since you seem to know more than me about who had planned to come or not, I was hoping you could pass this information along."

"Well, I—"

"Thanks, Zach," she said curtly and left his classroom, biting back a smile. That felt good. Both the perplexed look on his face, and the fact the matter with the cabin was now nicely settled.

Back in her classroom, seated behind her desk, she glanced at the clock on the wall. Still another twenty minutes before the first bell. She took out a folder from the desk drawer and browsed her weekly schedule, going over where her breaks were. She found herself frowning. Something was nagging at her. Specifically, why had Zach looked the way he had when she'd stopped by? It was almost as if she'd caught him with his hand in the cookie jar. Only he hadn't been doing anything except staring off into space. What had he been thinking about? What did people like Zach think about? Video games? Dungeons & Dragons? Screwing his siblings out of his parents' wills? Something about her?

That would explain why he had looked so guilty upon her sudden appearance. But just as soon as Katrina entertained that vain possibility, she discarded it. The world did not revolve around her. Certainly people did not sit around daydreaming about her. Even people like Zach. No, it was much more plausible he had thought she was going to let loose another verbal attack on him, especially considering how his attitude changed when she told him she wanted to apologize. Oddly, she found that explanation anticlimactic, as if she wanted a reason to get into it with him again. She usually wasn't like this, this petty, that's just how much he had gotten under her skin.

Students began to shuffle into the classroom, some chatting, others plopping down at their desks and falling immediately asleep. She was always mystified at where a child's energy went during the transition from elementary to high school. It was almost as if it didn't make the cut into teenage years, shoved out by hormones or something along those lines.

When the seven thirty bell rang, she roused everyone to attention, then started on about the importance of eliminating dangling participles. Throughout the lesson she experienced that floating sensation she'd been feeling off and on since waking that morning. Because after school, she was going to see Jack Reeves again, the man she barely knew but whom she couldn't stop thinking about. The list of items she'd decided she needed from the hardware store had been easy to compose, since she was beginning with next to nothing: energy-efficient lightbulbs, an extension cord and multipower outlet, an electrical heater for the bedroom because the old oil radiator took forever to heat up and the mountain autumn nights were already proving to be quite chilly, small kitchen appliances, and anything else she saw when she was there.

Who knew you could get so excited about shopping in a hardware store?

Her high spirits carried her throughout the remainder of the day, and before she knew it the last bell had rung and she was in her car heading down Front Street into the center of town. Her palms were damp on the steering wheel, her stomach churning with nervousness. She tried to tell herself seeing Jack again wasn't such a big deal. But it was a big deal. She had made it a big deal by thinking about him so much, the way those chocolate Advent calendars made Christmas an even bigger deal than it already was for kids by counting down the days of December.

She went over once more what she was going to say. Something simple about being new in town and would he care to show her around? Although that line had sounded perfectly plausible earlier, it now felt contrived, if not flat out ridiculous. After all, he didn't even know her. She was just another customer. She would be coming off as desperate.

She was approaching the hardware store on the right side of the street. She was tempted to drive right on past and return home, make dinner, and forget this mad scheme. But she knew she would regret doing that. So she pulled to the curb, checked her lipstick in the rearview mirror, and started down the sidewalk. She was still a good twenty yards away when Jack rounded the corner at the far end of the block and started toward her. Her mind chugged to a halt. Her step faltered. For a moment she entertained the notion, given the amount of time she'd spent fantasizing about him, she was superimposing his face on someone else, someone who resembled him. But she knew that wasn't the case. Not many men had tattooed forearms and a ponytail.

Should she pretend not to notice? Should she say hello?

The gap between them was disappearing fast. She figured he would turn into the hardware store, which was only a couple shops ahead of him. But to her surprise he walked straight past it. Straight toward her. His posture was proper, his chin up, and he seemed to be whistling to himself. His attention was focused on the park across the street, and he didn't see her. The gap between them had almost disappeared. Yes, he was whistling. She could hear him now. She decided to continue past him. She'd lost her nerve, she couldn't—

He noticed her at the last moment. The tune died on his lips. His face opened up in amused surprise. She tried to look surprised as well.

"Well, hello again!" he said jovially, stopping in front of her. "How are the hooks?"

All she could think of were pirates. "Hooks?"

"For your pictures?"

Katrina thought of them holding up the bed sheets over her windows. "Excellent, actually. Much better than nails. You're not working today?"

"You mean the hardware store?" He glanced over his shoulder at it. When he looked back, he was grinning. "I don't work there. I was just picking up a few things I needed yesterday. The owner had stepped out for a few minutes. Came back just after you left." She must have looked absolutely flustered, because he added, "Don't worry about the hooks. I paid for them. Like I said, a housewarming gift."

She was flattered. At least she thought she was.

"I was just heading down the street for a coffee," he continued. "Care to join me?"

"Um, yes, that would be nice."

He held out the crook of his arm. "Take it," he told her. "I'm working on being a gentleman. Doc's orders."

She took it. His appeal was irresistible. Best of all, she thought, he was doing all the work. She didn't even have to break out her prepared line. As they walked he tipped a nod or said a hearty hello to almost everyone they passed.

"Didn't you say you've only been here for a short time?" she said. "How do you know so many people?"

"I don't know a single soul," he told her, grinning again.

He took her to a place called Café Mozart, which was not a café but a private, upscale restaurant hidden away on the second floor of a building facing Front Street. Instead of sitting at one of the tables set with a bottle of wine and white folded napkins, he had the hostess take them to two elegant armchairs placed in front of a fireplace in which a small fire was burning. Off in the corner was a black piano, apparently so someone could play classical music when the place filled up. At the moment, however, they were the only customers.

"I thought you said you wanted to go for coffee," she said.

"This place has the best Joe in town."

Jack ordered two lattes, then settled back in his chair, crossing his legs. He looked right at home. She tried to relax as well. They made idle chitchat for a while, how-was-your-day? kind of stuff. Gradually they moved on to more personal questions. She asked him a few about his past, which he dodged. She didn't press the matter—she wasn't exactly eager to delve into her history either. When he told her he was only passing through Leavenworth, she felt her stomach drop three floors.

"So when do you think you're leaving?" she asked.

"I have no plans, really. But I'll tell you this much. This place is starting to grow on me. What are you doing for dinner?"

The question was so out of the blue, she stumbled for a response.

"Have you ever tried traditional Bavarian food?" he added.

"They serve that here?"

"I'm thinking of another place. Sausages, cider, kraut, Kettle Korn—it's great."

"Sounds interesting."

"So it's a date?"

He was either the most forward man she had ever met, or the most confident. "Yes," she said, unable to hold back a smile.

"Or should I say our second date?"

"What do you mean?"

"What would you call what we're on now?"

After the old-world charm of Café Mozart, Katrina had expected an intimate candlelit restaurant with tables set for two. Jack had other plans, taking her to King Ludwig's, a rowdy, family owned and operated place named after the eccentric Bavarian king whose claim to fame consisted of three fairytale castles he'd built before being allegedly murdered at the age of forty-one. Grand murals and magnificent hand-woven tapestries adorned the walls while couples danced on the dance floor and kids ran amuck. Katrina loved it, especially since the food rivaled the atmosphere. She had the *kassler rippchen* (hickory-smoked pork chops and red potatoes), *winekraut* (sauerkraut marinated in white wine), and *rotkraut* (red cabbage braised with onions, red wine, and applesauce). Jack had the duck with plum sauce. He kept their dark German beers topped, and it wasn't long before she began to feel a little tipsy. For his part, he might as well have been drinking water. The alcohol didn't seem to affect him in the least.

After the main course, Jack pulled her to the dance floor. He placed his hand firmly on the small of her back, drawing her close so her breasts pressed against his chest, and weaved her around the floor with only German accordion music to keep rhythm to. She had taken ballroom dance lessons years ago with Shawn, as well as a month-long course in tango, so she didn't exactly have two left feet. But her skill didn't compare with Jack's. He was an excellent lead who kept her moving with such fluidity she barely had to think about what she was doing. They quickly became the center of attention. When they'd had enough, half the restaurant gave them a standing ovation, clinking beer steins and howling approval. Katrina collapsed into her seat, her face flushed, and said, "I'd like to see you with some salsa music."

"*Gemutlichkeit*," Jack said, lifting his glass.

"What does that mean?"

"Good times."

She clinked glasses. "To good times." Then, "You know German?" For some reason that wouldn't surprise her at all.

"It was written on the menu."

She laughed, and Jack waved over the waitress, a young girl wearing a traditional dirndl dress, her blonde hair hanging down over her shoulders in long Goldilocks braids. He ordered them apple strudel for dessert, along with another pitcher of beer, then leaned back in his chair. The top three buttons of his shirt were undone, just enough to reveal his tanned chest and the tip of another tattoo. He looked more solid and real and handsome than ever. But if that was the case, then why did she think that if she closed her eyes for long enough he would disappear? For the first time in her life, that expression "Pinch me, I think I'm dreaming" related to her.

"I'm really enjoying myself," she said.

His black eyes sparkled. "I guess we were meant for each other. In fact, I know the perfect place we could go on our honeymoon."

Obviously he was kidding, but Katrina couldn't help but feel a tingle of excitement. She hadn't felt that invisible expiry date once all evening. "Hawaii? Guam? Mexico?" she said playfully, going along with it.

"Even better: Moose Lake. It's a small place just north of the border in British Columbia. Clean air, pristine lakes, rustic cabins. A little like Leavenworth, but without the tourism."

"Sounds lovely," she said, and it did. She thought anywhere with Jack would be lovely.

He winked. "Stick with me, kid. I'll show you the world. Speaking of this fine town, how are you finding it so far?"

She was about to say "great," that ubiquitous rejoinder, but when she saw the genuine interest in his eyes she decided to speak the truth. It would be good to confide in someone else about the whole cabin fiasco. Catharsis or what have you. "It started out a little rough, I have to admit."

"On a dark and stormy night—"

"Actually, it *was* a dark and stormy night. I was driving along Highway 2 when I passed this hitchhiker. I've never picked up a hitchhiker before. But it was pouring rain, and he was wandering around in the middle of nowhere."

"Where were you on Highway 2, exactly?"

"About twenty miles west of here."

"What was he doing out there by himself?"

"That's the thing. I thought maybe his car broke down, and that's what he said happened. But I don't remember passing any car. Oh—he was drunk, too."

"Ah," Jack said.

The waitress returned with their desserts and the fresh pitcher of beer. Ignoring Katrina's protests, Jack refilled her glass, then topped his as well.

"What does 'ah' mean?" she asked.

"Rainbow Roadhouse. It's a strip club out that way. I passed it on my way here." He held up his hands innocently. "Didn't go in. Scout's honor. But if this guy had been drinking, it would be the most likely place he could have been."

Katrina was nodding her head. It made sense. Zach had been too embarrassed to admit he'd been at a strip club, so he made up the story about the car. "He kept looking at my legs," she went on. "I was wearing a skirt."

"Short?"

"Sitting down, yes."

Jack grinned. "I probably would have done the same thing."

She lowered her eyes, embarrassed—and flattered. "But he was creepy," she said. "Not just the looking at my legs. But everything. The way he was acting, talking. I didn't think I could stand being in the car with him for the next thirty minutes, so when I saw this road sign announcing an upcoming turnoff to Lake Wenatchee, I told him I had a place there, which I don't. Guess what happens when we get there?"

"He tells you he lives there as well?"

"He asks me to go for a drink."

Jack feigned offense. "I feel like the schmuck now."

"You don't reek like booze and freak me out. Anyway, I told him no, but he wouldn't get out of the car."

Jack frowned. "What happened next?"

"Well, he finally got out and I drove off."

"At least you're okay."

"Wait—it gets more bizarre." Now that Katrina had started the tale, she found the words pouring out of her. Jack was a good listener. It was a relief to get this off her chest. "I saw him the next day here, on Front Street, just a few blocks down from where we are now. Turns out he's a teacher at Cascade High School with me. You should have seen our faces when the vice principal introduced us."

Jack turned serious for the first time. He leaned forward, eyes hard. "I hope his guy isn't still bothering you," he said, all levity gone from his voice. "'Cause if he is, I'll have a few words with him. I can be rather convincing when I want to be."

Katrina eyed Jack's powerful shoulders and chest, which his shirt could not mask, and his strong forearms and hands. She didn't doubt he could be "rather convincing," whatever that meant. "No, no," she said. "He's not bothering me. He's harmless, I've realized. Just a kid, really. When he's sober, he's actually quite smart and witty. Anyway, to make a long story short, that evening, after the first day of school, all the teachers went out for drinks for a kind of back-to-school thing. And then Zach—that's his name— he tells everyone about this lovely cabin I have on the lake. Next thing I know there's a party planned there for this weekend."

Jack let out a booming laugh.

"This isn't funny," she said sternly.

"Why didn't you just explain to everyone the truth? That this nutcase had scared the crap out of you, so you made it all up."

"I'm the new teacher. Slandering a colleague on my first day wasn't the first impression I wanted to make."

"Fair enough. So why didn't you say you didn't want to have a party?"

"You weren't there. It wasn't as simple as that. I was put on the spot."

"Am I invited?" he deadpanned.

"Very funny, Jack."

"So what are you going to do?"

"Well, it sort of worked itself out. I spoke to my sister yesterday. She's decided to come up this weekend for a visit. It's given me the perfect excuse to cancel. I told Zach to tell everyone the party's off."

"Can you trust this joker? Sounds like a sneaky bastard, if you ask me."

"If he screws this up," she said, "I'll kill him."

They finished their desserts—Katrina had another two sips of beer, but that was all—then they got the check. Jack pulled out his wallet, but she insisted she pay. He argued for a bit until she said he could pay for the next dinner.

Being rusty at the dating game, she thought she'd played that hand rather well.

Outside, the air was brisk but pleasant. The sodium-vapor street-lamps cast romantic pools of golden light on the sidewalk, while other lights lit up the profusion of colorful flowers that were every-where. A four-horse team came trotting up the street, pulling an old-fashioned wagon. The two drivers, dressed in traditional German clothing, waved at Jack and Katrina, who waved back. Katrina was grinning from ear to ear. "I think I'm going to like this town very much," she said.

"It's one of a kind. No question there."

She pointed east. "My car's that way."

Jack nodded in the other direction. "My hotel's *that* way."

His words zapped her like a shot of adrenaline. "Jack—"

"I know, I know. We just met," he said. "But there's something between us."

"I thought you were above clichés," she said lightly.

"I'm just telling you how it is."

"And how many women have you told that to before?"

Jack looked taken aback. She instantly regretted the words. "I'm sorry. I didn't mean it like that."

"It's all right. There's no pressure. How about I see you later this week?"

She hesitated. *Don't push him away. Don't do that. He's exactly what you need. Haven't you spent enough nights alone? It's time to let go of the past. Live in the present.*

"How far is it?" she asked.

Jack took her hand and led her down Front Street, past Café Mozart. They turned left on 8th Street and arrived at a quaint stucco-and-timber building called the Blackbird Lodge. He led her through the cozy lobby to his room on the ground floor. He fished his keys out of his pocket and opened the door. She stepped inside first. The lights were off, but silvery moonlight shone through the windows. She felt Jack's hands on her shoulders. Their touch was electric. They slid down her arms, slipped around her waist. He kissed her below the ear, his breath hot and sweet. Katrina had always thought she would feel awkward, guilty even, the first time she found herself in the position she was in now, a kind of betrayal of Shawn's memory. She didn't. All she felt was a powerful, burning longing, which instantly consumed her, stripping bare her thoughts, leaving only a naked, base desire. She turned around in Jack's arms and kissed him forcefully on the lips. They stumbled backward, into the door, slamming it closed. Then they were moving around the room with considerably less grace than they had on the dance floor earlier, a ball in a pinball machine, bumping furniture, tearing off each other's clothes in the process. By the time they dropped onto the bed, Katrina was feeling more alive than she had any time in recent memory.

They didn't get much sleep that night.

Around the same time Katrina was having dinner with Jack, Zach was in his basement, having a drink with a different Jack entirely. It was dusk out, the sky an otherworldly crimson. The fading light coming through the windows sketched the room in shades of reds and grays. Zach did not get up to turn on the overhead lights but remained on the sofa on which he had been sitting for the past hour. He raised the bottle of bourbon to his lips and took another swig. He was doing some soul searching which, for him at least, always went better with a cold beer or a bottle of booze. Specifically, he was debating about how to proceed with what he had begun to think of as the Katrina Vendetta. Should he continue harassing her about the cabin? Or should he drop the entire matter completely? He knew he should drop it. He'd already regained some of the face he'd lost out on Highway 2 by letting her know that he knew she was a liar. Now instead of him being in the wrong alone, they were both in the wrong, which sort of made the whole situation better. So what more was there to gain by continuing the harassment? Seeing her made the fool not only in his eyes but everybody they worked with? Sure, that would be satisfying. But was it really worth doing? Because she was becoming an obsession with him, and when something became an obsession, it could only lead to trouble. Last night was a perfect example. He still cringed every time he thought about what he'd done. But ironically, that was also precisely why he couldn't drop his beef with her. An obsession, by definition, was something occupying your mind which you couldn't brush aside.

So what to do?

Sometime later, Zach thought he had it figured out.

Chapter 9

Katrina was furious.

She could scarcely believe her eyes as she stared at the list of names on the pink piece of paper clutched in her hands. All in all it appeared as though twenty teachers had signed up—*signed up*—to attend the party at her cabin tomorrow night. There was even a little column for what they would bring. Some of the items listed included a fruit bowl, nachos, cake, pumpernickel bread, potato chips, and dip. A woman named Stacy Walters who Katrina didn't think she'd met yet wrote down in green ink a karaoke machine. She even drew a little happy face beside it, as if she thought Katrina would be thrilled. *Sure, Stacy. A karaoke machine. Why not? Why not bring along a busload of Japanese tourists as well? Sake anyone?*

Katrina's tunnel vision faded. She became aware of the rest of the office once again. The secretary, a blonde woman wearing very large hoop earrings, was regarding her with concern. She probably saw the bubble above Katrina's head filled with question marks and exclamation points and four-letter words. Katrina stepped into the hallway and checked the list one more time, specifically for Zach's name. As she'd expected, it was conveniently absent. Well, he was going to answer for his omission, as well as for his commissions. Right now.

She marched to his classroom, where he seemed to hide out during the day, never joining the others in the faculty lounge. Her heels rang purposefully on the tiles, like a war drum. Her anger— no, her incredulity he would try something like this—rose with each step so by the time she'd reached his room she not so much walked but blew in through the door.

Zach looked up from a stack of papers he was correcting, managing a surprised expression. She was sure he was anything but surprised.

"What did I tell you yesterday morning, Zach?" she demanded, stopping in front of his desk.

"What are you talking about, Katrina?" he said, setting the papers aside.

"Yesterday morning, Zach! I asked you to tell the other teachers the damn party was off."

"I did. I told them."

That admission surprised her. She hadn't expected him to be so bold, considering it would only take one phone call to another teacher to call the bluff. "You told everybody the party was off?" she said skeptically.

"Not yesterday. I got tied up with a few things. I did it this morning. Not everyone. But some. I figured word would spread."

She brandished the pink sheet the way a lawyer might brandish an important piece of evidence in court. "What about this—this sign-up sheet? I suppose you're going to tell me you've never seen it before?"

"No, I haven't. I don't even know what you're talking about. A signup sheet?"

Her confidence wavered a fraction. "Why did everyone else sign it, except you?"

"First, I'm still not sure what you're talking about. Second, I don't leave this classroom much. Don't use the faculty lounge." He shrugged. "I guess whatever that is never got around to me."

Katrina stared at him, weighing his words. He was good. Convincing. And she found herself wondering whether she had jumped the gun here. Was she biased against him because he had spooked her badly on the highway? True, he'd brought up the idea of the party in front of everyone at Ducks & Drakes. And, true, he went around telling everyone the party was on the next day. But she told him to cool it, to shut things down, and he said he had. To keep pushing this forward, out of pure malice, would be deranged. Was he deranged? That was still up for debate. Nevertheless, to be fair, to be unbiased, it was perfectly conceivable another enthusiastic teacher got carried away and created the sign-up list.

She clenched her jaw, the fight draining from her. She looked around the classroom, as if searching for a soft sofa to sink into and disappear.

"Listen, Katrina," Zach said levelly, "stop worrying about this thing. Just have the party. Bring your sister. Trust me, it'll turn out to be a lot of fun. No one cares whether you have furniture or not."

"It's more complicated than having furniture or not."

"What is?"

She hesitated. It would be so easy to come clean right now.

"Katrina?"

"Nothing."

"You can tell me." He was leaning forward, eager. A hard glint in his eyes had replaced the previous guilelessness, and she suddenly had the feeling he had been putting on a big show.

But she couldn't prove anything.

"I said it's nothing," she said tersely, then left.

Before leaving the school, however, Katrina stopped by the office to request a list of faculty phone numbers from the secretary. She knew there was only one option remaining to get out of hosting the party tomorrow night. She would have to do what she should have originally done instead of passing off the responsibility to Zach. Call up everyone individually and tell them the party was off, that her sister was coming up to visit tomorrow, and that the two of them would be busy all weekend. Still, even though that excuse had seemed fine and dandy yesterday, it no longer felt as justifiable, simply because the plans had since been set in writing, and it was now the eleventh hour.

Screw it, she thought with finality. *Screw what everyone thinks of me. They should have listened to me on Tuesday when I said I didn't want to host the damn thing. Let them bitch and complain if they want. I've had enough.*

That white lie she'd birthed exactly one week ago, that parasite that had been feeding off her insecurities, her narcissistic need to be liked and fit in, that goddamn lie which had become the foundation of the precarious house of cards she'd been living inside since she'd arrived in Leavenworth—that was going to die tonight.

As Katrina pulled into Blackbird Lodge on 8th Street, a flood of memories overwhelmed her, temporarily lifting her dour mood. Last night had been, well, magical. Not just the sex, though that had been very good. Everything, the whole package. She'd forgotten what it was like to fall asleep next to a man in bed, to wake up next to him, to *be* with him. There was no other experience like it, and it had taken abstaining from it for so long to realize how important it was. On the outside she still looked like the Katrina of yesterday. On the inside she felt like a butterfly that had just emerged from its chrysalis and had the entire world to explore with fresh, beautiful eyes.

She passed through the hotel lobby and knocked on the door to Jack's room. He appeared in the doorway dressed simply in black track pants. His bare chest glistened with sweat. She'd never seen the tattoos on his chest before, not last night because it was too dark, and not this morning because he'd been up and dressed and making coffee before she'd opened her eyes. There were a lot of abstract tribal designs done in the same green ink as on his arms. Two large colorful tattoos stood out above the rest: a wolf's head encircled by a dream catcher, and a bald eagle draped in the American flag. Native American meets patriot. Fitting. The tattoos added to his sex appeal, and she felt a tingling spread down her inner thighs. *God! I'm like a cat in heat around him,* she thought, pulling herself quickly together. She cleared her throat. "Sorry if I'm interrupting something," she said. "I should have called. I can come back."

"Nonsense!" he said with his usual gusto. "I was just finishing my workout. Come on in." He directed her to a chair, then pulled on a T-shirt. She wished he hadn't. The room was just as she remembered it, small but cozy and radiating tranquility. "So, you couldn't wait until six to see me, is that it?" he said, grinning.

"I wish it was that simple. I've had a pretty bad day. I just needed some advice, I guess."

"Fire away."

"I don't know where to start, exactly." She decided to pick up where they'd left off at King Ludwig's. "Remember what I told you about that teacher I work with? The party I'm supposed to be hosting tomorrow night? Well, apparently it's still on."

"That Zach guy didn't cancel it like you told him to?"

"Says he did. Maybe. I don't know. All I know is there was this flashy pink sign-up sheet in my teacher's box today after school with about twenty names on it."

"What are you going to do?"

"Call everyone on the list tonight and tell them it's off. They won't be happy."

"That doesn't seem so terrible."

"I just feel so fake. So wrong. I can't believe I've let it go this far."

Jack nodded, apparently thinking over what she'd told him, and she found by simply being in his presence the task at hand didn't seem as daunting as it had before. Nothing rattled him, it seemed, and that vibe and confidence was contagious. Although he hadn't done anything yet, hadn't even offered any advice, she suddenly felt very grateful to him, just for being there for her.

She was falling fast and hard for him. She knew that. Hell, a blind dog would know that. And perhaps she was falling *too* hard and fast. But she didn't care.

"Well," he said finally, "why not rent a cabin?"

She blinked. "Huh?"

"Rent a cabin on the lake for tomorrow night. It's off-season right now. A lot of people, I'm sure, would be leasing. They'll probably want a week or a month commitment, but I bet we could talk someone into just one weekend."

A ray of optimism broke through Katrina's gloomy state of mind, but only for a moment. She shook her head. "I can't," she said.

"Why not?"

"It's not right."

"I think it's a great solution."

"It'd be lying."

"Does that really matter at this point?"

"Yes, it does," she said. "If I'd been honest from the very beginning, we wouldn't be having this bizarre discussion."

"But we are," Jack replied. "So you have to do something, right?"

"I am going to do something. I'm going to call everyone tonight."

"Like you said. They're not going to be too happy about it."

"I don't care anymore."

"You sure then?"

"No more lying, Jack."

"You've already told everyone you have a cabin, so you're not really lying, are you?"

"Telling someone something and acting it out on a grand scheme is very different."

"Only if you get caught." He shrugged. "Look. You go and cancel, everyone's pissed. Maybe they start talking. Maybe they start thinking you don't really have a cabin after all. Or you go through with what I'm saying and everyone's happy. It's a simple decision, really."

Katrina was a little surprised by Jack's moral indifference in the matter, but she wasn't about to criticize him. He'd been much too kind to her already. And maybe he was right. What he was saying might not be the right thing to do in the ethical sense, but maybe it was the right thing to do in the practical sense. It reminded her of an incident that occurred during her first year of teaching at Garfield High. She'd caught one of her grade twelve students cheating on a midterm exam. The student had a bunch of thumb-sized cheat sheets in his fist. One had fallen to the floor, landing under his chair and slightly behind him. She picked it up as she patrolled the classroom without him noticing and confirmed what it was. Instead of pulling him out of the class and reporting him to the principal, which would have likely resulted in his failing the course and perhaps being denied the university of his choice, she asked to speak with him later in the day. When they met again she showed him the cheat sheet and explained to him the potential consequences. He went white, was on the verge of tears, apologized profusely—and most importantly—got the point. His name was Henry Vreeland, and he still kept in touch with her to this day. His last e-mail had been to tell her he'd graduated from Columbia Law School.

"Let's say I wanted to do what you're suggesting," she said. "I can't. Not really. I already made plans with my sister for her to visit."

"Bring her," Jack said. "There's only so much Bavarian-themed mini-golf and wagon rides you can take. She'd love it. Listen, you want this over with, right?"

"I just want my boring life back."

"Did you tell these other teachers you owned a cabin or were just renting one?"

She thought back. "Renting."

"Well," he said with a triumphant smile, "you're not really lying at all, are you?"

No, she supposed she wasn't. But she would still be lying to herself.

"You really want me to do this?" she said.

"Because I'm confident it will work. Besides, I was serious when I asked you if I was invited. I wouldn't mind a weekend away with a beautiful woman."

Katrina didn't say anything. *Right in the practical sense.*

"So?" he pressed.

"What if there aren't any places for rent?"

"Let's check right now."

The hotel room was furnished with knotty pine furniture, a fireplace, a king bed, a kitchenette, a cabinet holding a large TV, and a Jacuzzi tub built for two. There was no computer. Jack, however, had an IBM laptop, which he set up. He asked to use her Visa to pay the five-dollar fee for Wi-Fi access, saying he'd lost his card and was waiting for a replacement. He logged onto the Internet. While she made two coffees, he found a vacation rental site that listed cabins for rent in the area.

"Apparently Lake Wenatchee is a popular vacation spot," he said, scrolling through several pages of listings. "See anything you like?"

She shrugged. "Any one will do. It's not like I'm buying it."

Jack clicked on a link for a newly renovated luxury alpine villa. He began reading, "Outdoor hot tub, satellite TV, granite counters, cathedral ceilings, dishwasher—"

"Enough," Katrina said. "Next."

Jack shot her an incredulous look. "You kidding? This place is perfect."

"I told everyone it was just a cabin."

"Tell them you were being modest."

"I said there wasn't even furniture." She shook her head. "No, Jack. I can't. This one is ridiculous."

"It definitely would be romantic."

"This isn't a game," she said, a little more forcefully than she'd intended. "I still don't even think it's a good idea." But those were just words, and she knew it. The more she thought about what Jack had proposed, the more she believed it was an ideal solution. She placed a hand on his shoulder affectionately.

"Okay, okay," he conceded. "I hear you. How about this one then? Lakefront property. A-frame, true log cabin with loft. Open living/dining room with country kitchen, laundry cubby, and one bath. Nearby amenities: horseshoes, mountain biking, rock climbing, freshwater fishing." He looked up at her, eyebrows raised.

"How many bedrooms?"

"Just one. The loft."

"That sounds more like it."

Jack checked the availability. "You want it, it's yours."

"How much?"

He shook his head. "I talked you into this. I'll cover the expenses."

"How much, Jack?"

He clicked a link. "Weekly rates go from $740 to $850. And look at that—nightly rates. $120 midweek, $150 weekends. But like I said, I'll pay."

"You will not. This is my problem."

"Do you want it?"

She thought of a hundred reasons why she should say no.

"Okay," she told him. "Book it."

Later that night Katrina awoke bathed in sweat, jerked into a sitting position as if from an invisible hook. A scream too big for her throat never made it out of her mouth. All that emerged was a strangled cry. The world seemed to tilt before righting itself. She was breathing hard and fast as she recalled the gruesome images that had been crawling through her head.

It was the same nightmare that had plagued her sleep ever since Shawn had passed away. In it she and Shawn were chained to a wall in a dirty, windowless dungeon. The big wooden door would creak open ever so slowly, as if the person on the other side was taunting her with the suspense. A faceless man would appear. She would watch in frozen horror as he cut and pulled Shawn apart like a chicken on a cutting board. The images were so disturbing she didn't know where her mind could have dredged them up from.

She heard the ticktock of a wall clock, loud in the otherwise silent room. *Ticktock-ticktock-ticktock.* It went on and on, perfect and indifferent. Slowly the overwhelming sense of dread drained from her body, leaving in its wake a bottomless despair.

"You okay?"

Katrina started. She had completely forgotten she was in Jack's bed. After they'd booked the cabin, he'd taken her to dinner—this time to a wonderful French restaurant—then they'd returned to his hotel where they'd made love with, if possible, more passion and abandonment than the first time. She looked at him. The blinds were open a crack, and enough glossy moonlight seeped into the room for her to make out the strong lines that delineated his face. Handsome and strong and, God, so attractive. He was lying on his back, propped up on his elbows, his head cocked toward her. He'd taken his ponytail out earlier, and his hair now fell down over his shoulders like a silky lion's mane. He reminded her of the blacksmith in the romance novel she was reading. Only Jack was infinitely more interesting and complex. Knowing she was not alone, the emptiness in the bottom of her stomach vanished. "No, I'm fine," she told him. "Go back to sleep."

"Bad dream?"

"Yes," she admitted.

He sat up next to her and took a hand. "Want to talk it off?"

"No. But thank you."

"I'm a good listener."

She knew he was. "Thanks, Jack. But go back to sleep." The veil of darkness made her feel secure, like she could tell him the deepest secrets of her heart. But she remained hesitant about opening up to him. She wasn't ready to talk about Shawn yet. Soon, maybe, if their relationship continued along the same light-ning-fast track it had been on. But not yet. "You've already done so much for me," she added. "More than you know."

"Remember," he said. "I'm here for you."

She nodded but didn't say anything more. She didn't trust her-self to speak. Those last four words were the most reassuring thing he, or anyone for that matter, could have told her. She felt like a castaway who had not only finally hit shore, but had found some-one waiting there on the beach for her.

She lay back down, pulling herself against Jack's hard body so they felt like one, and vowed she would always be there for him as well.

Chapter 10

Saturday morning.

Katrina was sitting on her front porch, drinking a freshly brewed cup of coffee, trying not to think too much about the evening's upcoming event, when her cell phone rang.

It was Zach.

"Just a quick question," he said cheerfully, almost cockishly. "I went ahead and chartered the school bus. But I need to give the driver directions to your place."

"Aren't you the go-to man?" she said, allowing sarcasm to edge her voice.

"Yeah, well, someone had to do it."

"Did you find out who made that sign-up sheet?"

"Nope. I asked around. No one knew."

"Guess I'll never know."

"Guess not."

"So you want the directions?"

There was a moment of stunned silence.

"Uh, yeah." She could almost hear him frowning. "If you have them."

"Why wouldn't I, Zach? It's my cabin, right?"

She gave him the directions.

"All right, cool," he said hesitantly. "So we can show up around seven?"

"That's fine."

"Okay. I guess that's it then."

"That's it."

"See you tonight, Kat."

"I told you not to call me that."

"Er, right. Later."

They hung up.

Although certain friends had called Katrina "Kat" her entire life, she hadn't liked Zach calling her it back on the highway, and that fact still hadn't changed.

She finished her coffee while watching a yellow warbler foraging on her front lawn, then went back inside and rinsed her mug out in the kitchen sink. She was trying to decide whether she was hungry or not when a car horn honked outside. She returned to the living room and peeked through the front window. A beetle-black Porsche was parked behind her Honda. It was sleek looking with a swoopy nose, those distinctive headlamps, and a discreet rear spoiler. She'd noticed the same car parked out front the Blackbird Lodge yesterday, but she'd never suspected it belonged to Jack. He was a surprise that kept getting better and better.

The driver's door opened and Jack stepped out, dressed in chinos, a white linen shirt beneath a cream-colored cardigan, and boat shoes a shade lighter than his brown leather belt. He looked like he'd just stepped off a yacht docked in Monte Carlo.

Katrina rubbed the top of Bandit's head. He was lying in the middle of the floor, sulking. When he'd noticed her packing earlier, he'd worked himself into a frenzied excitement, assuming they were going on another road trip together. When he didn't see his leash go into the suitcase, his frantic energy dissipated, and he began making heartbreaking whining noises. "I'm only going to be gone for one night, buddy. You got all the food and water you need in your bowls. But *no* chewing the furniture. Got it?" That was a bad habit of his, a way of letting her know he was not happy being left on his own. "Come on, give Mommy a kiss."

She lowered her cheek to his snout. He gave her a halfhearted lick.

"That's a good boy."

She grabbed her suitcase and stepped out the front door. Jack was now on the porch, leaning against the banister. He might be dressed like he'd just stepped out of a James Bond movie, but he looked very relaxed and casual at the same time, as if he'd thrown on the first thing he'd pulled out of his wardrobe. She couldn't say the same for herself. She'd put on her makeup, washed it off, and put it on all over again, to get it perfect. Then it had taken her nearly an hour to decide on her present outfit, a three-quarter-length dress with butterflies and matching butterfly jewelry.

Jack complimented her on how she looked, which made her light up. He took her suitcase and stuffed it in the Porsche's tiny trunk.

"Pretty impressive wheels," she said.

He opened the door for her. "320-horsepower 3.4-liter flat six. I'm a car guy."

"And a gentleman," she said, slipping inside.

Katrina had never been in a Porsche before—the closest thing would have been Shawn's Lexus—and she quickly realized why people who had the money bought one. The engine purred with effortless ease, and the ride down Wheeler Street was smooth as silk, making any other car she'd been in seem a laboring beast in comparison. They made a tight right onto Ski Hill Drive. The tires bit into the road while the snug sports seat held her firmly in place. When they made a right onto Highway 2, Jack kept to the speed limit as they passed a Howard Johnson and a Best Western and all the other hotels positioned at the westernmost point of town to be the first to greet visitors coming in from Seattle. As soon as they passed Icicle Road and there was nothing around them except hills and trees, he stepped on the gas. The sports car bulleted forward.

"Any preference for music?" Jack asked her, taking a pair of Ray-Bans clipped to the sun visor and putting them on.

"What do you have?"

He nodded at the digital interface on the dash. It was touch-screen and synced with his iPod, which he told her was stowed away in the center console. Pretty neat. It made her want to trade in her Honda. She scrolled through the exhaustive list of artists.

He had a little bit of everything and a lot of classic rock, which suited her mood. She tapped a Buffalo Springfield song, and the opening chords came through the speakers.

She said, "So this guy—Charlie?—is meeting us at the cabin when?"

"Supposed to be there at nine. We should be right on time."

The morning was crisp and blue, the sun a gold coin burning brightly in the east. The countryside was sprayed with a fiery blast of autumn colors: a field of orange huckleberry bushes, mustard-yellow alpine larches and aspen, deep-red vine maple. The towering sugar-peaked mountains remained rooted in the background, unmoving, millennium-old monoliths seemingly impervious to human concepts of time and speed.

"So you must be doing well to buy toys like this," she said, patting the leather seat of the sports car.

"I'm actually between jobs right now." He shifted to fifth and overtook a green sedan. They must have been doing more than seventy miles an hour, though Katrina felt perfectly safe, which was due either to the well-engineered car or Jack's assertive driving. Probably a little bit of both.

"What did you do before?" she asked. "No—let me guess. Bank robber? International assassin? Treasure hunter?"

"Nothing so glamorous, I'm afraid. I used to own a small gym. A ring, some punching bags, weights. When I retired from that, I made some decent investments. They paid off well."

Katrina was slightly disappointed by the mundane revelation. Jack had been an enigma to her. Uniquely handsome, larger-than-life personality, a drifter. All the ingredients for intrigue and mystery. The fact he was an ordinary guy with an ordinary background seemed anticlimactic. Almost like finding out your favorite movie star was a foot shorter in real life. Nevertheless, she had to admit she was partly relieved. There was no future with a man who lived a secret life, but there was with one who paid taxes, obeyed laws, and perhaps even went to church.

Future? she thought, feeling a warm buzz inside her that was equally wonderful and frightening.

"Do you go to church?" she asked.

He glanced at her. She could see a tiny version of herself reflected in his mirrored lenses. "That's out of the blue."

"It just popped into my head."

"As a matter of fact, I do."

"Catholic? Protestant?"

"Whichever one goes to midnight Mass on Christmas."

She smiled. Two out of three wasn't bad.

"So you owned a gym," she said, wanting to glean some more information out of him. "Does that mean you know how to box?"

"I'm no Mike Tyson." He held up a tattooed forearm. "I'd have to get one of these on my face if I was. But sure, I box. Started with karate, actually. Did some judo. Then got into kickboxing and boxing."

"A fighter? I never would have guessed." He had the physique for it, no question. But he seemed too refined, too articulate and worldly to once have been involved in such brutal sports.

"Don't underestimate anyone," he told her. "I learned that the hard way."

"But why fighting?"

In a thick Rocky Balboa accent he said, "Because I can't sing or dance." They laughed. He asked her, "What about you? Have you always been a teacher?"

She nodded. "I love kids. Always have." For a moment a cloud passed in front of her sunny disposition as that nesting instinct took hold inside her once again. The one thing she wanted most in life—a child of her own—still seemed so impossibly far away.

"Even the older ones?" Jack asked. "They don't drive you crazy?"

"You just have to know how to handle them. It's not their fault they're teenagers." On the stereo "For What It's Worth" finished and was followed by "Mr. Soul." "You know what? I don't even know where you're from."

"You're very inquisitive this morning."

"I'm sorry. I—"

Jack dismissed her apology with a wave, took off his sunglasses, and jumped into his life story. He was born in Colorado to an Ojibwa mother and a Caucasian lumberjack father, who'd been a violent drunk. At the age of two, Jack was diagnosed with leukemia. For the next few years he grew up in a hospital ward where, day after day, he was subjected to the crying of mothers over their dying children. "It was pure grief," he said, uncharacteristically subdued. "I mean, there was grief everywhere. I learned not to make friends because they would probably be dead the next day or week. But I beat the cancer. I think I must have been about five when I left the place. I was the only one in my ward who survived."

"God, Jack."

"You think it would get better after that, right? Things could only get better? Well, they didn't. Not really. My mom and pop fought all the time. Screaming, calling the cops on each other, you name it. Sometimes it got ugly. I mean, bloody ugly. For seventeen years that's pretty much all I heard. I'd been hearing grief all my life, I guess you could say. But if there's a bright side to any of it, it's that their constant fighting was the impetus that got me into karate. I needed to get out of the house. More than that, I needed to get all my anger out. The therapy became an addiction. When I got a bit older, I started getting into tournaments, some legal, some not. I made some money, opened a gym. You know the rest."

"I had no idea," Katrina said, breaking the trance she'd been under. "I didn't mean to pry."

"Don't worry about it," he said with a wink. "It was a long time ago. I was a kid. I'm as good as new now." That trademark wink of his, she thought, was as much a part of him as his long hair and tattoos. It made an intimidating rock of a man approachable, the way a popular uncle could always break the ice with his nieces and nephews. It also summed up his outgoing personality more than any words could, and it erased any awkwardness she'd felt about pressuring him into revealing his past—a past he might want to keep private.

"Did you like it?" she asked. "The fighting?"

"Quick and easy answer, no. I didn't like beating up on guys. Didn't like the destruction. I'm a sensitive guy, believe it or not.

When I saw an opponent after a fight, all bloodied up and everything, I felt bad for him, really bad. I did it because I was good at it."

"But you left it."

"Doing something you don't like for a bit is okay, I think. You learn from it. Learn what you like and don't like. But then you move on, take that knowledge with you, and apply it to a different situation. If you don't, well, if you don't that's a little sad. You got one shot at life. Why waste it? I'd rather live my life regretting certain choices I made rather than regretting choices I *never* made, if you get what I mean?"

She thought she did.

"I have to tell you though," he went on. "I don't usually get caught up talking about the past. So if you have any more questions, I suggest you ask them now while I'm on a roll."

"Just one. Why Leavenworth? Why are you here?"

"Like I said. I was just passing through."

"Where are you going?"

He shrugged. "Haven't decided."

Katrina wanted a better answer than that, but he'd just revealed so much about himself, while she'd yet to tell him anything about her past. She figured it would be best to wait for another time. And perhaps, on some level, she didn't want him to tell her what his plans were, because there was a strong possibility, given how short a time they'd known each other, those plans didn't include her.

That thought shook her, hard.

Twenty minutes later they passed a fun-looking place called Squirrel Tree Resort, then turned right onto State Route 207. They took this all the way up into Lake Wenatchee State Park, where they turned down some rutted back roads, which were definitely not made for low-riding sports cars. Eventually they pulled up to the A-frame log cabin. It was in a little disrepair, but it felt like a cabin should feel, as opposed to the multimillion-dollar cottages that were popping up all over the country—or the alpine villa, for that matter, which Jack had tried to talk her into renting.

Jack pulled up beside a silver pickup truck parked out front, and they got out of the car. Katrina breathed deeply the fresh mountain air. She didn't think she'd ever tire of doing that. An elderly man dressed in black cords and a black turtleneck and leaning on a polished cane limped out the front door. His thinning gray hair was cut close to the scalp, and a few liver spots stood out on his skin. He peered at them through rimless eyeglasses. Katrina's first thought was of Steve Jobs in his last few months. "You made it," he announced, then broke into a coughing fit.

"We did," Jack said, crossing the distance between them and shaking hands. "I'm Jack Reeves. This here is Katrina Burton."

"Howdy," the man said. "I'm Charlie. I don't got much time. Got to get me to a goddamn funeral. Seems like I'm going to more 'n' more of 'em each year. Soon it's gonna be me. Who's gonna come? No one, cause they're all fuckin' dead. But come in, I'll give you the tour. Don't mind your shoes."

The cabin was rougher around the edges than the Internet advertisement led prospective renters to believe, but Katrina liked it. A wagon-wheel chandelier hung from the cathedral ceiling above the open living/dining room, which featured a stone fireplace, an uncomfortable-looking patched sofa, and a rocking chair with ottoman. Mounted on one wall was a stuffed deer head, its beady eyes staring off into nothingness. The kitchen contained the bare necessities: scarred fridge, ancient stove, stainless-steel sink, and two sets of cupboards. Katrina poked her head in the bathroom and discovered an unremarkable toilet and sink along with an old-fashioned, claw-footed tub, which made her think momentarily of her bathroom back in Leavenworth, and the creep who'd been looking in. A narrow flight of dangerously steep steps led to the second-floor loft. It was stuffed to capacity with a queen bed and a small night table on which sat a blinking alarm clock. The smell of old wood and old blankets hung over everything, musty but not unpleasant.

"This little baby's been in the family for years," Charlie told them. "Grandpa built it, oh, say, must've been just after the Depression. I came up here all the time as a wee pecker, and when the folks went knockin' on heaven's door, it came to me. That's Bob Dylan, ain't it? Anyway, it's the only thing they left me worth two shits. I don't got no brothers or sisters. Glad not to." He whipped out a handkerchief to smother a coughing fit that left him looking shaky. "Fuckin' cold," he explained. "That's why I'm renting. We live in Skykomish. The missus don't want me out here in the fall or winter. No insulation. No central heating. Holy shit. Thinks I'll get pneumonia. Get yourself pneumonia, she says, and you best go sleep in your grave 'cause you'll be dead soon enough. Goddamn women. Can't stand 'em. No offense, ma'am."

"None taken." Katrina handed him the one hundred and fifty she'd withdrawn from the ATM last night.

Charlie counted it, then frowned. "Didn't I mention the deposit?"

"What deposit?" Jack asked.

"Hell if I didn't," Charlie said reflectively, scratching his bald head. "Can't trust my memory no more. I need another hundred deposit. Never used to ask, but last year I rented her out to two college boys over Memorial Day weekend. Said they just wanted to do some fishin', hikin'. I don't care, I said. Just as long as I get my money. You know what them kids end up doin'? Havin' a big old party. Twenty friends, I reckon. Helluva mess. Goddamn beer spilled over the floor, cigarette butts everywhere you looked, bottles behind every rock 'n' tree. Probably pissed wherever them little peckers wanted to, I bet. Kids nowadays got no damn respect for nothing. Not even the dead. Am I right? Sure I am. Thank the Lord they didn't burn the fucker down. But I learned my lesson, I'll tell you that. Don't rent to no snot-nosed kids no more. That's why all the questions last night."

"So no parties, huh?" Jack said lightly but cautiously.

"Hell no! But you look like a respectable fella, am I right?"

"The best." Jack took two fifties from his wallet and gave them to the old man. "All we have in mind is a little romantic weekend. Here you go. One hundred for the deposit."

Charlie took the money and stuffed it in his pocket. He gave them a final, lengthy appraisal before handing over a single key and bidding farewell. He limped down to his pickup truck, hiked himself inside, and drove off with a toot of the horn.

"Why'd you do that?" Katrina said to Jack as they watched the truck disappear into the trees.

He looked at her. "Do what?"

"Tell him it's just us here? We should have told him we're having some friends over."

"You heard him talk. He's a crazy bastard. He might have told us to go to hell. Besides, what does it matter? He's never going to know if we have people over or not. And we're not a bunch of rowdy college kids throwing some big bender. I'll keep an eye on everybody. Afterward I'll make sure the cabin is spotless before we leave."

What he said made sense. Despite his assurances, however, a bad premonition had stolen over her, sending a chill down her spine. She eyed him speculatively.

"It's no big deal," he insisted.

"I don't like it, that's all."

"What's not to like? Look around. Smell the air."

"It's just another lie," she said, and she almost wanted to laugh. She felt like someone waist deep in quicksand. The more she struggled to free herself, the deeper she sank.

"You're worrying too much," Jack told her, taking her hand. "Everything is going to be fine."

Katrina hoped he was right.

Chapter 11

It was seven thirty p.m. and the sun was dipping behind the mountains in the west, throwing long, scarlet streaks across the sky. The yellow school bus bumped and chugged its way down a back road bordered by towering aspen and moss-covered maple trees. Inside it the atmosphere was buzzing and upbeat and expectant. The female teachers were lumped up by the driver, gossiping and chatting about whatever women gossiped and chatted about on buses. Dolly had a guitar and sometimes she would strum a few chords and get everyone singing. The men were grouped together in the middle of the bus, separated from the women, like they were at a high school dance and afraid of catching cooties. They were telling ribald jokes and popping beer cans, each trying to get a word in over the other. Big Bob was winning, commanding the most attention as usual as he reminisced over past ice-fishing trips to Lake Wenatchee.

Zach was sitting at the very back of the bus, watching all this with an odd combination of contempt and envy. It was the feeling you got when you were looking at something from the outside in. He didn't fit in with them, didn't really want to, to be honest, but still felt a mild longing. He would have felt better if the not fitting in was his decision, not theirs. But whatever. They were all a bunch of country, go-nowhere hicks. He didn't want to hang out with them anyway. He cracked open his sixth Beck's and took a swallow. Cold and good. He'd had four before he left his house—no way was he getting on a bus with thirty people stone sober; he'd likely have one of his panic attacks inside of five minutes—and then two more on the road, including this one.

He thought again about the phone conversation with Katrina earlier this morning. He'd been walloped by the fact she really did have a cabin. When he'd hung up, he'd been embarrassed as well—so embarrassed he'd considered not coming tonight. He'd felt how Donald Trump likely felt when the president released his birth certificate. Still, he decided to come because he couldn't not come. His obsession with Katrina didn't end because it turned out she hadn't been lying. In fact, that only made his obsession stronger—because it meant she hadn't kicked him out of the car because she thought he was a drunk and a freak. She'd genuinely taken him as far as she could.

Did that mean it was time to finally bury the hatchet? Yes, he thought it did. Maybe then they could even become friends. And maybe if they became friends, they could become more than friends—

In the middle of the bus, Graham Douglas stood and started making his way down the aisle toward the back. He was grabbing each seat for balance, resembling someone wading through waist-deep water. He took the seat across from Zach, leaned forward, unzipped his pants, and pissed into an empty beer bottle. "There's no toilet on this thing, man," he said to Zach without looking at him. "What the fuck do they expect you to do? Piss out the window?" He did up his pants, stuffed the full bottle in the crack where the seat met the side of the bus, then reached across the aisle and snagged one of Zach's Beck's.

Graham worked with Monica in the Music Department and was one of the more popular teachers at the school. He sang in some garage band that apparently played the occasional gig around the state. He was older than Zach, maybe twenty-six or seven, and with his red afro, mustache, and muttonchops he was one of the ugliest fuckers Zach knew. He dressed like he was from the seventies as well, with tie-dye shirts and bell-bottoms. Zach always thought he looked like he'd just stepped out of the Fleetwood Mac lineup. He twisted the cap off the beer, took a swig, and said, "How dope is tonight going to be, Zachy-boy? Bob-O brought a couple fishing rods. See if we can't catch some pike. You fish, Zachy-boy?"

Zach merely shrugged. He hated that nickname. It was a dig at him, a condescending reminder he was by far the youngest teacher at the school.

"What's wrong, Zachy-boy? Cat caught your tongue? By the way, why the hell are you sitting way back here by yourself? We're missing your deep philosophy shit. Seriously. You're a whack kid, you know that? Who else knows so much about the next stage of evolution, right?"

Graham was making fun of him. Zach would have known that even if the smug amusement wasn't written all over Graham's face. At a party last year, Zach had gotten pretty drunk and he'd somehow gotten sucked into a discussion about evolution with Henry Lee, a science teacher at the school. Zach had gone on about how human bodies were replaceable if not altogether obsolete, how the next step in evolution was going to be a hive-like interconnection of cyborgs in a metaconsciousness, a necessity step to outcompete the super-intelligent robots mankind will create à la *The Matrix*. "If you can't beat computers and robots, then join them!" he must have slurred half a dozen times. A group of teachers had formed around him, and he'd thought they were genuinely interested in what he was saying. They weren't. They'd been mocking him, egging him on, like Graham was doing now. He discovered that the following Monday at school by the looks he got, the laughing behind his back.

"Fuck off, Graham," he said.

"Whoa, man! What's up with you? I'm telling you the real deal. We're missing you up there. After all, we got you to thank for organizing this little shi-bam, right?"

Zach felt a shot of panic. "What are you talking about?"

"The RSVP thing. That was you, wasn't it?"

"No," he said immediately. "Why do you think that?"

"No one really knows her yet, except you. Hey, is she single?"

"Who? Katrina?"

"Does she have guns?"

"What?"

"What the hell's wrong with you, Zachy-boy? Jugs, cannons, norks, gunzagas. *Tits*, Zach. What do they call 'em on your planet? She has a thing for suits and I haven't gotten a good look. Sexy all right. But a little prissy, if you ask me."

Suddenly Zach felt extremely protective of Katrina. "You don't have a chance," he said.

Graham grinned, looking a bit like a clown. "We'll see, won't we?" He patted Zach on the shoulder, then headed back to join Bob and the others in the center of the bus.

Zach watched him go, and all of a sudden he felt queasy and lightheaded. His eyes started to water and blur. He groped at the window and yanked down the upper pane of glass, letting in a sharp gust of wind. He breathed deeply and steadily, counting to ten, then twenty. He began to feel better again. He looked up the aisle. Thankfully no one had noticed his episode. They didn't know he suffered from agoraphobia and panic attacks. They would have assumed he'd drunk himself silly before the party even started again.

Assholes.

A short time later the bus shuddered to a halt. This was accompanied by a rising buzz of excited chatter. Zach peered through the window. A small log cabin was ahead of them, facing the shadowy expanse of a lake. He grabbed his six-pack of beer, which now only had three remaining in it, and his knapsack, which contained his harder booze, then followed the noisy procession off the bus. He started toward the cabin but stopped abruptly when the cabin's front door opened and Katrina appeared to greet everyone. Because right behind her was some macho-type guy with long dark hair and a big white smile. He hooked an arm around Katrina's shoulder and welcomed them all to the party.

Chapter 12

It didn't take long for the party to get bopping. Crystal, who Katrina and Jack had picked up from the bus station earlier in the day, after meeting Charlie, cranked up Janis Joplin—cottage music, she said—as soon as the bus arrived. The teachers came inside in a wave, stuffing the fridge with beer and mixers and laying out hors d'oeuvres and other food on the kitchen table. Soon you couldn't hear yourself speak. Not surprisingly, Jack had no problem socializing with a roomful of strangers. In fact, with his hearty greetings and easygoing charm, his ability to work the room and make everyone feel welcome, he quickly became the center of attention. He was currently swapping fishing tales with Big Bob, who didn't look so big anymore standing next to Jack. Katrina already had three female teachers poke her naughtily or give her a you-sly-dog-you expression. Monica was the most blunt, saying, "My God, he's a big block of sex wearing pants," as her eyes gobbled him up.

Katrina bit back a smile and thought she was the luckiest woman in the room that night. For something she'd been dreading all week, it seemed the party might just turn out okay after all, and she was amazed to find she was even having fun.

Crystal made her way over holding two drinks. She handed one to Katrina. "Vodka soda with lime," she said. She bore a striking resemblance to Katrina, even though she had brown hair and chestnut-colored eyes. Katrina had always thought this. So did most other people who knew them both. It was likely the shape of their faces, which were both hearts with pointed chins. The biggest difference between the two of them was Katrina was thin while Crystal was more on the plus side. Crystal called herself plump—not fat, she would acknowledge, but plump, like a cute baby, a little too soft around the thighs and hips and waist to feel comfortable in a bikini. Katrina always assumed this negative self-image Crystal lugged around was one of the reasons she had become such a recluse after their parents' death, and why she now had an aversion to college, where image was paramount.

She sipped her drink. "Not bad. I hope you're not going to drop out of school and take up bartending?"

"No," Crystal said. "But it doesn't sound like a bad idea."

"It's just going to take a couple weeks to adjust. Once it does, you'll have a fantastic time."

"I know. But I can't say I'm going to miss it this weekend. This cabin is awesome."

Katrina gave her a stern look. She and Jack had already explained to Crystal everything that had happened to lead Katrina to rent out the cabin and pass it off as her own. They'd warned her not to say a word about it, to anyone. She'd seemed intrigued by the subterfuge and had promised to keep it a secret.

"Okay. Okay," Crystal added. "Don't worry. I get it. So where's this crazy Zach guy anyway?"

Katrina had been wondering that herself. She'd glimpsed him briefly out by the bus when everyone had arrived, but then she'd been swept up in a mob of greetings and had completely forgotten about him. She looked around the room and spotted him through one of the front windows, outside, standing on the porch. "There," she said, nodding.

Crystal's eyes widened. "You didn't tell me he was so good looking."

"He's not," Katrina said flatly.

"Sure he is. He looks like—I don't know. Someone famous."

Wasn't that what she had thought too? A young Rod Stewart or Ronnie Woods? "Don't even think about it, Chris. He's not your type." Watching Zach, Katrina realized she should go have a word with him. After all, she'd pulled off this grand scheme mainly for his benefit. It was important to see whether he was buying it or not. She said, "I'm going to go talk to him for a second."

"Can I come?"

"Listen, Chris. You're to stay away from him. Don't even talk to him. Got it?"

"Why?" she said saucily. "Is he *dangerous*?"

"You heard me."

Crystal seemed as if she was about to protest, but she merely took a sip of her drink and shrugged. Katrina went outside and joined Zach on the porch. He was wearing jeans and a long-sleeved shirt. A cigarette was parked in the corner of his mouth, a beer bottle in his hand. The sixty-watt lightbulb dangling a pull chain glowed in the dark above him, attracting a fury of moths.

"Hi, Zach," she said. "I didn't know you smoked."

He glanced sidelong at her, shrugged.

"What are you doing out here—"

"Who's the Indian?"

She blinked, surprised by his directness. "His name is Jack Reeves. He's half Ojibwa."

"Looks like he just escaped from jail." He flicked the cigarette away into the night, then turned toward her for the first time. Sharp shadows hollowed out his cheeks and blacked out his eyes, making the orbits appear to be two dark pits. "Are you dating him?"

"I don't know if that's any of your business, Zach."

"He looks like he rapes little boys."

"That's enough, Zach," she said, realizing it was a mistake to come out here.

"What about me?"

"What about you?"

"Would you ever date me?"

The comment rocked her. *Date you?* She couldn't have been more astonished if someone had told her she had a twin sister. She'd been under the very clear impression that he *hated* her, not *liked* her. But now that the question had been raised, it took on a reality very quickly, and she realized maybe it shouldn't be such a shock; maybe it had been staring her in the face the past few days, and she just hadn't been looking. After all, those two emotions—

like and hate—were probably more interchangeable than any other two. How many guys had she despised when she was younger after they'd broken her heart? How many guys had she felt bitterness toward because they were out of her league?

"Zach—" she said, not knowing what else to say.

Suddenly he stepped toward her, closing the space between them in a single stride. The shadows fled from his face, and she could see his eyes clearly. They were glassy, the way they'd been a week ago in her car. For a moment she thought he might hit her. Although the intensity that radiated off him frightened her, it was not the white terror she'd felt when she was trapped alone on the highway with him. Then, she hadn't known him, and there hadn't been anyone to rescue her if things turned bad. Here, if he tried something, she might get a bruise, maybe even a black eye or a bleeding lip, but all she had to do was yell. Someone would hear.

"Answer me," he hissed. "If you weren't fucking that Indian, would you go out with me?"

"Zach, you're far too young—"

Before she could finish, however, he shoved past her. He yanked open the front door and disappeared inside, swallowed by the buzz of many conversations and the blare of music. Katrina rolled her eyes, then started after him. It seemed he was heading toward the laundry, where everyone had stored their jackets and bags.

She reached out and touched his shoulder. "Zach, wait—"

He spun, rolling his shoulder as if her fingers were acid. "Don't touch me," he growled.

She held up her hands defensively and tried to think of the best way to get him to calm down. She became aware that everyone had stopped talking and were gawking at the two of them. Someone turned down the stereo. A hush fell over the room. It was as if Butch Cassidy and the Wild Bunch Gang had just sauntered in through the batwing doors of some old Western saloon. Zach didn't seem to care. He continued to glower at her with unchecked rage.

"Come outside," she said softly, hoping this wasn't going to turn into an even bigger scene yet knowing it was. "We'll talk out there."

"About what? About *Jack*? Where is he?" He looked around the room.

Jack appeared, cool and collected. He had a faint smile on his face, as if he was amused by the happenings. He glanced at Katrina, tipping her an imperceptible nod that seemed to say, "I'll take care of this." He stopped in front of Zach. "I think you and I should go outside, friend."

Zach swung the beer bottle in his hand. Foaming ale sprayed in an arc, splashing those standing closest to him. A woman shrieked. Jack didn't flinch. He brought his right hand up with amazing speed and caught Zach's wrist about a foot from his face. He twisted the wrist sharply. Zach grunted and dropped the bottle, which smashed on the floor. He thrust his arm under Zach's armpit and grabbed a fistful of his shaggy hair. "Let's go, pal," he said.

"Let go of me!" Zach shouted. "Get your motherfucking Indian hands off me!"

"Jack," Katrina said urgently. "Be gentle. Please."

But Jack was already shoving Zach roughly forward, toward the front door, like a bouncer escorting a drunk from the club. Zach continued to spew off more curses, but he couldn't free himself. Both men disappeared outside. The door slapped the frame with a loud, flat crack. Silence hung in the air until someone snickered. Katrina saw it was Graham.

"That kid is so friggin' messed up it ain't funny," he said.

"No, it's *not* funny, Graham," Katrina told him, glaring at him until he wiped the smile off his face and looked suitably ashamed. She went toward the door, people parting before her. As soon as she stepped outside, she heard the voices behind her raise as one in a swell of excited babble. The music was turned up again.

Jack was standing down at the bottom of the porch steps, by himself. Past him Katrina could make out the silhouette of Zach as he stumbled in the direction of the school bus. She started to follow, but Jack gently restrained her.

"Leave him," he said.

"I need to talk to him."

"He needs to be alone. Sober up a little. What was that about anyway?"

She shook her head. "It seems he's a little jealous of you."

"Jealous? You mean he *likes* you? You made him out to be your archenemy."

"I guess it was a little more complicated than I thought."

"Well, that adds a twist to things, doesn't it?"

"I really think I should go talk to him."

"Later," Jack said decisively, and took her hand. "Now come back inside. You're missing your own party."

Chapter 13

Crystal Burton was stretched out on an adjustable sling chair down at the dock where the party had migrated after the scene with Jack and that Zach fellow inside. A couple of people were fishing off the end of the dock, but everyone else was sitting cross-legged in a circle, playing loud drinking games with a deck of cards. Apparently there was an "Asshole" and a "President," but that was the extent to which she was paying attention. One woman had become so obnoxiously drunk she was poison to listen to. She kept cackling like a witch at everything, only it seemed she was the only person who thought what she was hearing was funny. Across the lake pinpricks of light floated in the darkness—the lights from what Crystal assumed were other cabins, maybe a campground or two. To the west, a rocky point prickling with trees blocked her view, but along the eastern shore she could make out the shadowy form of another dock jutting out over the water. She could also see the outline of the corresponding cabin. Given the noise everyone was making, she hoped it was unoccupied.

She sipped her Seagram's Cooler and thought about what had happened earlier. She felt bad for Zach. After Jack had taken him outside, and Katrina had followed, everyone had erupted in conversation, some chastising Zach, most mocking and pitying him, saying he was a drunk and a joke and so on. Crystal had listened to it all with a grim look on her face. She knew what it was like to not fit in, to be the outsider.

Katrina thought her off-and-on isolation was self-imposed, a result of psychological scarring from their parents' death, a fear of making close friends because they might just disappear one day, or some Jungian mumbo jumbo like that. Perhaps it was true. All Crystal knew for sure was she'd never been good at making friends. She was not skinny enough for others to want to hang around her. Not confident enough to command attention. Not witty enough to be funny. Not chatty enough to be a mingler. That had been her high school story, and it seemed it was going to be her university one too, given she'd already failed to join any of the quickly forming cliques. It was pretty damn depressing. Everybody had friends. She didn't even have unpopular friends. Well, maybe Mary Wenders. They'd known each other since they were twelve, but Mary was in Texas now, attending college there.

Crystal sighed, sipped her drink, and saw a small flash of light on the neighboring dock. She squinted. Yes, a glowing red dot. The tip of a cigarette? Who could it be? The neighbors? Not likely. There were no lights on in the adjacent cabin, no glow lamps leading down to the dock. Someone from the party? But why would they go way over there—?

Zach, she realized. Probably counting down the minutes until it was time to head home.

Crystal returned to the cabin to grab another cooler. Jack and Kat were inside on the sofa, beneath the stuffed deer head. Jack had an arm around her shoulders while Kat had her knees pulled up to her chest.

"Hey guys," Crystal said. "How come you're not down at the dock?"

Jack said, "I have all the company I need right here."

Kat slapped him playfully. Crystal smiled. It was good to see her sister happy again after everything she'd been through with Shawn.

"What are you doing up here?" Kat asked.

"Just getting another drink. Want anything?"

She declined as Jack raised a bottle of white wine that had been sitting on the floor by their feet and refilled both their glasses. Crystal went to the ice box in the corner and took the last cooler from the four-pack she'd brought. She also snatched one of the numerous beers that were floating in the cold water. She crossed the living room to the front door.

"Since when do you drink beer?" Kat asked.

"I'm out of coolers," Crystal replied simply, then she was outside. She didn't return to the sling chair and the others but made her way east, toward where the school bus was parked. The night thickened around her as she left the light from the porch. She entered a copse of trees that blocked out most of the sky, so it was nearly completely black. She slowed but continued on. She assumed if she went far enough along the road, staying parallel to the lake, she would come to the neighboring dock. It turned out she was right. Fifty yards on the trees thinned. She could once again see the flat expanse of the lake and the neighbor's dock. This close she could make out the person she'd spotted earlier. She'd been right. It was Zach.

She followed a worn path down a rocky slope to the dock. Twigs snapped under her footfalls and small pebbles rolled into the water. She definitely wouldn't have made the cut at assassin school.

Zach heard her approach—he'd have to be deaf not to—and turned around. "Who's there?" he asked.

"My name's Crystal. Hi." She stopped next to him.

"Is this your place? I didn't think anyone was home—"

She shook her head. "No, I'm Katrina's sister. I came with her earlier."

Even in the poor light, she could see the surprise on his face. "You're her sister?"

"Heavier, I know. But a DNA test will prove it."

"No, it's not that. I just didn't realize—" His voice hardened. "Did she send you here to talk to me?"

"No," Crystal said quickly. "I was on the other dock and saw you light a cigarette."

"And?"

"And nothing," she said. "I just wanted to talk."

"Why?"

"I don't know. Do I need a reason?" She held forth the beer she'd taken from the fridge. "Want it?"

He hesitated, but accepted. There was a crack-sigh as he twisted off the cap.

"Sit down," he said. "You're making me nervous just standing there like that." She sat and he studied her. "How old are you?"

"Nineteen."

"That's a big age difference between you and your sister."

"Thirteen years, two months, fourteen days."

He took out a pack of Marlboros and offered her one.

"I don't smoke," she said.

"Me either. Quit last year. Found these on the bus. Thought what the hell." He took one out and lit it up. "I'm surprised your sister didn't warn you to stay away from me."

"Actually, she did."

He stared at her, long and hard. Then he shook his head. He didn't say anything more. Crystal was worried she'd put her foot in her mouth, so she said without thinking, "I heard you think we're all going to turn into cyborgs."

Zach's mouth dropped open. The cigarette almost fell out. "Are you kidding me?"

"What? No. I . . . I just overheard someone say that."

"Did they send you over here? Is this a goddamn joke?"

"What? No. Seriously. I'm so sorry." *Why was he so angry?* "Someone said something. I thought it sounded cool. I like that kind of stuff. Sci-fi, you know?" She almost jumped to her feet, to run away, but then Zach chuckled to himself. The chuckle became genuine laughter. He took a drag from the cigarette and laughed some more. She felt a bit more relaxed.

"I'm sorry," she apologized again. "I didn't know it was a sensitive subject."

"Whatever." He tossed the smoke into the lake. "I believe you."

"Can you tell me about it?"

He gave her a look that seemed to be assessing whether she was being genuine or not. Apparently he thought she was because he said, "You really want to know?"

"Like I said. I like that stuff."

So Zach told her his theory of evolution—or someone's theory, at any rate. It was pretty out there. It was also pretty cool. They talked a little bit about it, then got onto movies, then books, then movies again. It turned out they had a lot in common. And Zach wasn't what she'd imagined at all. He was funny and intelligent and, when you got past the walls he threw up, sweet even. She couldn't understand why nobody liked him.

"How's the party over there?" Zach asked, changing gears.

"Boring. I felt weird hanging out with teachers—I mean, I know you're one. But you're different."

Voices and laughter continued to float across the water, loud and brash. Someone had brought a portable stereo, and Eminem started rapping about what it was like to be white trash.

"Different?" he said. "What do you mean?"

"To begin with, you're not a dinosaur."

"Youngest teacher at the school. So people keep reminding me."

"How old are you?"

"Twenty-two."

"Yeah?" she said, knowing she was preparing herself to do something, though she wasn't sure what. "That's good. It's not too old."

"Too old for what?"

Crystal leaned toward Zach, thrilled and amazed—and terrified—by her sudden confidence. Her lips touched his. The thrill and amazement remained. The terrified part went up in smoke. She kissed him lightly, hesitated briefly, then kissed him harder. This was her first real kiss, and an explosion of relief rocked her as she realized she'd crossed the barrier. She was *doing* it. What had the big deal always been? Why had she always thought everything would have to be perfect? Perfect guy, perfect place, perfect evening? She was sitting on a dock with someone she'd just met, someone whom everyone else thought was a weirdo, but she was absolutely content.

Zach's hand brushed through her hair. It felt good. His hand slipped down her cheek, down her neck, and cupped her left breast. That felt even better.

In the distance she heard the engine of an approaching car.

Zach broke apart, looked toward the road, and frowned. "Who the hell's that?"

She blinked, a little fuzzy. *Who cares?* she wanted to say. *We were kissing!* "Someone who lives down the road?" she suggested.

"Isn't your cabin the last one on this road?"

"My cabin?"

"Whatever. Your sister's."

"It's not her—" She bit her lip.

Zach frowned. "Not her what?"

"Nothing."

"Not her cabin?"

"No, it is."

His frown deepened. "What's going on here?"

"Nothing. I told you."

"Why don't I believe you?"

"It's true."

The sound of the car grew louder. The high beams illuminated the nearby trees, turning them a ghostly gray. They both watched as the car—a light-colored pickup truck—passed by.

Zach shoved himself to his feet. "I'll be back in a minute."

"Where are you going?"

"To check it out."

"Why? Who cares?"

But he had already left, hurrying to catch up to the truck.

Chapter 14

Katrina and Jack both heard the vehicle approach. They looked at one other, each thinking the same thing. Who could it possibly be?

"I'll take a look," Jack said, going to the window.

"Who is it?" Katrina asked.

"You're not going to like this."

"Why? What?"

"Charlie's back."

Charlie? Old man Charlie? No-party Charlie? "God!" she exclaimed. She jumped off the sofa and joined Jack at the window. "What's *he* doing here?"

"I'll go find out."

Jack went out onto the porch. Katrina followed. Charlie slammed the truck door closed and limped, scowling, toward them. "You!" he spat, stopping at the bottom of the porch steps and waving his cane at Jack. "What did I tell you about havin' no goddamn parties?"

"A few people stopped by," Jack said evenly as the old man clumped up the steps. "They're all teachers from Cascade High School. Responsible folk. You have nothing to worry about. The place will be as good as new tomorrow morning."

Charlie pointed his cane toward the shouting and music coming from the lake. "Responsible folk, you say?" He almost spit the words out. "That don't sound like responsible folk to me. Sounds like a wagonload of college bastards. Am I right? Hell, yes! That's what the neighbors said. Ron calls me up and says, 'What the bloody hell is goin' on, Charlie? There's a roaring bender goin' full blast over at your place.' And he lives three cottages down, so I know whatever the fuck a bender is, it's somethin' loud enough to wake the dead, God rest 'em. I says, 'Don't worry, Ron, I'll take care of it.' And so I would. Got in the truck and came straight up here just as fast as I could. And I'm bleedin' glad too! Outta my way!"

Charlie whacked his cane at Jack's shins, then lurched past like a pirate walking with a peg leg. He shoved open the door and entered the cabin. Katrina and Jack followed. Looking around, Katrina wished she'd had time to clean up. Glasses and beer bottles were left haphazardly on every available surface. So too were paper plates stacked with leftover food. The table they'd brought from the kitchen to serve as the buffet was a mess. A pile of CDs was fanned out on the floor, next to a box of vinyl records someone had found and rifled through. A maze of dusty footprints led every which way. But it was the spot where Zach had broken his beer bottle that seemed to centerpiece the room. They'd picked up the larger pieces of glass and did their best to get all the smaller shards, then they'd soaked the beer out of the beech floor with a damp cloth. Katrina thought it would be fine in the morning, but at the moment the big dark puddle-shaped stain did not look fine at all. It looked like someone had urinated on the center of the floor.

"Mother of all hell!" Charlie exclaimed breathlessly, sounding like a man who'd just witnessed his own death. He cranked up the volume, "You've turned this place into a fuckin' pigpen!"

"I'd say that's a slight hyperbole," Katrina said.

"Hyper what?" Charlie whirled on her. "You some college smart ass too? Sure you are, and these are all your whore friends. Just 'cause you're young you think you got God's good grace to do any fuckin' thing you want. Well, I ain't going to take it. No sirree. I want you and all them friends of yours outta here. And don't you even think about askin' for your deposit back. Got that, sugar tits—"

Jack grabbed Charlie by the shoulder, pressing down on some pressure point. The old man cackled and bent sideways. With his eyes bulging and his mouth gaping, he looked like a man in his death throes. "Watch what you say to the lady," Jack warned him.

"Let him go, Jack!" Katrina said. "You're hurting him."

Jack released his grip. Charlie stumbled free, bringing his hand up to massage his shoulder. "That's assault, you son of a bitch!" he gasped. "And don't think I ain't gonna report it. I am. Lock your ass up in the slammer. You'll probably like that, won't you, you big ape? Trade this bitch in for—"

This time Jack had Charlie by the throat. He marched him toward the front door, keeping him at arm's length, like he was a leaky bag of garbage. The old man tripped over his own feet as he was shoved backward. He swung his cane wildly, hitting Jack a couple times, but Jack didn't seem to notice.

"Jack!" Katrina said. "Where are you taking him?"

"Stay inside," he told her over his shoulder. "I just want to have a little talk. Won't be a minute."

Charlie gurgled something unintelligible.

"No, Jack," she said. "Let him be. I'll go tell everyone to leave."

He paused at the threshold to look back. "And what reason are you going to give?"

"I don't know. I'll think of something."

"Wait here," he said, and his tone left no room for debate. The door closed and he was gone from sight.

Katrina brought her hands to her mouth, forming a steeple. She took a deep breath, playing over the confrontation. Jack had manhandled Charlie. An old man. True, Charlie was sexist and vulgar. But that didn't give Jack the right to treat him the way he had. It had scared her. Especially after he'd done the same thing to Zach less than an hour earlier.

She shook her head. Later. She'd talk to him about it later. Right now she had to clean up the cabin. She hurried to the kitchen, grabbed a plastic bag, and began collecting all the empty bottles and dirty plates, wondering the entire time what Jack was talking to Charlie about, and what else could possibly go wrong.

The simple answer, she would soon find out: everything.

Chapter 15

Jack strong-armed the struggling old man down the porch steps, all the way to the silver pickup truck. Charlie's eyes were wide and feral, showing something between fury and fear. When Jack figured he was far enough away from the cabin Katrina could not overhear him, he released his grip. This time old Charlie didn't have any fighting words. He doubled over, rubbed his throat, and tried to catch his sputtering, ailing breath. Jack grabbed him by the collar of his shirt and tugged him upright, so he could make eye contact. "I've been easy on you so far because there was a lady present," he said in a low, dangerous voice. "But it's just you and me now. And if I hear anything I don't like, I'm going to hurt you. Bad. Got that, compadre?"

Charlie glowered and rubbed his neck and didn't say anything.

"See, this night is special for me and my friend in there," Jack went on. "And I don't want anything or anybody to ruin it for her, especially a dirty old prick like you. So this is what I'm going to do. You and I are going to walk over to my car, like two civilized human beings. I'm going to get my wallet and I'm going to give you an extra two hundred dollars for your trouble of coming all the way down here. And then you're going to get into that nice Ford F-150 of yours and you're going to drive back home and you're going to enjoy the rest of your evening while we enjoy ours. I'll talk to the guests on the dock and tell them to keep it down. And tomorrow I'll personally see to it that this place is as new as it can be. Now what do you say? Do we have ourselves a deal?"

For a moment Charlie seemed like he was about to say something, and by the look on his face, it wasn't going to be something nice. But he reconsidered and began limping toward the Porsche. Jack joined him. The sound of Jim Morrison singing about a whiskey bar echoed up from the lake. Jack opened the sports car's front door, popped the glove compartment, and took out his wallet. As he was twisting out of the car, he saw the old man's cane slicing through the air. Pain exploded across his face in a firecracker show of blazing light. He staggered to one knee. The cane came again. This time down on the back of his skull. No stars. Just a soupy murkiness. He lost his balance and fell to his side.

"This ain't about no money, you goddamn monkey," he heard Charlie say, though the old man's voice was small and seemed to be coming from a place very faraway. "It's about respect. Ain't your daddy ever teach you about that? But I do believe I deserve somethin' for haulin' ass all the way up here. Holy Jesus! Look-ee here! I'd say five hundred just about covers it. Now, I'm going to go tell all your no-class friends to get off my fuckin' property. And maybe, if you're lucky, one of 'em will help you get your sorry ass together."

Silence. Bolts of pain throbbed behind Jack's face. It felt like someone had shoved a handful of searing needles up his nose. He could taste gritty, coppery blood—blood mixed with dirt. He tried moving a hand. It responded. He brought it to the back of his head. A golf-ball-size lump. He felt his face. It was tender to the touch. Anger burned inside him, burned away the blackness. He opened his eyes and saw he was facedown in the mud. He summoned all of his strength to push himself to his feet. He stood straight, almost toppled over, didn't. His vision was swimming, but he could see enough to make out old Charlie, twenty feet away, heading for the dock. Jack started after him, almost delirious in his zest for payback. With each step his strength returned. By the time he was looming tall behind Charlie, his eyes were inhuman in their intensity and manic anticipation.

Charlie turned too late. "Oh shit no—"

He never finished. Jack's hand shot forward, fist open, so the heel of his palm connected squarely with Charlie's nose. Cartilage crunched, making a popping sound, like when you crack your knuckles. Blood spurted. Charlie flew backward, lifted clear off his feet. He landed on his back, probably cracking one or two of his brittle bones in the process. Jack wasn't done with him. He wasn't thinking, wasn't able to stop himself. He stepped over to where Charlie lay in a crumpled heap and kicked him as hard as he could in the ribs. This time bones definitely broke, a whole bunch of them. He kicked again and again until the rib cage became soft and mushy. Charlie was moaning, spitting up blood, whole mouthfuls of it. One of those moans might have been a word, maybe a plea. Jack didn't know, didn't care. He was seeing red, in his own world. He kept kicking long after Charlie had ceased twitching.

Jack finally got ahold of himself. He stared down at the broken body frosted with moonlight, panting more from rage than exertion. The reality of what he'd done began to sink in. He felt for a pulse.

Charlie was dead.

Jack swore to himself. Then he swore again, louder. He looked to the cabin, half expecting Katrina to be standing on the porch, watching him in horror. She wasn't. He turned toward the dock. No one had come up. No one had seen what he'd done.

He heard something, leaf litter crackling. He snapped his head in the direction of the noise. The road disappeared into a copse of trees. All was quiet.

"Hello?" he said.

The only answer was the whistle of a breeze and the shiver of leaves.

Jack returned his attention to Charlie. He grabbed the old man by the scarecrow ankles and dragged him into the nearest bushes.

Chapter 16

Katrina finished sweeping the floor, thinking the place looked respectable, almost how it had been earlier in the afternoon, minus the dark beer stain. That continued to stand out like a scratch on a new car two hours off the lot. But there was nothing to be done about it except to let it dry on its own. She set the broom aside and was about to go looking for her glass of wine when the door opened and Jack entered. She froze in total shock. His nose, mouth, and chin were dripping with blood. Crimson splotches stained his cashmere cardigan.

"Jack! Oh my God!" she cried. "Are you all right? What *happened?*"

He brushed past her and grabbed a bottle of bourbon off the buffet table. He filled a tumbler to the rim and knocked half of it back in a single mouthful.

"Talk to me, Jack. You're scaring me."

"Bastard whacked me with his cane." He finished the drink and poured another.

"Who? Charlie? For God's sake, why?"

"I tried to pay him off. Offered him two hundred bucks to go home. I went to the car to get my wallet. I was turning around, getting out, when—*bam.* The coward kinged me right in the face. Before I could clear the fuzz, he smashed me again, on the back of the head."

Katrina was dumbstruck. "You need to go to the hospital. Dammit, where's my phone?"

She started to turn away when he grabbed her wrist. "You're not calling anyone."

"Don't be ridiculous, Jack. Look at you! Your nose is likely broken."

"Just fetch me my bag from the laundry, will you?"

He went to the bathroom to clean up. Katrina didn't move, a dozen questions screaming inside her head. She considered ordering him to go to the hospital with her, but she knew it would be futile. He would do what he wanted to do. She hurried to the laundry and retrieved the black overnight bag he'd brought with him. She set it on the middle of the living room floor and was unzipping it when the front door clattered open and Graham Douglas strolled in. At the same time Jack emerged from the bathroom, bare chested. He'd washed his face and looked better than he had before, but his nose was still a mess, leaking a rivulet of fresh blood.

"Jesus tits!" Graham exclaimed. "What the hell happened to you, man?"

Jack shrugged, and Katrina could tell he didn't have time for Graham right then. "Went to take a piss out back. Ran into a tree branch."

Graham seemed about to laugh but thought better of it when he saw the look in Jack's eyes. Jack took the white shirt Katrina was holding in her hand, then disappeared back inside the bathroom.

"Some tree," Graham mumbled as he crossed the room to the ice box. The smell of marijuana trailed behind him, green and skunklike. He stuffed two beers in his pockets and opened a third. "I thought your sister was up here with you."

"Chris?" Katrina said, surprised. "She's down at the dock with you guys, I thought."

"Not last time I checked. By the way, whose truck is that outside?"

Charlie's pickup? she wondered. Had he stuck around? After beating the crap out of Jack? No way. Not unless he was crazy—or unless he hadn't had a chance to leave.

Her blood turned cold.

Graham was watching her with interest. She zipped up the bag and stood. "One of Jack's friends stopped by," she said lightly.

"Where is he?"

"I . . . I don't know. Around somewhere. Out back, maybe."

Graham seemed to buy it. "Oh—I was supposed to ask when the bus is leaving?"

She checked her watch. It was nine thirty. "Eleven, I think. Lance is probably sleeping inside it right now, if you want to ask him. Or you can confirm with Zach. He organized everything."

"Yeah, I'll do that," he said, heading toward the door. "Keep your cool on—and tell Jack-O to watch out for those branches."

He left, humming a song to himself. Katrina hurried to the bathroom door. "Jack?" she said urgently. "Charlie's truck is still here. Why hasn't he left? Where is he?" The door opened. Jack was wearing the shirt she'd given him. He'd plugged his nostrils with toilet paper and he really did look like a boxer right then— a boxer who had just gone twelve rounds with the defending champ. "Where did Charlie go?" she pressed. "If he talks to—"

"He's dead," Jack said simply.

She blinked. "He's what?"

"Dead."

"What are you telling me? You killed him?"

"That's what I'm telling you, yes."

"That's not funny, Jack."

But he didn't smile. Didn't say, "Gotcha!" In fact, he didn't show any emotion at all. And just like that Katrina knew it was true. She must have gone into shock because when Jack handed her a glass of bourbon, she was no longer by the bathroom but sitting on the sofa.

"Drink it," he told her.

Katrina looked at him. She felt surreal and hollowed out and utterly confused. She was still waiting for the punch line, still clinging to that gossamer strand of hope this was all one bad joke taken way too far. But it wasn't and she knew that. She knew that the same way she knew her name was Katrina. Not with thought or effort. She just knew it. Charlie was dead and there was nothing she could do to change that horrible fact. Dead—the word didn't seem real. It seemed connected to an abstract idea, not a concrete thing. Not a person. Not Charlie.

And Jack had said he'd *killed him?*

It didn't make sense. Nothing was making sense.

For a moment she thought she was going to be sick, but the sour sensation passed. A fury of fresh questions wanted to leap out of her mouth. Only one—the most important one—made it. "How?" she mumbled. "How did he die?"

"It was an accident."

"What kind of accident?"

"Like I said, he bashed me with his cane. I guess he thought I was out for the count. Probably should have been. But I got up. He was heading to the dock. I came up behind him. Last minute he turned around and I punched him. I didn't mean to hit him so hard. But he'd just played baseball with my head, and I wasn't thinking too straight."

Katrina dropped her face into her hands, still feeling spacey and unreal. She couldn't accept they were talking about this. You had conversations about the weather and your job and your friends. You didn't have a conversation about how you killed someone.

"Where's his body?" she asked, the last word causing her to swallow hard.

"I moved it to the bushes."

Finally emotion and gut reaction gave way to reason. She began thinking in terms of cause and effect. "You shouldn't have moved him."

"Of course I should have. Someone would have seen him if I hadn't."

"But when the police find him, they're going to be suspicious—"

"Whoa-ho-ho," Jack said, recoiling from her. "We're not calling the cops."

She stared at him as if he'd spoken another language. "What are you talking about, Jack?"

"What do you think I'm talking about," he snapped. "I just *killed* a man. They'll haul me off to jail."

"No," she said, shaking her head, not wanting to hear what he was saying. "It was an accident. You didn't know one punch was going to kill him. Besides, all they have to do is look at you, your face. It was obviously self-defense."

"Right, Katrina. Look at me. I'm six one, two hundred pounds. Charlie was an old man. Must've been at least seventy. Throw in my fighting background, how's that going to look?"

He was right, she knew. But she also knew they had to call the police. It simply wasn't an option to conceal a murder.

Christ. Was that what it was going to be called?

Murder?

Her initial denial was already becoming acceptance, and with that, horror.

Jack was going to jail. That was the cold reality of it.

"This is all my fault," she said. "If I hadn't lied—if I had just told everyone the truth—"

"Stop it," Jack told her. "What's done is done. Now we have to focus on the future and decide what we're going to do."

"Jack," she said severely, speaking with quiet conviction, "we have to call the police."

"Goddammit, Katrina!" He shot to his feet and winced, bringing a hand to the back of his head, as if the sudden movement had jolted his injuries. "We're not calling the police!"

"We have to," she insisted. "So maybe we can't call it self-defense. But it wasn't premeditated, for God's sake. We can prove that. Charlie came *here*. We didn't know he was going to do that. And what reason would you have to kill him? Right? So we bite the bullet and plead second-degree manslaughter. It happens. Accidents like this. Bars. Sports games. Fistfights break out. People get hurt. Sometimes fatally. What's that for a first-time offense? Probation? Six months?"

Jack began pacing back and forth in front of her. "Then everyone finds out you lied about this place."

She made a noise that would have been laughter under more regular circumstances; right then it was just a noise. "I don't care anymore," she said.

"You'll have to leave your job."

She frowned. "Because I lied?"

"No, because your 'boyfriend' killed someone. It won't matter to anyone you've only known me for a couple days. They think we're together. That's all that matters. You can't go on working at some place where they think you're a liar and your boyfriend is a murderer. Especially not at a school. Think about what the kids will say. It's the hard truth."

Katrina felt as though she was watching her life fall apart in slow motion. Jack was going to jail and she was going to lose her job. She was numb with sadness. But if that's what had to happen, that's what had to happen. There was simply no way she was covering up a murder. She couldn't believe Jack was trying to convince her of that route. Just yesterday she'd thought she knew him so well. Now it was as if she hardly knew him at all.

"So, I move then," she said.

Jack was shaking his head. "You just got here. You told me you liked it. You're not packing up and moving because of something stupid I did."

"That's my decision to make."

"You're not listening to me."

"You're not listening to *me*."

"I said no cops," he said firmly.

"There's a dead man in the bushes!"

Jack stopped pacing. He spent a long moment looking at her, appraising her. His face was lined in thought. He said, "Listen, it's not so simple."

"What are you talking about?"

"There's something I haven't told you." He poured himself another drink from the bottle on the buffet table. "It's about my past. When I told you about my fighting, I didn't tell you everything. I mentioned I competed in tournaments. Some legal, some not. What I didn't tell you was that the illegal ones were *really* illegal. Pit fighting stuff. I became involved with a bad crew down in California. Links to mobsters, corrupt businessmen. They set up the fights and I fought them. Always won. I became a black-market celebrity of sorts. Then there was this one fight, my last one. Some muaystyle fighter fresh off the boat from Thailand. He was a prizefighter of a wealthy nightclub owner who had ties with the Russian Mafia over on the East Coast. I knocked the guy out in the first round. The thing is, he never got up."

Katrina hadn't thought this could possibly get any worse, but it just had.

"You killed him," she stated in a flat voice.

"I elbowed him in the face. Only my elbow hit him in the eye. There was this sound—Anyway, his eye socket shattered, sending shards of bone into his brain. He dropped to the ground. Was pronounced dead at the scene."

Katrina opened her mouth and closed it. She didn't know what to say.

"The next week the police busted up the fighting ring," Jack went on. "My promoter, one of the first people arrested, ratted me out. But I'd already packed up and quit fighting. In fact, I'd just come up the coast to Washington when I heard what happened. It was all over the news. I stuck around Seattle for a few weeks, then started east, for Michigan or maybe Massachusetts. While passing through Leavenworth I liked the vibe and decided to stick around for a couple days. And then, well, and then I met you."

Katrina was shaking her head, feeling sickened and staggered all over again, like she was on a nightmare rollercoaster that wouldn't stop to let her off. Jack had killed two people in his life. She should have known he was too good, too perfect, to be true.

"So you're on the run?" She wanted to laugh. She wanted to cry.

Jack shrugged, finished his drink. "If that's what you want to call it."

"The police know you killed that fighter?"

"My promoter sung like a canary. They know everything. You see the problem I'm in here? I tell them what happened with Charlie, my name goes in the system. Bulletins pop up."

Katrina stared at Jack for a long moment, then looked away. She wasn't mad at the deception, she realized. All she felt was drained. "I'm having a hard time accepting all of this, Jack."

"We call the cops, Katrina, and I'm going to jail for a long, long time."

"But they were both accidents," she said stubbornly, angrily.

"A judge or jury isn't going to have much sympathy for someone who's killed two men with his bare hands, accident or not."

"So what do you propose we do?" she said in challenge, knowing by asking this question she was getting pulled over the line to his side in this marathon tug-of-war. "We can't just leave him in the bushes. The neighbors know he came here. His wife probably knows as well. When he doesn't return home, she'll call the cops. We'll be the prime suspects. Last people to have seen him alive."

"We make it look like an accident."

"But it was an accident."

"No, I mean a real accident. A car accident."

Katrina looked at him skeptically.

"We put his body in the pickup," Jack explained, his eyes alight, as if he was reinvigorated by her partial acquiescence. "I'll drive. You follow in the Porsche. Charlie said he lived in Skykomish. That's just west of here. When we get near the town, we make it look like he ran off the road."

"He just drives off?"

"Maybe he falls asleep? Maybe a deer runs in front of him? It doesn't matter. The cops have no reason to be suspicious. They won't think of asking us. It'll be over."

Katrina was silent. Was she buying into this mad scheme? If she did, she would be an accomplice to murder. If she didn't, Jack would go to jail. For an accident. Something that was already done and couldn't be undone. *Dammit!* she thought. There were so many gray areas. She needed more time to think things through. But she didn't have the luxury of that option. There was a dead man in the bushes and a couple dozen teachers down at the dock.

"Katrina," Jack said calmly but resolutely. He sat down beside her and took her hand. "Charlie's dead. There's nothing we can do to change that. But we can change the future. Either we report the death and your life here gets ruined—not to mention I go to prison—or we do what I'm suggesting. No one will be any the wiser, and that will be that."

"We'll get caught," she protested. "Something will go wrong."

"Nothing will go wrong."

"How can you be so sure?"

"You just have to trust me."

"Dammit, Jack."

"Trust me."

She went silent, frantically searching for a last-minute exit but finding none. Suddenly she was consumed by a deterministic feeling she was being swept up in something larger than herself, something she could do nothing to prevent, and that terrified her more than she could have imagined.

Jack tilted her head so they were looking into each other's eyes. "Will you do this for me?" he asked.

No! Tell him he's on his own.

Abruptly Katrina thought of Shawn, gaunt and weak, a skeleton on his deathbed. She recalled the helplessness she'd felt, the frustration at her utter powerlessness. The vow she'd made to herself to never let someone in need down again. Then she flashed back to last night, lying in bed beside Jack, the bond she'd felt between them. He'd been a rock for her so far. He'd listened to all her crap. He'd pursued what he'd thought was the best course of action to get her out of her sticky lie. And he'd asked for nothing in return. Not a thing. What was it he'd said? *I'm here for you.*

Katrina understood that what Jack was proposing wasn't the right thing to do, and that he wasn't the perfect man she'd thought him to be. But sometimes the right decision wasn't always the best decision, and perfect or not, she still did have strong feelings for him. And she knew with a growing certainty she wasn't going to be able to sit idly by while another man's life slipped through her fingers. Not when she could do something about it.

Her choice, it seemed then, was inevitable.

"Yes," she said softly, almost to herself. "I'll do it."

Chapter 17

Zach was pressed against the trunk of a tree, still as a tombstone. Blood was thumping in his ears and his legs felt rubbery, like they might give at any moment. Jack had already returned inside the cabin, but Zach was too terrified to move. When he'd shifted his weight earlier, making noise, he'd been convinced Jack was going to come over to investigate. If that had happened, he'd been ready to run and just keep running. Because Jack had not just killed that old man, he'd demolished him—and he would demolish Zach as well if he knew he'd witnessed the entire murder from start to finish. Nevertheless, he could no longer remain where he was. He had to check on the poor sucker. There was no way he could be alive, no way, not after all those bone-breaking kicks that soon became wet, fleshy kicks. But he had to check, just the same.

He looked around the tree trunk. All clear. He crept over to the bushes where Jack had dragged the body. He took a few steps into the thicket, pushed aside some shrubs, and flinched, even though he had known what to expect. The old man's face was a scarf of blood. His nose was crushed. It almost looked out of place, as if it had moved a few inches to the left. His mouth was open, revealing a black, toothless hole. Maybe he didn't put in his dentures today, but more than likely his teeth were lying in the dirt over where he'd been beaten silly. Cold moonlight reflected in his upward-gazing eyes, which shone like two silver coins—the ferryman's fare for the trip across the river. As horrible as his face was, it was his body that caused true horror in Zach, because it wasn't natural. It looked like a doll's body—something stuffed with beans and as supple as a noodle. It was in the shape of a badly drawn *S*, scrawny arms at its side, knees together. And the chest—that was the worst part. It looked deflated, empty, like an alien in a horror movie had just burst free from it, leaving a womblike cavity behind.

He was dead. No question. *Demolished* was the word Zach had thought before and the word that came to his mind again. He stumbled away, feeling the first squirming of self-loathing. He'd stood by and watched Jack murder a defenseless old man. He'd remained hiding behind a tree when he could have done something. But what could he have done? It had all happened so fast and unexpectedly. He couldn't have anticipated that first palm strike or whatever the hell it was. Then Jack was kicking the old man as soon as he'd landed on his back. By the time Zach had gotten his wits about him, it was over. Five, maybe six seconds. That's all it took.

Zach's first impulse now was to whip out his cell phone and call the police, or even run down to the dock and tell everyone what Jack had done. But he hesitated. He didn't know all the facts yet. Didn't know why the old man had attacked Jack, or what was going to happen next. Because maybe Jack was going to turn himself in, and Zach wouldn't have to get involved at all. Or, better yet, maybe Katrina would turn Jack in. How sweet that would be. Talk about poetic justice. So, yeah, maybe he would just wait and see how things played out, say in the next ten minutes or so—

The cabin door opened and Jack and Katrina appeared. Zach stiffened, as if he was going to bolt. But he didn't move. They would see him. He might be thirty yards away, but any movement would draw their eyes. They'd know he had seen the body. Jack would come after him and catch him before he could call the police or reach the others. So very slowly and quietly he lowered himself to his chest and crawled deeper into the tangle of bushes, moving away from the old man's body. Then he stopped and remained perfectly still. The rich, earthy smell of the soil filled his nose. He scarcely allowed himself to breathe.

"Where?" he heard Katrina say. She sounded shaky.

"Right there." Jack. He didn't sound shaky at all.

They pushed into the patch of bush where Zach was hiding.

Shrubs snapped and rustled. They couldn't have been more than ten feet away.

"Oh, Jesus," Katrina said, barely a whisper.

"Try not to look at it," Jack said. Not *him* anymore. Just an *it*—a clump of meat and bones that if skinned and hacked to pieces wouldn't look out of place in a butcher's window.

"There's so much blood. Why's there so much blood? You said you only hit him once."

"I did. Right in the nose. All the blood's from his nose."

"What's wrong with his body? It looks—floppy."

"That's because he's dead. Muscles loosen."

Loosen my ass, Zach was thinking. *It's because you broke every rib in his chest and probably every bone in his arms as he tried to defend himself.*

"I thought they stiffen," Katrina said.

"Not for a few hours. Now stand back. I don't want you to get any blood on you."

There was a much louder crackling of vegetation: Jack dragging the body free, all the way to the pickup truck, which was twenty feet away. Zach pushed himself to his knees so he could see what was happening. Jack lifted the old man effortlessly into the bed of the pickup. He took something from Katrina—a sheet, Zach realized—and flung it over the corpse.

"I really don't feel comfortable with you driving the truck," Jack said.

"There's nothing to do about it. I can't drive manual."

"I know. I know." He handed her the keys. They chimed as they switched hands. "Stay right behind me until I pull over. Then pull over in front of me. Got it?"

"Yes."

"Stay calm. And don't touch anything aside from the steering wheel and the ignition key."

Katrina climbed in the truck. Jack got in the Porsche. With a roar and a purr, the two vehicles revved to life. The headlights seared holes through the darkness. Dirt crunched beneath the rubber tires as they swung onto the narrow road. Zach ducked as the two sets of headlights swept past him. Then they were gone, and it was quiet once more. Zach remained right where he was, flabbergasted.

Katrina was helping that jackass!

A fresh swarm of jealousy buzzed through him, stinging his pride, because he knew she would never risk herself, her freedom, for him. Nevertheless, he stuffed those feelings aside and focused on what was important. The murder. He would have to report it now, wouldn't he? He'd waited to see how it played out, and it had played out horribly. He had no qualms about ratting Jack out. But that meant he'd have to rat Katrina out as well, explain how she'd helped him get rid of the body. Could he do that? Because this wasn't a game anymore. This wasn't busting her for a lie she told. This was busting her over accessory to murder.

But what other option did he have?

He took out his phone and dialed 9-1-1.

Chapter 18

Katrina remained a few car lengths behind Jack's Porsche as they made their way west on Highway 2 toward Skykomish. They were passing along the stretch of road where she'd picked Zach up eight days before, and a number of taunting questions popped into her head. What if she'd left Seattle Friday afternoon rather than Friday night? What if she'd taken a different route, following I-90 until Highway 97 and going north to Leavenworth from there? Or what if she'd simply never stopped for Zach? All those parallel-world scenarios inevitably led to the same conclusion: she would not have tipped the first domino. She would not have lied to Zach about where she lived. He would not have mentioned the make-believe cabin in front of everybody at Ducks & Drakes. There would have been no sign-up sheet, and she would not have rented the cabin to justify what never should have had to be justified in the first place. Consequently, Jack would not have been attacked by Charlie, and he would not have done what he had done. In fact, in that rose-colored reality, Katrina would probably be back at her bungalow with Crystal, maybe cooking together, or maybe watching a movie with the lights dimmed and a bowlful of popcorn and talking about sister stuff.

In the distance the lights of a small town came into view. The taillights of the Porsche flashed red. Katrina slowed also. The highway cut straight through the center of the town. They passed kids on their skateboards loitering out front of a convenience store, a family strolling down the sidewalk, and an old man with a long beard sitting on the bench out front of the post office, not doing much of anything. The normalness of it all made Katrina realize just how nice normal was. In contrast, she was all too aware she was driving a stolen pickup truck with the owner's bloody corpse sprawled out in the flatbed under a sheet. The last time she'd felt this depressed, this lost and confused, had been after the doctors had told her and Shawn that Shawn had less than six months to live.

Death, she realized grimly, made you pay attention to living.

They emerged on the other side of the town and sped up once more. Katrina hardened her resolve. She would get through this. Jack was right. They could make Charlie's death look like a car accident. The police would have no reason to suspect foul play. Car accidents happened all the time. They would wake up tomorrow morning and read about it in the local paper: old man falls asleep behind wheel and dies in fatal crash. The sun would set and rise and life would go on. Come Monday morning she would be back at Cascade High School, plowing through her daily routine.

It would be over.

But then what would happen between her and Jack? Jack was a renegade. On the lam. One of society's ghosts. Could she be with someone like that? Never knowing if his past was going to catch up with him? Always wondering if today was going to be the day he wasn't there when she got home?

Katrina shook her head. She was being a hypocrite.

After all, she was now a felon too.

Roughly twenty minutes later they were approaching the outskirts of Skykomish. Jack swung to the shoulder and watched as Katrina rolled past him, stopping ten feet or so ahead, as they'd discussed. He hopped out of the Porsche and met her as she got out of the truck. Crickets chirruped from the cheatgrass and coyote willow that lined the road, creating a wall of sound. Other than that, the night was silent. "We have to be quick," he told her, throwing the sheet off Charlie. He lifted the old man out of the flatbed, carried him around to the truck's driver's side door, and shoved him in behind the wheel. He was still flippety-floppety. Rigor wouldn't set in for at least another hour.

"Why are you putting on his seat belt?" Katrina asked.

"Because I don't want him to fly through the windshield."

"But that would be good, wouldn't it? It would explain the blood on his face."

"Corpses don't bleed," he told her. "He would have a bunch of fresh, bloodless cuts all over his face. The coroner would know he'd been dead before the crash. And dead men don't drive trucks."

Jack noticed Katrina blanch at what he was saying. Likely wondering if she hadn't thought of that, then what else had she failed to think about? He hoped she wasn't going to crack under pressure.

"So how do you explain the blood?" she asked.

"I know what I'm doing here," he snapped. There was no time for how-to-fake-an-accident 101. Not now. Someone could drive past any minute. "Go wait in the Porsche. I'll be done here in a minute."

She left, looking relieved to be going. He reached inside the cab and twisted the key in the ignition. The engine turned over. He went to the side of the road and kicked around in the grass until he found a large stone. He returned to the truck, put the transmission in neutral, and set the stone on the gas pedal. The tachometer needle shot up to 4,000 rpms. He counted to three, then shoved the gearstick into drive, jumping clear as the truck lurched forward. The truck roared down the road in a straight line, picking up speed. It angled to the left, crossed the broken yellow line, then reached the far shoulder, where it shot off the road and collided head-on with a black cottonwood tree. The crash sounded oddly quiet.

Jack ran back to the Porsche, got behind the wheel, and tipped Katrina an A-OK nod. He drove to the destroyed truck, careful not to spin his tires and leave any kind of skid marks on the macadam.

"Was it supposed to do that?" she asked. "Go to the left?"

"Doesn't matter. If Charlie had fallen asleep, or swerved to avoid an animal, then he could just as easily have gone either way, left or right." He stopped parallel to the truck. "I have to check it out. Keep an eye out for cars. You see any lights coming, you honk the horn."

Jack waded through the cheatgrass to the truck. One headlight had blown, while the other one shone a beam of light into the forest. The smoking engine was partly obscured by a patch of prickly phlox, but he could see enough of it to know it had taken a good licking. He opened the door and examined the interior of the cab. Charlie's head was slumped limply against his chest. His arms hung at his sides. His wrinkled and bloodied face was turned toward Jack, his mouth open, and he almost appeared to be laughing, as if he'd died while thinking about one last crude joke.

Remembering the old man's foulness eliminated any pity Jack might have felt for him now. He retrieved the rock from the foot well, turned his head away to protect his eyes, then hurled it upward against the windshield, hard, just above the steering wheel. The glass spider-webbed around the point of impact. Satisfied, he lobbed the rock away into the trees. Next he wiped down the steering wheel with his shirt, took Charlie's hands, and pressed them on the wheel at the ten and two positions. He believed what he'd told Katrina when he said the police would have no reason to be suspicious of a car accident. But it was better to be safe than sorry. If an investigator took fingerprints and found none on the steering wheel, he would be scratching his head for a little but would eventually figure it out. Lastly Jack undid Charlie's seat belt and shoved him forward so his head was up between the top of the dashboard and the windshield. He studied his handiwork. An auspicious feeling he'd overlooked something nagged at him. But on the drive here he'd gone over the plan from every angle, and he knew the unease had to be paranoia. Besides, he had to move.

He returned to the Porsche, slipped behind the wheel, and pulled a U-turn so they were now traveling back toward the direction of Charlie's cabin and Leavenworth. Beside him Katrina was ashen-faced, her arms folded across her chest. She was looking straight ahead. Eventually she said, "Where do we tell everyone we were?"

Jack shrugged. "Maybe no one will have noticed we were gone."

"By the time we get back it will be almost eleven. The bus will be waiting to leave. Surely people will be wondering where we are."

"I doubt they'll notice my car is gone."

"So?"

"So we tell them we walked up to the point. Let them fill in the rest."

She didn't say anything more.

"What's wrong?" he asked her.

"What do you think, Jack?"

"I mean, right now."

She didn't answer.

"Tell me."

"Nothing."

Jack didn't press her. She'd been through a lot. One hell of a lot. And considering the risk that had been involved—that was still involved, at least until they saw how tomorrow unfolded—she was so far handling herself admirably. He didn't know another woman quite like her, and he felt more attracted to her than ever. He reached over and squeezed her thigh reassuringly. He felt her flinch slightly. He let go. Time, he thought. That was all she needed. A little more time.

He shifted into fifth. He was eager to get back to the cabin and thus tempted to speed. But the last thing he wanted was to be written up for speeding, an indisputable record he and Katrina had been near the scene of the crime. He kept up a steady sixty-five miles an hour.

"It's just another lie," Katrina said quietly as they were passing a rest area.

He glanced at her. "What is?"

"Telling people we were in the bushes making out."

"Come on, Katrina. In light of the big picture, who cares about that?"

"Don't you see?" she said, and her voice was hard. Cold. "It was a stupid white lie that got me into this whole mess. It led to another lie, and another. And look what's happened!"

"It's the last one."

"No, it isn't. There's no last one. I know that now. This will follow us around forever."

"It will be all right," he said. "Have faith. I know what I'm doing."

"Shit!" Jack said, slamming on the brakes. The car fishtailed as it skidded to a stop.

Katrina, who had been staring out the side window, snapped her head forward, wondering whether in some cruel twist of irony they'd hit an animal, just as Charlie was supposed to have done. But there had been no impact. Nothing lay sprawled on the road in front of them.

"What happened?" she demanded.

He didn't reply.

"Jack? What is it? What's wrong?"

"I knew I had forgotten something."

"Know what?" she said, working herself into a panic. "What are you talking about?"

"You stupid, stupid son of a bitch," he mumbled to himself.

"Jack! You're scaring me. What's wrong?"

He looked at her, as if just registering she was sitting beside him. "The blood," he said, shaking his head. "I forgot about the blood."

"What blood?"

"The blood all over Charlie's goddamn face."

"What about it? You said you knew what you were doing." She didn't know what he was talking about, but she nonetheless felt as though his supposedly unsinkable plan was springing a gaping leak.

"Back at the truck I smashed the windshield, to make it look like Charlie hit his head, causing the blood. It didn't matter if it was dry, because it would be a while before the cops reached there anyway. But I forgot about the other blood."

"What other blood?"

"The blood splatter—the blood that was all over my cardigan. Because if he really collided with the windshield, then the blood from his wounds should also be splattered around inside the cab."

Katrina was silent as she let this new revelation sink in. "Is that really a big deal?"

"Think about it, Katrina. There's a dead man back there in that truck, his face a sheet of blood, which magically didn't get on anything else. Yes, it's a big deal. A big fucking deal. Even these hick cops aren't going to miss that."

Springing a leak? she thought, and she felt a crazy laugh bubble up her throat. *It seems we've just hit a goddamn iceberg, Captain.*

"So what does this mean?" she said. "What do we do? What *can* we do—?"

"We have to go back."

"Absolutely not, Jack! We've been lucky this far. It's not going to last."

"No cars have come toward us yet. Maybe none have come behind us either."

"If we go back, we're going to get caught." She said that as a statement.

"Dammit, Katrina. Not now."

She felt what little there was left of her self-possession slipping, and she thought she knew how someone standing in the path of a tsunami felt. Hopeless. Like there was nothing you could do to prevent the oncoming disaster.

"We can't go back," she insisted stubbornly.

"What do you suggest then?" he demanded.

"I don't know. God, I don't know."

"If someone has stopped, then we keep driving. That's it."

"And if no one has stopped, what do we do?" she challenged. "Slit our wrists and spray the cab with our own blood?"

"Burn it."

"The truck?" she said incredulously.

"What else?"

"I don't know about you, Jack, but I've never heard of a car exploding into a ball of flames because of a collision. Maybe in the movies, if one happens to career off a cliff. But not running into a tree."

"I'm not talking about a big explosion. Just a fire."

"You can't just set the seats on fire with your Zippo. Investigators can tell where a fire starts."

"That's why we make it look like an *engine* fire. Leaking fluids, spilled oil, short circuits, faulty carburetors, catalytic converters—these all start engine fires. And the odds skyrocket during an accident. Usually if a fire breaks out, people turn off the engine and call for help and stop the fire before it gets out of control. That's why you don't hear about it much. But if a fire started, and no one knew about it, and it was allowed to burn, enough heat generated, well, there'd be nothing left but a metal skeleton sitting on melted tires."

"And if someone comes by and puts it out?"

"How many people do you know who drive around with fire extinguishers in their cars? Rig drivers, maybe. But it wouldn't matter. We just need enough of a fire to tamper with the evidence. That way, even if the cops get suspicious, nothing short of a confession or an eyewitness could convict us."

Apparently the decision was made, because Jack wheeled the car around and sped back the way they'd come. He pushed the speedometer up over ninety miles an hour. It was the first time she felt the Porsche breaking a sweat. The engine whined like a torpedo and the trees outside flashed past in one continuous blur. It was also the first time she'd seen Jack break a sweat. He wasn't sweating, per se. But he was sitting straight, both hands on the wheels, staring straight ahead, intense, like a man on a mission. That should have been a comforting sight—Jack in control, Jack determined to make everything right—but in truth it freaked her out. Because up until this point, he had been as cool as a cucumber—snappish sometimes, yes—but in general treating the whole situation like someone who knew exactly what he was doing and couldn't do wrong. Seeing him if not nervous then at least concerned was like seeing your pilot searching for a parachute in rough turbulence.

During the suspense-laden trip back to the scene of the accident, her mind began exploring what would happen if they were caught. Funny enough—or more appropriately, narcissistically enough—it wasn't the jail time she would serve that bothered her the most. It was what everyone she knew would think of her. Old friends back in Seattle. Relatives. Crystal. Even the students she used to teach, and the ones she was just getting to know now—kids who looked up to her as a role model. For the first time since her parents' death, she was glad they were not around. She could not bear them to witness her humiliation and disgrace. Eventually, though, she did begin to wonder about jail time. What was the sentence for covering up a murder? Or, as the lawyers would put it, conspiracy to obstruct justice. Five years in a state prison? Eight? She wasn't sure. But both those sentences seemed like an eternity. Cold cement cell. Tasteless food. Menial jobs. Lack of communication with the outside world. Worse, when she got out she would have a criminal record. She could never teach again. What would she do with herself? There was never anything else she had wanted to do besides teaching.

She glanced at Jack. What would happen to him? Or, specifically, between her and him? She had to be realistic about that. They could write to each other for the first few years. When she got out, she could visit him. But was she just being romantic? Did she really want to spend twenty years visiting a man she could never be with? Never grow old together with? No, she would likely not visit him. Not even once. She would have to make a fresh break. She would have to look for a new man yet again.

Forty-year-old woman, convicted felon, jobless, and more than a little damaged seeks man to settle down with and raise children.

Yeah, right.

She was going to grow old and die alone—

"You okay?" Jack asked, noticing her eyes on him.

She glanced away, ashamed to be thinking such thoughts. They were not caught. Not yet. They were still very much free. And together. "I'm okay," she said.

"I hope you're not still thinking we're going to get caught. We're not. We're almost there and there hasn't been a single—"

Up ahead, Katrina made out a set of headlights. She felt as though she'd been punched in the gut with a steel gauntlet. "Someone's there," she said unnecessarily.

Jack slowed to eighty, then sixty-five, the speed limit. A blue Buick sedan was parked off to the side of the road, beside the crashed pickup truck. A man ran out onto the road, waving his hands. His face was stark white in the headlights. Jack slowed a little more but continued past without stopping. Katrina saw the man's expression morph from distress to disgust.

"He's alone," Jack said. Before Katrina knew what was happening, he'd looped the Porsche around in a tight turn and was heading back.

"What are you doing?" she demanded. "We can't get involved now! We'll have to give a statement. We'll have to explain what we're doing way out here!"

"We're not going to stick around. I'm just going to talk to him."

Katrina didn't like what she heard in his voice. She didn't know what it was, only that it frightened her. "Keep driving past," she said.

The man saw them coming back and was waving them over. Jack pulled up behind the Buick. Katrina was furious he'd blatantly ignored her, but there was nothing she could do. He was in the driver's seat.

"Stay in the car," Jack told her, then climbed out.

Katrina watched him for a moment, then flung the door open and got out as well.

Jack shot her a glance but didn't say anything. He turned his attention to the man, who was short and potato-thick with a weather-seasoned face framed by a red beard and a wild mane of matching hair. "What happened here?" Jack asked, with just the right amount of curiosity and concern.

"Damned if I know," the man said, stroking his beard nervously. "I went down there to see the damage, give some help, you know. But, sweet Jesus, I'm positive the poor sucker's dead. I didn't find a pulse."

"Did you call the police?"

"Don't got my phone with me. You got one?"

"No."

Katrina knew Jack had his phone in his pocket. Her ominous feeling deepened. "Jack," she said, "come back to the car. We'll go to Skykomish. Get help."

Jack ignored her once more. "Let's you and me go take another peek," he said to the man. "Maybe he isn't as dead as you say."

"I ain't never seen a dead person before. Once or twice in a coffin. No real dead person, you know what I mean? But I'm sure this guy's gone. I told you. I never found a pulse."

"Let's just make sure." Jack put a hand firmly on the shorter man's shoulder and guided him toward the crashed truck.

"Jack!" Katrina shouted.

Both men turned to look at her.

"What are you going to do?" she asked cryptically.

"Go back to the car."

"What are you going to do?"

"Go back to the car, Katrina." There was an iron timbre to his voice. But she would not be cowed.

"Let's go to Skykomish," she said. "Get help there. Don't do this." *Do what?* she wondered. *Kill him? Was that was she was thinking? That Jack was going to kill the man?* She had no idea. She had no idea about anything anymore. Only that she wanted to get the hell away from there—far, far away.

The man with the red hair stiffened. He glanced from Katrina, to Jack, then back to Katrina. He looked like a man who had heard something he wanted no part of. "Maybe I better go for help myself." He turned toward his car, but Jack tugged him back. He lost his balance and fell to the ground. "Hey!" he protested.

"Shut up!" Jack said.

"Jack!" Katrina cried, taking a few steps forward. *Yes, he was going to do it. She believed that now. He was going to kill that man.*

"I'm not going to say this again," he told her. "Get back to the car."

"Don't touch me!" the man gasped, and began scrambling away on all fours. "Stay away!"

Jack started after him, huge and looming, like a polar bear about to pounce on an injured seal. Aware she had only a few seconds to act, Katrina did something she had never done before in her life: she leapt onto a grown man's back, wrapping her arms around Jack's throat. His knees buckled from the added one hundred and twenty pounds, but he didn't go down. Then the next moment she was airborne. He'd shaken her free as if she'd been nothing more than a pesky child. The impact with the ground came fast. She landed in the tall grass and made an "oomph!" sound. She raised her head and was immensely relieved to see she'd provided the man vital seconds to escape. He was back on his feet, charging recklessly into the dark pine forest.

She turned her attention to Jack. He was looking at her with not so much anger but pity, as if he'd been betrayed. Crazily she waited for him to say, "Et tu, Brute?" But he didn't say anything. Then he was off, disappearing into the trees.

Katrina knew the man with the wild red hair didn't stand a chance.

Chapter 19

Bruce Heinrich ran deeper into the forest. His arms were crossed in front of him in the form of a crucifix, as if to ward off the branches from raking him across the face. He heard the crazy son of a bitch right behind him, coming fast. Bruce's mind was pumping on all cylinders as he tried to figure out what he'd stumbled into the middle of and what he could do to escape. He was no coward, that was for sure. He considered himself strong and in shape, largely due to the last thirty years he'd spent as a contractor up here in these parts, and ten years in northern Oregon before that, building houses and cottages and such, doing most of the hard manual labor himself. But he was no idiot. The man on his ass cleared six feet and two hundred pounds and looked about as strong as an ox. So no stopping and fighting his way out of this. No sir, no way. He'd have to hide. Get a lead, lose the bastard in the dark.

A pagan branch found a gap through his crucifix and clawed his face, drawing a painful line beneath his right eye—an inch higher and he would have been halfway to blind. He stumbled, shouldered a tree trunk, then staggered on. He didn't slow. It was pitch-black, but he didn't slow. He could hear the man behind him, closer than ever.

Who the hell were these people he'd waved over? he wondered manically. Fugitives on the run? If so, why would they stop? Why would they want to kill him? The dots didn't add up. The only thing that connected him to them was the dead man in the pickup. But they couldn't have been responsible for that. They'd been driving past—

Unless they'd killed the man, maybe ran him off the road, then had to come back for something. Maybe there was a suitcase with a million bucks in the pickup—

Bruce slammed into another tree. Something sharp went right through his hand, below the padded, fleshy lump of the thumb. Red pain screamed, hot and sizzling. It reminded him of the time he'd slipped while shingling a roof, impaling his hand on an up-ended, rusty nail.

What had it been? A branch? The tip of a branch?

The crazy son of a bitch finally caught up and grabbed Bruce's shoulder. Bruce let out a startled cry. He flailed an arm wildly to break free and connected with what he thought must be the bastard's face. The man let go. Bruce lumbered forward, cupping his injured hand with his good one. He made it about ten paces before an intense heat exploded in his right ear. He dropped to his knees and brought his good hand up to his ear. Blood was gushing from it, streaming down his cheek, slippery and smooth. *I've ripped it in half. I've ripped my fucking ear in half.* He teetered on the brink of unconsciousness.

Something slammed his back. The pain was like a cannonball. He fell to his side, instantly aware he couldn't move. His arms, legs, neck wouldn't respond.

Lord, was he dead? But if he was, then why was he still conscious?

Bruce realized he was probably paralyzed.

Before he could consider whether being a quadriplegic was any better than being dead, there was a sharp tap to his temple and he didn't have to wonder any more.

Chapter 20

Jack stared down at the dark, lifeless shape of the man he'd killed. He'd driven his foot into his back and heard the spine snap. Then he'd kicked him in the right temple, where a major artery and nerve were located, to make sure the job was done. The smartest thing to do now, he decided, was to leave the body where it was. He knew if he brought it back to the car, and Katrina saw it, she'd never help him dispose of it properly. In fact, he was pretty sure she would go straight to the police. Besides, nobody was going to find it out here anyway, not in the forest alongside an unremarkable strip of highway. No hiking trails nearby. No Ski-Doo trails. The only thing that would find the man with the red hair was something with a good nose—a nose for blood. Likely a black bear or a coyote. And that was ideal. No medical examiner could comb over a body that was in the belly of a bear. There would be bones left, but that would be all. By next spring they would be buried beneath a new carpet of leaf litter and fresh ground vegetation.

Jack searched the corpse for a wallet and keys, which he found. He made his way back to the highway, quickly but not nearly as recklessly as the mad charge in. He pushed past some sagebrush, then was clear of the haunting trees. Katrina was by the Porsche, arms folded across her chest, pacing back and forth. Thankfully, no more cars had shown up. Katrina spotted him, froze momentarily, then ran over, looking like someone who had just escaped from a loony bin. Her eyes were wide and stormy, her face drawn and pale. "What have you done, Jack?" she sobbed, pounding her small fists against his chest. "What in God's name have you done?"

"Get a grip, Katrina!" he said. "What's gotten into you? You scared the shit out of that guy with all of your cryptic talk. You made it sound as if I'd been planning on killing him!"

She continued to pound. "Did you?" she demanded. "Did you kill him? I know you did. Don't lie to me. I know you did."

"Are you serious?" He grabbed her wrists. "You're not making any sense. You're hysterical."

"You killed him!"

"I just had a talk with him."

"Liar!"

"It's true."

"Where is he then? Where is he right now?" He felt her wrists tremble in his grip, as if she wanted to yank them free or start hitting him once again. He held on firm.

"He's thinking about the talk I had with him. The talk I had planned from the beginning before you jumped on my back and almost let him get away." He finally let her go and glanced down the highway both ways. "I'll explain everything to you very soon. But not now, not here. We have to get the hell out of here before someone comes along."

Katrina swayed, as if suddenly dizzy. A hand went to her mouth.

"Don't throw up!" Jack said, fearing she was going to contaminate the crime scene. "Hold it back!" He tore off his T-shirt and held it like a horizontal sail in front of her. She vomited into it, retching over and over again. Jack's eyes went back to the highway. No headlights. Not yet. But soon. Their luck was going to run out very soon. He felt like they were playing Russian roulette, not with bullets but with each second that slipped by. When Katrina had finally finished, he knotted the shirt so it became a small pouch, carried it to the Buick, and tossed it in the backseat.

Katrina was right behind him, a shadow. "What did you say to him?" Her voice was raspy from the gastric acids that had visited her throat. She still looked as furious and scared as she had before, but now there was something else in her eyes: doubt. She was doubting her previous conviction he'd killed the man with the red hair, and right then Jack knew he had her. He could coach her through this.

"I'll explain everything later," he said softly, gently. "I promise. But right now we have to finish this. Someone's going to come by any minute."

"I don't care," she said. "I'm done with this."

"Goddammit, Katrina. You'll be throwing away your future. Your life. Do you understand that?"

Leaving her to dwell on that, Jack ran to the pickup truck. He shoved aside the bush of prickly phlox and yanked up the hood, which had already come unhinged by the collision with the tree trunk. The engine was still running, like he'd left it. He unscrewed the oil filter. It was hot and singed his hand. He shook the excess oil onto the scorching manifold and exhaust, then rescrewed the filter, leaving it a little loose so if the fire was investigated it would appear to have been loose before the crash, or to have been a product of the crash—either way explaining the leaking oil and, consequently, the fire.

The oil bubbled, creating a smell of rotten eggs that almost gagged him. Blue smoke billowed into the air in thick, greasy clouds. There was a whoosh as the entire engine burst into flames. Seconds later the blaze leapt higher as other fluids ignited.

Jack felt a flush of pride before telling himself this was not the time for back patting.

He returned to where Katrina waited. "You're going to have to drive the Buick," he told her, holding forth the keys while anxiously checking the highway yet once more.

"You said you only talked to him," she said, confused.

"I did. I talked to him. I threatened him, yes, but I only talked to him. I took his driver's license and told him if he ever said a word about any of this I was going to come for him and his family." When he saw the look of horror on her face, he added quickly, "It was just a threat. An empty threat. But a threat that had to be made to keep him quiet." Eyes to the highway again. "Look, we can discuss the ethics of this later. After you've thought it through rationally, from every angle. After you've done that, if you still want to give up, or turn us in, or whatever, then okay." That was a lie. He would never allow her to do that. "But right now we need to move.

Don't ruin your life because in the heat of the moment you let yourself be swayed by your emotions. You'll regret it every long night you spend in prison."

"Where is he?" she persisted. "Why do we have to take his car?"

"I wanted him to walk home. Have a good long while to think about what I told him. Know I was serious. And his car can't be here when the next person drives by."

What seemed like an eternity passed before Katrina held out her hand. Relieved, Jack gave her the Buick's keys.

"Follow me," he said. "I know a place—"

In the distance, coming from the east, a set of headlights appeared.

Chapter 21

Katrina watched in horror as the car approached. Time seemed to slow down; her thoughts sped up and took on a fresh clarity.

When Jack had emerged from the forest, and she'd been convinced he'd killed the man with the red hair, she'd been numbed, once again unable to think straight or fully accept what was happening. It was as if she was a member of an audience, watching a drama that was her life unfold. She could see herself pounding Jack's chest, could hear herself accusing him, but didn't seem to be in control. All she could do was watch from that spectator's seat as she refused to go along with what Jack was saying, because by denying him she'd thought she could somehow deny any of this was really happening. But, of course, it was happening. Cold reality had sunk in when Jack told her she was risking her future on an emotional decision rather than an intellectual one. Yes, she felt appalled at what she'd become a party to. And yes, she and Jack deserved whatever punishment a judge and jury could throw at them.

However, there was another part of her as well, the part Jack was appealing to, which did not want to lie down and give up. And if she was to listen to that preservation instinct, there could be no more hesitating or debating or doubting, no more blurring the distinction between wrong and *really* wrong. The fuzzy line outlining moral culpability had been quickly etched in stone. She was either with Jack one hundred percent, or she was against him. That was the reason she'd accepted the Buick's keys, and in doing so sealing her complicity in the fate of the man with the red hair—regardless of whether she truly believed he was alive or not.

And now that she'd made that decision to do whatever it took to see this thing through, she was as terrified as ever at getting caught.

Jack was already running to the Porsche. "Go! Go!" he shouted at her. "But don't turn on the headlights."

Katrina jumped into the front seat of the Buick. She fumbled with the keychain. There were about ten keys on the damn thing! She jammed the biggest into the ignition. Fit, but didn't turn. Probably for the trunk. She tried another big one. No go. *Come on. Come on!* She tried a third, convinced it wasn't going to work either. The engine caught. Jack pulled up beside her and was saying something. She buzzed down the window.

"Don't use your brakes either," he said, then peeled off into the night.

She followed, spending about as much time looking in the rearview mirror as she did straight ahead. The jumping flames of the blazing fire had now consumed the entire pickup truck. The headlights of the fast-approaching vehicle merged into one bright streak of light. She prayed she was far enough ahead to have escaped their reach. Then the inferno disappeared behind trees as the road began to bend slightly. The headlights vanished as well. Apparently whoever was behind her had indeed stopped to investigate the blazing wreck.

The dizzying rush left her, but she still felt as if she was jacked up on speed. For the first time she became aware the car stank like vomit, and she remembered Jack had tossed the puke-filled shirt in the backseat. God, how had he remained so cool under pressure back there? She'd been pacing and punching and puking while he'd been efficient and restrained and rational and maybe a bit emotionless. And that wasn't exactly right, was it? To remain emotionless in a pressure-cooker situation like that?

Katrina focused on the road ahead. She could make out the shape of the black Porsche, but only because she knew it was there. When Jack flicked on his headlights, she did the same, and her thoughts turned to how such a pleasant evening could have gone so terribly wrong. She replayed the choices she'd made and tried to decide whether she could have or should have done anything differently. But even with the benefit of hindsight, she believed she'd made the best choices she could have at the time she'd made them given how limited her range of options had been. Fate or God or really bad luck had simply intervened and screwed everything up, which was not something she could have predicted and thus prepared for.

An old philosophical question came to mind. You're in a room with a gun, five old people, and a child. Someone tells you if you shoot and kill the old fogies, the kid lives. You kill the kid, the fogies live. So which is it? Red or black, all or nothing? Obviously both choices are abhorrent. The point is, you have to choose. And more, you have to choose between the lesser of two evils. Likewise, if Jack had purposely and maliciously killed old man Charlie, or if he had murdered the red-haired man, she would have notified the authorities the first chance she got. But Charlie's death had not been viciously planned and acted out—it had been an accident— and the Good Samaritan, while likely scared senseless and worried sick for his family, had not been harmed. Jack, it could be argued then, was only guilty of manslaughter in the second degree and of being one scary asshole.

Like he told her, however, his past made his predicament much more complicated than that, and a judge or jury would probably not be so sympathetic. Especially after he tried to cover up the murder. So if she turned him in, she would be responsible for condemning him to a long time behind bars. And he was not meant to be caged. Nobody was, but him especially. He had too much zest for life, too much of that electric something that distinguished a stallion in the wild from a domesticated, gelded one. In a sense, she would be sentencing him to a slow and painful death. And she had already watched one man she loved go that route. She could not in good conscience let that happen again—especially not when all she had to do was keep her mouth shut.

The lesser of two evils.

A place called '59er Diner rolled past on the left side of the road. There were a few cars parked out front, even at this late hour. Jack slowed to make the turn onto State Route 207, toward Lake

Wenatchee State Park. Katrina frowned, wondering where he was leading her. She hadn't thought about that yet. She'd assumed he would be going to the red-haired man's home to drop off the Buick. But up 207? Did the man not live in a nearby town, but in the forest? With his family? Unlikely. Was Jack not going to the man's home then? Was he returning to the cabin? That would be crazy. She wished she had brought her cell phone so she could call him up and ask what the hell he was thinking. But her phone was in her handbag, back in the cabin, in the laundry room.

They continued north for three miles until they reached Wenatchee River, which they crossed. Jack took the back road toward Charlie's cabin. She could recall the way well, even in the dark. Everything about this evening, every detail, would likely be ingrained on her brain for years to come. Jack made a right turn down a narrow road with a "Road Closed" sign nailed to a tree. He stopped in a small clearing. She parked next to him and got out. The area offered a clear view of the moon-dappled lake. She figured this was a lot someone had purchased and cleared with plans to build on it.

"I thought you were taking us back to the cabin," she said.

He nodded at the Buick. "Not with that."

"How did you know about this place? Why are we here?"

"I saw it earlier when we came in. And to answer your second question—we're leaving the Buick here until tomorrow. I'll come back and drive it to our red-haired friend's house then."

"What if he decides to tell someone? What if, once he gets his car back, he goes to the police?"

"He won't."

"How can you be so sure? Nobody keeps secrets forever. Especially secrets like this one."

"They do if they're smart. Think about it. A big crazy son of a bitch threatens to hurt him and his family if he ever says a word of what he saw tonight—an old man dead in his car, an old man he doesn't even know. Would you risk your family over that?"

"No," she admitted.

"Katrina," Jack said, resting his hands on her shoulders, "you know I would never touch his family. It was a threat, to keep him quiet. That's all. You believe that, don't you?"

With his strong jaw set and engine fluid marking his face like war paint, his bare chest chiseled and tattooed, he looked almost savage. But his eyes sketched a different picture entirely. All she could see in them was understanding and concern for her. As if reading her thoughts, he smiled, a slight lifting of the corners of his lips.

"Yes, Jack," she said wearily. "I do."

"I couldn't have done this without you. You know that, don't you?"

She nodded.

"Thank you."

Katrina was about to respond but found she didn't have anything to say, or didn't want to say anything. She'd been through too much. She was overwhelmed. She was angry and mixed up and scared. She simply didn't want to talk anymore. Tears came instead.

When Jack pulled her close, she leaned into his strong embrace.

Chapter 22

It was 10:47 p.m. when they finally returned to the cabin. They parked a fair way down the road so no one would see or hear them pull up and walked the rest of the way. Jack was once more wearing his white T-shirt. They'd washed it in the lake where they'd left the Buick, and now it was damp-dry and faintly smelly. He was holding Katrina's hand. The light from the cabin's porch shone through the fence of trees. "I Want It All" by Queen was playing, and Katrina thought back to when her sister had called on Wednesday to say she wanted to visit. That seemed like a lifetime ago.

Someone screamed, then laughed. More ruckus followed.

Old Charlie would be rolling over in his grave, Katrina thought. If he had one.

They passed the school bus, which was idling, getting ready to leave. The driver, Lance, spotted them and honked the horn.

"You're back!" Monica said. She was sitting on the porch steps, a beer beside her.

Suddenly Jack and Katrina were the center of attention, everyone coming out of the cabin or off the bus, asking questions, making jokes.

"We just went for a walk," Jack said. "Sorry to hold up the caravan."

"Sure you did," Monica said with a smirk.

"You know there's a bedroom upstairs," Graham added.

It was just as Jack had said, Katrina realized. No one suspected a thing. The knot in her stomach loosened. She began to breathe a little easier.

"Well, thank you all for coming," Katrina said, wanting to change the topic. "It was a lovely time." The falseness of that last statement made her almost laugh out loud.

"Hey, listen," Monica said. "I assume you and Jack are staying the night. We cleaned up most of the stuff inside already, but you're still going to need to clean up in the morning. When it's light again. Give a final dusting or whatever. Am I right?"

"Yes," Katrina replied, wondering where Monica's rambling was going.

"Well, would you mind if a few of us stayed as well? I know Bob and Steve are still down on the dock fishing. And I'm not really ready to pack it in yet. What do you say? We won't be loud. Have a drink with us. It will be fun. So?"

Katrina would have preferred for everyone to have gotten on the bus right then—herself included—so she could put this ghastly night behind her. But she couldn't do that. Monica was right. She and Jack would have to clean up in the morning. So she supposed it wouldn't hurt to have a few others stay as well. It would seem suspicious to say no. Besides, it would also give her and Jack an alibi for the remainder of the night, if it ever came to them needing such a thing.

"Okay, sure," she said.

Monica squawked happily. Then all the teachers who were leaving began saying their goodbyes, telling Katrina she should have another party real soon. *Yeah, right,* she thought. Maybe when cows fly and frogs sing and hell freezes over, defrosts, and freezes again. Maybe then, but not likely. Once the bus was loaded and the doors hissed closed, Jack, who was standing next to her, gave her shoulder a reassuring squeeze. She cupped her hand over his. *My partner in sin.* With another honk of the horn and a billow of smoke, Lance maneuvered the bus around, got it facing the right way, then chugged down the dirt road, branches slapping at the bus's high roof.

"Where's Crystal?" Katrina asked the remaining small group.

"With Zach," Graham said.

Katrina thought he was joking and told him so.

"Alonzo saw them earlier," Monica explained. "They came by the cabin for a minute. Got some drinks. He said they looked pretty comfortable together, whatever that means. Then they disappeared again. No one has seen them all night. Strange, you know. Like, where would they go?"

"I thought she would have had better taste than that dude," Graham said.

"Ha!" Monica said. "Like *you*, you mean?"

Katrina frowned. "So nobody knows where they are?"

"Probably in the bushes. Seems to be the place of choice for tonight."

"Do you want to go look for them?" Jack asked her.

Katrina couldn't believe Crystal had gone off with Zach, especially after she'd warned her to stay away from him. But after all she'd just been through, she couldn't get worked up over it. "No," she said. "Let them be. Right now I wouldn't mind a drink." She and Jack excused themselves and went to the kitchen, where Jack poured them both brandy on the rocks.

"You were right," she said. "About no one—"

He held up a finger to his lips. "Not now. Later."

When they returned outside, Zach and Crystal were strolling up to the porch. Guilty-aloof expressions were stamped on their faces, like they knew they'd been doing something they weren't supposed to be doing but didn't give a damn. Maybe they were even a little proud of it too.

"Get some action, Zachy-boy?" Graham said, tipping back his beer.

"That's my sister, Graham," Katrina told him sternly. "Watch what you say."

"We were just down at the dock," Crystal explained. "It's really nice. You can see all the stars."

Katrina said, "You can see all the stars from here."

Graham laughed.

"Christ, Graham, you're obnoxious," Katrina snapped. Her words were met with stunned silence. She quickly added, "I didn't mean that. It's just that I . . . I have a bad headache."

"I apologize about what happened earlier," Jack said to Zach. "No hard feelings, right?"

Zach looked at him, then looked away.

"Who came by a little while ago?" Crystal asked.

"Nobody," Jack said.

"We saw a car drive past." She turned to Zach. "It was a pickup truck, wasn't it?"

"Maybe." He shrugged. "I don't know."

"Sure you do," Crystal pressed. "You followed it."

"No I didn't. I told you. I went to take a leak."

Crystal looked at Katrina expectantly.

"We didn't see any truck."

"What mushrooms are you eating, man?" Graham said. "You told me a friend of Jack's stopped by."

Katrina had forgotten Graham had mentioned the truck earlier, while she'd been looking for a shirt for Jack to wear. Her mind reeled for an explanation.

"Don't worry, you can tell them," Jack said, intervening. "It was someone I'm doing a project with. I needed to sign some papers. I told him to swing by so he could mail them off first thing Monday morning. I asked Katrina to keep a lid on it because I hate guys who mix work with pleasure. Hope no one's too offended."

"So that was *you* who left with him," Crystal said. She turned to Zach again. "I told you it was his car."

"You left?" Monica said. "Where did you go?"

"Zipped back to Leavenworth." Jack said it nonchalantly, but Katrina knew he must be furious their story was being picked apart at the seams. "We had to get some documents my pal forgot."

"Did you go too?" Zach asked Katrina.

"Yes," she said, hoping it was the right answer. It probably would have sounded more plausible had she said she'd stayed behind. But she was too worried about saying something more that could be contradicted.

"That's a pimp ride you have," Graham told Jack. He searched the parking area. "Where is it? The 911?"

"Down the road a little."

"Why—"

"I'm going to the dock," Katrina cut in. "See how Bob and Steve are doing." Her throat was cotton dry, her heart fluttering. She and Jack needed to get out of there. Right away. They'd just dodged a number of bullets, but they wouldn't be able to keep it up for much longer.

She set her drink on the porch railing and took Jack's hand. They crossed the road and wound their way down the shrub-bordered dirt path, which was dotted with the occasional piece of flagstone. She stopped between a massive western white pine and a blue elderberry, the berries purple and ripened and looking like bunches of tiny grapes. She checked behind them to make sure no one had followed their lead. No one had.

"Damn your sister," Jack whispered.

"She didn't know," Katrina said.

"Our story has gone out the window."

"You said we wouldn't be suspects."

"We won't. But it was nice to know we had something to go on if it came to that. Now it's full of holes and loose ends."

Down at the dock Katrina could hear Bob telling some tale, his voice echoing out over the water, though he was too far away for her to make out what he was saying. Steve was laughing loudly.

"What do you think about Zach?" Jack continued.

Katrina frowned. "What do you mean?"

"Do you think he saw anything?"

"What makes you think that?"

"Your sister said he followed the truck."

"He said he went to relieve himself."

"And who do you believe?"

Katrina didn't reply. She tried to think of whether it was possible Zach could have followed the truck back to the cottage and watched Jack hit the old man. There was a chance. But it was unlikely. Why would he have cared about a passing vehicle? Especially if he had been off somewhere making out with Crystal? Still, the fact he might have seen something chilled her more than the lakefront wind. She made a mental note to ask Crystal exactly what had happened when she got her alone tomorrow.

"Besides," Jack said, "I was getting a vibe from him."

"What kind of vibe?"

"Nothing specific. But he wouldn't look me in the eyes."

"You threw him out of the party, Jack. What do you expect? A warm hug? If I was him, I wouldn't feel comfortable around you either."

"Maybe. But I don't trust him."

"That doesn't mean he saw anything."

Jack studied her for a moment, his eyes searching hers. Then he bent forward and kissed her on the lips. He was still holding his drink. She could hear the ice cubes clink. When he pulled back, Katrina smiled at him, but it wasn't a real smile, because she had experienced none of the feelings she had the night before.

Chapter 23

Just after sunrise, while everyone else was sleeping, Jack drove the Porsche through the early morning fog to the clearing where he and Katrina had abandoned the Buick. The blue sedan was where they'd left it, though with the addition of a coat of dew that misted the windows as if two teenagers had been making out in the backseat all night.

Jack put down all the windows, put the transmission in neutral, then pushed the car onto the slab of rock that led to the lake. He gave it a strong shove. It rolled away from him, bouncing down the slope, the undercarriage scraping against the rock, throwing up a sheet of sparks. It splashed into the water, which washed over the hood and flooded the interior. The car floated in one spot for a while, defiant, until the engine dragged the front end down. Then the entire thing sank from view. Jack watched the spot where it had once been until the trapped air had stopped bubbling to the surface and the water became mirror smooth once more.

All evidence of what he'd done in the woods the night before magically erased.

In the vaporous calm that followed, he returned to the Porsche, satisfied with his work so far.

Chapter 24

When Katrina woke up light was shining through the bedroom loft window. She could hear sprightly voices floating up from the lake. Her first thought: rise and shine, time to get packed and clean up the cabin. Then the events of the night before hit her like a slap across the face, only this slap numbed her entire body. Charlie's bloodied corpse. Jack chasing the Good Samaritan. The truck on fire. For a long, dazed moment, Katrina tried to tell herself it was all a bad dream, and she half convinced herself of it. But her memories were far too elaborate to be any dream. It was reality, cold and brutal. She made a sound that wasn't quite a word, but the emotion was crystal clear. Misery. She wanted to curl up into a ball and pretend last night never happened, but she couldn't do that, couldn't run or hide from this, so she sat up, placing her feet on the floor. She took a steadying breath. She had to face the day. Oddly, she realized she was almost excited to do so. Today they would discover whether or not the police suspected foul play in Charlie's death. By the afternoon she would either be in police custody or free. She felt like a gambler who had just placed her entire life savings on one bet. Terrified, slightly nauseous, but excited nevertheless.

She climbed out of bed—still fully clothed, she noted—and went downstairs. Monica was in the kitchen, boiling water on the stove's ancient burner. "Where's Jack?" Katrina asked right away.

"No idea," Monica said. "I've been up for about an hour and haven't seen him. Must be an early riser. But you don't know? Didn't you?—well, it's none of my business. But I thought that

maybe you two would have both slept upstairs? Did you sleep separately?"

The truth was Katrina had no idea where Jack had slept,
whether with her or on his own. After the kiss halfway down to the
lake, she'd told him she was going to get some water. She'd wanted
some space. She hadn't been ready for the kiss. Not then. Not until
she'd sorted her feelings out better. Once alone, she'd gone up to
the loft and, emotionally drained, was out in seconds. "I drank too
much," she told Monica by way of explanation. "Was out like a
light. I'm not sure where he slept. What about Zach and Crystal?
Are they around?"

"They took off again last night. I'm not sure where. Where's
there to go, right? It's crazy. Like they have some secret love nest.
Oh, I'm sorry! I shouldn't say that. I wouldn't want Zach dating
my little sister either. Dating? No—I didn't meant that either! I'm
sure they're just friends."

Katrina merely nodded, realizing how trivial such concerns still
felt. The water came to a boil. Monica made them both mugs of instant coffee. Katrina's mug had the red-and-blue Esso logo on it,
below the words "Thankful Tankful '87." Probably a promotional
giveaway from the gas giant. She wondered if it had meant anything special to Charlie, had any sentimental value? A profound
sadness welled up inside her.

Monica withdrew a box of Special K from her backpack, along
with a carton of UHT milk. She offered Katrina a bowl, but Katrina
declined. She was far too upset to stomach anything. While Monica ate her cereal, they made small talk, mostly about the party—
apparently a couple teachers had gone skinny dipping—but
Katrina wasn't listening. Her mind was a million miles away.

At half past eight, Jack came through the front door, carrying
two brown paper bags from McDonald's. Katrina greeted his arrival with conflicting emotions. Relief he was back from wherever
he'd gone. Pity for him that she'd dragged him into this god-awful
mess. Even fear, mild and uncertain, but there nonetheless. It
wasn't a fear for him but a fear of him. The way he'd acted last

night—his calm coolness, his rational persuasion, his apparent lack of remorse at what they'd done—it was not normal and thus somehow frightening. Nevertheless, more than any of that she felt a burning curiosity. Had he spoken to the Good Samaritan? Was their secret still safe? Was the red-haired man going to hold up his end of the deal?

She saw the newspaper rolled up beneath his arm and her breath caught in her throat. *Had the media reported the car accident? What was the verdict?*

"Hope you two haven't eaten." Jack said, grinning, and he seemed as upbeat as usual. He looked around the empty room. "Where is everyone else?"

"Down at the dock," Monica said. "Apparently morning is the best time to fish."

"Tell them there's food here if they want it." He looked directly at Katrina. She couldn't read anything in his eyes. "Want to come outside for a minute, Kat? I have something to show you."

It was another beautiful day. The sun was burning brightly in the cobalt-blue sky, lighting the timbered slopes of the Cascade Mountains a brilliant emerald green. Puffy clouds drifted lazily overhead on unseen currents. There were a few canoes out on the lake, as well as a motorboat, sounding like an ambitious bee in the otherwise still morning air. Jack stopped when they were a safe distance from the cabin and held up the paper that had been beneath his arm. It was the *Leavenworth Echo.* "Nothing in here," he said with a triumphant smile.

"Is that good?" she asked hopefully.

"Accidents aren't newsworthy."

"But that's just the *Echo.* Isn't there a Skykomish paper?"

"I didn't see one. But I also have the *Everett Herald* and the *Wenatchee World* in my car."

"And nothing?"

"Zip. I went through every page."

"Do you think it just didn't make the morning edition?"

"It's possible. But I doubt it. Whoever we saw behind us last night would have reported the burning truck. Editors would have had all night to get the story together. As for that other loose end, I returned the car to our red-haired friend. I repeated my threat. His lips are sealed. He won't be saying a thing. Trust me on that."

It's over then, Katrina thought, overwhelmed with relief, although the relief was tainted with the guilt of knowing they'd gotten away with something very wrong.

"So what does this mean?" she asked, wanting Jack to confirm what she had just concluded.

"It means," he told her, "last night never happened."

Zach was stretched out on the rocky outcrop to the west of Katrina's cabin. Or whoever's cabin it belonged to. He'd pressed Crystal about that slipup the night before, but she hadn't given him anything more. She was beside him now, her head on his chest. The morning sunshine was warm on his face. There was a refreshing breeze coming off the water. It should have been a pleasant Sunday morning. A picture-postcard morning. But it wasn't. How could it be after what he'd seen? He'd witnessed a goddamn murder. A murder he'd never reported. He'd been close. Very close. He'd pressed 9-1-1 into his phone, but he'd backed out before he'd pressed Send. Why? He'd asked himself that a dozen times since, and he kept coming up with the same answer.

Crystal.

He liked her a lot. It was crazy, but he did. He'd known that as soon as they'd started talking down at the dock. It wasn't because she was Katrina's sister or anything like that. They simply connected. And therein lay the problem. If he turned Katrina and Jack in, he could kiss whatever he had going with Crystal goodbye. Girls weren't so interested in guys who sent their older sisters to prison. It was a selfish reason, he knew. But the truth was he didn't know that old man from squat. If he reported the murder, he would be alienating the first person he truly liked—and who liked him—in years. Besides, it wasn't as if he was going to keep the murder a secret forever. He was just going to be prudent about what he knew. Justice might be delayed, but it would be served eventually, he was pretty sure about that. What was that old expression by

Pope? *Wise men say only fools rush in?* No—that was Elvis. *For fools rush in where angels fear to tread?* Yeah, that was it. Zach was no angel, but he was no fool either.

So what was his next step then? He didn't know. But he would have to figure it out. And soon.

"What are you thinking about?" Crystal asked him, pushing herself up on an elbow.

"You," he said.

She smiled. "Really? What about?"

"Just stuff."

"Me too."

"What kind of stuff?"

She shrugged. "You know. Like what's going to happen when I go back to college. Because, you know, you're still going to be here. What are we going to do?"

Despite his attraction to her, Zach knew he couldn't pursue anything with Crystal right now, not until this mess with Jack and Katrina was resolved—if he didn't turn out to be the bad guy and she still wanted to see him, that is. "We should get back to the cabin," he said, sitting up. "Your sister probably wants to leave, and I have to see if I can catch a taxi with someone."

"I'm going to be at Kat's all day. Why don't you come by after you get back?"

"I better not."

"Oh." She looked at him for a long time, reading between the lines. She got to her feet. "I think I should go."

"I'll go back with you."

"No. I'm fine."

Zach watched her walk away, wondering what the hell he was doing.

Katrina glanced over her shoulder at Crystal, who was crammed into the backseat of the Porsche, looking out the window. She'd been unusually quiet all morning. "Anything wrong, Chris?" she asked.

Crystal seemed about to shake her head, but then she said, "You were right about that Zach guy. I should have stayed away from him."

"What did he do?" Katrina demanded. The last thing she needed was for Zach to start screwing up her sister's life as well.

"Nothing." She frowned. "I mean, we got along fantastic and everything, right? I know you said he's weird, but he's not. Not really. He's nice. Then this morning we went for a walk, hung out at the water. I asked him about, you know, about what's going to happen with us later on, because I'm at school and everything. And, well, he sort of brushed me off."

"I told you—"

"I know what you told me. Okay? I don't need you to remind me."

"Sorry, Chris. It's just that— Oh, I don't know. Forget it."

"He has a few marbles loose," Jack said.

"That's what you say," Crystal said. "I don't think so. The thing is, I think I really liked him."

"The best thing you can do, Chris," Katrina told her, "is to forget about him. You're at college. It's a big place. You'll find someone else in no time."

"Yeah, I know. I guess." She didn't sound too convinced or happy about the prospect. "By the way, where are we? How much farther?"

"Almost there," Jack said. "Another twenty minutes."

Katrina asked, "What time is your bus again?"

"Whenever. They leave pretty regularly. Just drop me off at the station. I'll wait around."

"You don't want to stay for dinner? We can make it early."

"Nah. It's okay. I have all my stuff I brought with me anyway. I'll come back and visit again. I think I just want to go back to campus now."

"I have a question for you," Jack said, lifting his eyes to the rearview mirror. Katrina knew he'd been waiting the whole car ride to spring this. "It's about last night. When you and Zach met us back at the cabin, just after everyone else had left on the bus, you said something about Zach following my friend's truck. But Zach said he was relieving himself. Which was it?"

"Why?"

"It's not a big deal. I'm just curious about something."

"What?"

"It's complicated, Chris," Katrina said. "Just tell Jack what he asked."

She shrugged. "We were sitting down on the dock—the neighbor's dock—and this truck drove by. I thought Zach said something about seeing who it was. Maybe he didn't though. Maybe he just needed to use the bathroom. I can't remember."

"Why would he have wanted to see who it was?" Katrina asked.

"I have no idea. Wait! That's not true. I just remembered something."

"What is it?" Katrina turned farther in her seat, so she could watch her sister closely.

"Umm. I might have let it slip that the cabin wasn't really yours."

"*What?*" Katrina said, incredulous. "To Zach? What did you say?"

"I'm not sure. I can't remember everything. I was drinking."

"Try to remember, Chris."

"I don't know! He was talking about the cabin like it was mine. I told him it wasn't. He said yeah, yeah, your sister's place, and I started to say it wasn't yours either. I tried to stop myself, but it was too late."

Katrina noticed Jack clench his jaw tight. "So he might have wanted to find out what was going on?" he asked.

"Maybe. Who cares? What's the big deal?"

"How long was he gone?" Jack demanded.

"Not long, I don't think. Like a couple of minutes, maybe."

Katrina realized this was turning into an interrogation, but she didn't care. The implications of Crystal's revelation were staggering. If Zach had seen Jack murder the old man, well, he was *Zach*. The only person he likely despised more than Katrina herself was

Jack. He wasn't going to keep quiet, not in a million years. He was going to sing like a canary on a world tour, and he was going to do it with a big smile on his face.

Had he already? Would the police be waiting for her back at her house?

Katrina and Jack exchanged glances. She saw skepticism in his eyes, and that's probably what he saw in hers. She asked, "What did he say when he returned?"

Crystal shook her head. "Nothing. He didn't say anything." Her voice became petulant. "Are you guys going to tell me what the big deal is? You're acting really weird, you know that?"

"Someone keyed my friend's truck," Jack told her smoothly.

Katrina studied Jack for a moment, torn between admiration and apprehension by how easily he could tell a lie. On the one hand, she was very happy he was on her side. All she seemed to be doing when she opened her mouth was digging holes, while every time he opened his, he was getting them out of those holes. Yet at the same time she knew nobody should be so good at telling lies. It was like being good at being bad, and it made her wonder if he had told her any lies. About his past? About old Charlie? About the Good Samaritan?

"Oh my God!" Crystal exclaimed. "You gotta be kidding?"

"All along the driver's door," Jack said. "We don't know who did it."

"Why would Zach do anything like that?"

"He's not exactly my best friend. Not after I showed him the door."

"Why wouldn't he just scratch your car then?"

"I'm not saying it was Zach. I just want to rule him out."

"Well, he didn't do it," Crystal said matter-of-factly.

Jack didn't press any more. Katrina didn't either. Crystal was a dead end; she knew nothing more helpful. To lighten the mood, Katrina changed the topic to what Crystal had planned the following week at school, and they continued on that track until they pulled up to the Kwik Stop on the corner of Highway 2 and Icicle Road at the western edge of Leavenworth. Crystal went inside the service station to check the Greyhound bus schedule and returned a minute later to inform them a bus would be arriving in forty minutes. Katrina offered to wait with her, but she said she had a book to read and would be fine by herself. So they hugged, said it was good to see each other again, and promised to catch up again soon.

As Jack pulled back onto Highway 2, Katrina said, "Are we going to my place?"

"You have somewhere else in mind?"

"No, but what if Zach already called the police? What if they're at my house, waiting?"

"They won't be."

"How do you know?"

"Because he hasn't told them anything—yet."

"But how can you know?"

"If he had, he would have done it last night. The cops would have come up to Charlie's cabin right away to investigate. We're talking about a dead body here. The fact they didn't means he never called them."

The python that had been tightening around Katrina for most of the trip slithered away. "God, I was so worried. So that means Zach didn't see anything?"

"Maybe," Jack said. "I really don't know. But I'm going to find out."

She frowned. "What do you mean? You can't just go up and ask him whether he saw you kill someone. That's ridiculous."

"That's exactly what I'm going to do." He made a left onto Ski Hill Drive.

"But what if he didn't see anything?"

"What if he did?"

"Then he would have called the police by now, right? Or he would have at least said something to one of us. You saw him last night. He certainly didn't act like he saw something."

"I told you I got a bad vibe from him."

"And I told you he had good reason to be uncomfortable around you."

"Because I kicked him out of the party? Or because he saw me hit Charlie?"

"No, Jack." She was shaking her head. "I'm going to see him tomorrow at school. I'll be able to read him. Let me deal with it."

"Dammit, Katrina. He might be considering calling the police right now. I'm not waiting around for a day to see what he decides to do. Now listen." He swung left onto Wheeler Street. "After I drop you off, I'm going to drive over to his place and have a little chat with him. A friendly chat. I won't come right out and say anything incriminating. But I want to feel things out. I should be able to tell whether he knows anything or not."

Jack pulled up to her long driveway. No police cars waiting out front with their gumballs flashing. Katrina released the breath she'd been holding, but she didn't get out of the car.

"How are you going to explain an unannounced visit to his house?" she asked. "You don't think that will look suspicious?"

"I'll tell him I want to apologize."

Katrina hesitated, thinking it through. She said, "Okay, fine. But I'm coming too."

"Out of the question," Jack said immediately. "You'll make him nervous."

"I'll make him nervous? You're the one he's scared of."

"It will be strange, the two of us going there."

"No stranger than you showing up alone."

"I'm not arguing this, Katrina. And we're wasting time."

Katrina shook her head angrily. Trying to change Jack's mind, she'd found out through trial by fire over the past fifteen or so hours, was about as easy as moving a mountain with a shovel. "Fine," she snapped. "Do what you want. You'll do it anyway." She was halfway out for the car when she had a terrible thought. "Jack," she said, looking through the open door, "you're only going to talk to him, right?"

"Jesus Christ, Katrina. What do you think I'm going to do? Break his knees?"

She didn't know. Break his knees? Or something worse? "Promise me you're only going to talk to him."

Jack scowled. "I promise I'm not going to kill him. You satisfied?"

"That you won't touch him."

"I'm not going to lay a hand on his fucking precious body, okay?"

Katrina flinched at the acid in his words.

"Sorry," he said, his face softening. "But I need to go, get this sorted out."

Katrina closed the door and stepped to the curb. Jack wheeled the Porsche around in a tight U-turn, then roared off down the street. Long after he'd disappeared from sight, she remained where she stood, arms folded across her chest, trying to make herself believe his promise.

Chapter 25

Zach was sitting on the sofa in the basement he was renting, sipping from a bottle of Glenfiddich despite it only being noon, when there was a knock at the door. He frowned. Nobody ever came by his place. He waited. Sure enough, another rat-tat-tat. Loud and sharp, like whomever was knocking was wearing a ring, and that's what was doing the knocking. His landlady? He wasn't behind on any bills.

More knocking. No ring finger this time. A fist.

Zach's frown deepened. Maybe it was those Jehovah's Witnesses. They'd come around last week, a jolly looking old lady and a skinny girl dressed like Punky Brewster, both grinning at him like Armageddon was right around the corner and only they knew how to be saved. They read him some crazy passage from the Bible and asked him if he believed it. He asked them if they believed in Smurfs, then promptly swung the door shut.

Wham-BAM.

Zach started. That definitely did not sound like a meek, God-fearing knock. Curiosity peaked, he went up the stairs, knowing he shouldn't be answering the door but answering it anyway, like the guy in a horror movie who has to see what that thump was coming from his closet even though there was blood splattered all over his bedroom. He pushed aside the curtain that covered the window in the door and was shocked to discover Jack the Indian standing there. A wild impulse to lock the door and return downstairs swept through him. But he got ahold of himself and opened the door, trying to manage an air of nonchalance. He even leaned casually against the doorframe. "Yeah?" he said, just as cool as James

Dean before his Porsche slammed into the oncoming Ford Custom Tudor.

"Hiya, Zach," Jack said, flashing a big Cheshire grin. "How you doing, champ?"

"What do you want?"

Jack's smile stayed in place, but his black eyes were unreadable. Zach felt like they were peeling away his false bluster layer by layer until they had a good look at the truth inside—a kid who was scared senseless and way, way out of his league. "I think we need to have ourselves a little talk," he said. "Just you and me."

Zach's worst fear was immediately confirmed. Somehow Jack knew he had seen him murder the old man. In which case opening the door had been a very big mistake.

"It won't take long," Jack added, and stepped inside.

Zach was forced to retreat backward. There wasn't much room to maneuver on the small landing, and he stumbled down the stairs, almost falling on his ass.

"Why are you so jumpy, Zach?" Jack said, staring down at him. "What's the matter? Do I make you nervous?"

"This is trespassing."

Jack closed the door behind him. He turned the deadbolt, which made a solid click as it slid home. He came down the stairs, still smiling, like he was having a good old time. "Trespassing, you say? Really? I thought you said come in."

Zach backed up across the basement, putting the sofa between himself and Jack. "Do you want something to drink?" he said. "Tea? Orange juice?"

"Shut up, Zach."

"Why are you here?"

"Like I said. Just to talk." He stopped on the other side of the sofa so there was about three feet separating the two of them. He nodded to one of the armchairs. "Take a seat, why don't you?"

"I'd prefer not to."

"*Sit down, Zach.*" His voice was steel. Zach sat in the chair farthest from Jack. "That's a good boy. I think you're catching on. When I say something, you listen. Now, we're going to have that talk, you and me, and you're going to answer some questions truthfully. Got that?"

Zach nodded mutely. Jack watched him for a moment, drilling him again with those black eyes. He nodded to himself and strolled a circle around the room, as if he was taking a leisurely walk in the park. Eventually he stopped in front of a framed photograph of Zach's parents that was sitting on a shelf screwed into the wall. He picked it up and examined it thoughtfully. Zach glanced at the stairs, wondering what his chances were of getting up them and out the door before Jack got him. Slim, he knew. Especially with the deadbolt in place. Still, he seriously considered trying. Because Jack was a goddamn crazy murderer—a crazy murderer who was now standing in his home, looking at a picture of his parents.

Zach stood up. Not to run. He wouldn't make it, he'd decided. But because he couldn't sit any longer. The suspense was killing him.

"Sit your ass back down," Jack growled at him.

"Get the hell out of my house."

Jack laughed, pleased, like a hunter who'd realized his prey might put up a fight after all. Still holding the picture, he came over to Zach, grabbed a fistful of his shirt, and pulled him close, so their faces were inches apart. "I can break you in half," he said softly, threateningly. "Remember that, champ." He shoved Zach backward, so he collapsed into the chair.

"A friend of mine is coming by in a couple of minutes," Zach bluffed.

"I was under the impression you didn't have any friends."

"His name is Robert. He lives down the road."

"You know," Jack said, clearly unfazed, "originally I came by to apologize to you."

Zach frowned, wondering if that could be true. He quickly dismissed it as wishful thinking. Jack apologizing to him was about as likely as a hungry shark passing up an easy meal. "Apology accepted," he said, regardless.

"No, my friend," Jack said, shaking his head. "I'm afraid it's no longer quite so simple as that."

"Why not?"

"Because the situation has changed."

"How?"

"Actions speak louder than words."

Zach did his best to look clueless.

"Don't bullshit me, Zach. I'm good at sniffing out bullshit. Real good. And you stink of it."

"I seriously don't know what you're talking about."

"I saw the look on your face when you opened the door. You were scared. Why's that, Zach? What reason do you have to be scared of me?"

"Because you're crazy, and you tried to beat me up last night."

"Good try, Zach, but no. If I had wanted to beat you up last night, you wouldn't be standing today. You wouldn't even be sitting. You'd be lying in a hospital bed begging the doctor for more morphine because you hurt so bad. So that's not the real reason. We both know that." He glanced at the picture in his hand, hefted it, as if testing the weight of the silver frame, then sat down in the armchair opposite Zach's. He even folded his goddamn legs, like he was in a private room in an upscale club about to light up a cigar. "Let's talk about Katrina's sister Crystal, why don't we? I'm still not clear on what she meant when she said you followed my friend's pickup back to the cabin. Would you care to elaborate for me?"

"I was taking a piss," he said, poker faced.

"That's not what she said."

"She's wrong."

Jack smiled again, but it didn't reach his eyes this time, which remained cold, black chips. It seemed to say, "Go on, prove it."

"Why would I care about a stupid pickup truck?"

"Let me tell you why," Jack said, leaning forward. "I think you were pissed off with Katrina because she wanted nothing to do with you. I think when Crystal let it slip that the cabin wasn't Katrina's, you thought you could use that to get some dirt on her. And I think you followed the truck to see what you could dig up. Are you following me?"

"I don't know what you're talking about." It was all he could think of to say.

"Don't dick around with me here, Zach. I *know*. Get that through your fucking thick head. So what we've got to do now is decide what we're going to do about this little predicament we're in."

He wants to cut a deal? Zach wondered, amazed and incredibly relieved. Given the direction the conversation had been headed, he had been thinking he was never going to leave his basement alive. "It's not a predicament," he said immediately. "I'm cool with it."

"How so?"

"I won't tell anyone anything."

"And I'm supposed to trust you?" Jack was speaking conversationally, had been for most of the interrogation, and there was something about that which flooded the ventricles of Zach's heart with ice water. It was the way someone spoke to you before they shot you in the back of the head. "You already told me you don't like me," he went on. "I bet the first thing you're going to want to do is tell someone what you know. And then they'll tell someone. You know how it goes."

"I won't tell anyone anything."

"When you're drunk?"

"No, I swear."

"And what about the cops?"

"No, never."

"This isn't a game. You know that, Zach, don't you?"

"I know. Trust me, I know."

Jack leaned so close Zach could see a hairline scar on his chin and smell the musky-woody scent of his cologne. "Because if you ever tell anyone," he hissed, "even hint at it, I will track you down and kill you, do you understand that?"

"Yes."

"Louder."

"*Yes.*"

"Good." He sat back. "But I'm not satisfied yet."

Zach groaned inwardly.

"You know why I'm not satisfied?" Jack said. "Because you're a sneaky little rat. I can tell that. Everyone can. It's something you have to work on, Zach. I know how fucks like you work. I bet you think you can report me, then go and lay low somewhere until I'm arrested, isn't that right?"

"I wasn't thinking that."

"Sure you were, Zach. Because you're a sneaky little rat." Jack stood suddenly. He still held the photo in his hand. He focused on it. "Your mother. She's pretty. What does she do?"

"She's a lawyer." Zach thought that may distress Jack. It didn't, not in the slightest.

"You don't want to see any harm come to her, do you?"

"Leave her out of this!"

"Because if something were to happen to your lovely mother, it would be your fault. You would be responsible. You do know that, don't you, Zach?" He paused to let what he was saying sink in. "I have a friend. I'm going to call him when I leave this dump of yours. I'm going to tell him to kill her if I ever go to jail. Run her down while she's crossing the street out in front her law office, maybe. Rape and murder her in a park, maybe. Something like that. My friend, you should know, is very creative. And you should also know he's just gotten out of jail. Seven years, he was in there for. Needless to say, he doesn't like lawyers too much."

Zach wanted to tell Jack his mother was a corporate lawyer, that she didn't deal with slime like him or his friend. But that wouldn't help his situation any. Jack might lose it and punch him the way he'd punched that old man. Then he might rip out the gas line to the stove and shove some newspaper in the toaster. Blow the entire house, and his landlady upstairs, to smithereens. Zach wouldn't put that past Jack. He wouldn't put anything past the lunatic.

"Are we clear?" Jack asked. "Do we understand one another?"

Zach nodded.

Without taking his eyes off him, Jack dropped the picture to the floor. Glass shattered. He picked the frame up, shook away the jagged shards, and peeled the photo out.

"I'm going to keep this," he said. "For reference."

He turned and left.

As soon as the side door banged closed, Zach was up the stairs and bolting the deadbolt. He returned to the basement and began pacing back and forth because he was too worked up to sit. His heart was beating like a hummingbird's. His head felt like it might explode.

Did Jack really have a friend who would kill his parents?

Zach swore to himself, angry. That was the thing. He could never know. Nor could he take the risk and call Jack's bluff. If it was just his life on the line, he might have done as Jack so aptly suspected, going into hiding, then reporting Jack to the police. But there was no way he could tell his parents to do the same. His mother was a partner in her law firm. She couldn't simply stop working, pack up, and move across the country all because of him. Even if she did, she would have to return at some point—her friends were here, her life was here. Since no one knew who this real or fictional friend of Jack's was, she would never have any peace of mind.

Run her down while she's crossing the street out in front her law office, maybe. Rape and murder her in a park, maybe—

An epiphany froze Zach to the spot. Had Jack threatened Katrina the way he'd just threatened him? Had he forced her to help dispose of the body and keep quiet about it? If he had forced her, that meant she was not in on it with him, not a coconspirator. She was on Zach's side, a prisoner of circumstance and fear. He could talk to her, figure out what to do next—

There was another knock at his door.

Chapter 26

After Jack left to speak with Zach, Katrina went inside the bungalow and made green tea, thinking it would calm her nerves. It
didn't. She ended up tossing it down the sink after two sips. She
took up pacing around the house aimlessly, finding the unfurnished rooms a reflection of how she felt inside. Barren. Lonely.
Empty. As if her insides had been dug out like a pumpkin's a week
before Halloween. This was the first time she'd been alone since
Jack had told her that Charlie was dead, that he needed her help
to make his death look like an accident, and his iron steadfastness
and confidence had left a vacuum in his departure, which was
quickly filling up with growing despair and self-hatred. What had
seemed like a bad idea to begin with seemed utterly unthinkable
now. How had she ever gone along with Jack's plan? The dam of
lies they'd built was straining under the pressure of the enormity
of them all. Each time they repaired a crack, another one opened
somewhere else. It didn't take a rocket scientist to know that
sooner or later the whole thing was going to explode.

Then turn yourself in, she told herself. *Stop protecting Jack. He's a
murderer. And a liar.*

She shook her head. Was he? Was he really? Or was he simply
a decent man doing what anyone in his position would have done?

She stopped pacing when the picture of Shawn on the fireplace
mantel caught her eye. She looked at her one-time fiancé with sad
nostalgia. *God, I wish you were here, Shawn.* Jack and Shawn were complete opposites. While Jack was a walking magnet, his presence in-
escapable, Shawn had been Mr. Everyman: average height, build,
looks. Never the life of a party but always polite and interesting.

Steady, stable, and reliable. On paper he didn't seem extraordinary in any way, especially when compared to Jack. But she had been very comfortable with him, happy. Isn't that all that mattered? Because she'd been a contestant on the "Jack Show" for less than a week, and she had become an absolute mess. Of course, she had been placed in exceptional circumstances, but that was just the point. Shawn would never have let her be put in those circumstances.

During his annual physical a little more than two years ago, Shawn had complained to the family doctor of an increasing loss of memory and muscle coordination. The doctor had referred him to a specialist, who'd ruled out common forms of dementia such as inflammation of the brain or chronic meningitis. When there was still no clear diagnosis, more tests were performed, including a spinal tap, an EEG, and a computerized tomography. Finally an MRI scan revealed patterns of brain degeneration that led the specialists to believe Shawn was suffering from variant Creutzfeldt-Jakob disease. Shawn and Katrina's perfectly happy life was flipped upside down. CJD, they learned, was a very rare and fatal brain disorder that affected but a sliver of the population. The physicians—and they had gone to see a number—all told them Shawn had roughly six months to live. The illness progressed quickly. Shawn soon began suffering from involuntary muscle jerks and went partially blind. He lost the ability to move and speak before falling into a coma. Katrina didn't want him to spend his final days in a hospital bed, so she converted the first floor of the house they'd recently purchased—and renovated to accommodate a nursery—into a dreary sickbay, where she served as his full-time nurse. Eleven days after he came home, he died.

Katrina turned away from the picture, wanting to clear those haunting thoughts from her mind. She noticed Bandit standing by the stereo, staring at her, likely sensing the string holding her together was getting ready to snap. She decided to take him for a walk, simply to do something until she heard back from Jack and learned how his "talk" went with Zach.

"Come on, buddy," she said, grabbing the leash from where it hung on the key hook next to the front door. "Let's get some air."

He smothered her with rough licks while she attempted to link the leash to his collar. Once she had it secured, she grabbed a three-quarter-length wool jacket from the closet and went outside. Dark storm clouds had drifted in front of the sun while she'd been inside, and the bright afternoon sunlight had been filtered to a gritty gray. The temperature had dropped as well. It felt more like late October than early September. As she walked Bandit down the street, she thought about fast-approaching Halloween. She decided an appropriate costume for her would be one of those black-and-white-striped prison uniforms, with the plastic ball and chain manacled around an ankle—that is, if she wasn't wearing a real prison uniform by then.

A little ways down Wheeler Street she stopped when she spotted Our Lady of the Snows Catholic Church across the road. It was a sprawling white building with a portico and a blue roof. Parents and children and the elderly were filtering inside. Katrina stared at the building for a long moment. Then she knotted Bandit's leash around a utility pole and crossed the street. As she climbed the church's front steps and entered the narthex, she had the irrational thought she would instantaneously combust, her skin bubbling and sizzling and melting under a ball of flames while families looked on in horror. That didn't happen, of course. She took a seat in a pew and waited for everyone to get settled and for Mass to commence.

She hadn't been to church for years, and nothing seemed to have changed. It was, after all, one of the oldest institutions in the world whose evolution had taken centuries, not decades, or even years or months. The high ceilings dwarfed the congregation. The light filtering through the stained-glass windows was a brilliant red and icy blue. A hushed silence layered everything, what you only experienced in churches and libraries and, perhaps, the waiting room at the dentist's office.

The opening hymn began. The priest, dressed in a white-and-purple cassock, made his way down the center aisle, followed by his entourage. "Welcome to Sunday Mass," he began in a loud, clear voice when he reached the altar. "My name is Father O'Donovan, and thank you all for joining us today in our time of worship."

For the next hour Katrina followed the familiar ritual of Mass: standing, sitting, kneeling, praying, singing. Throughout it all she found herself thinking about the past. When she was six or seven, before Crystal had been born, she had been unlike most of her other friends in that she'd always looked forward to attending church. For one, she liked the dressing up bit. But more than that, she liked the Sunday school where all the younger kids were ushered after the initial hymn was sung. She enjoyed the tales of miracles and adventures she learned about in the picture Bible, and when her teacher once told her that Jesus watched down over everyone, she'd spent the entire afternoon that day in the backyard, looking up into the sky, hoping to catch a glimpse of Jesus, or even God, peeking over a cloud. Years later, in grade nine, she received the top mark in her religious studies class for a paper outlining the existence of God using St. Anselm's ontological argument.

The Good Girl, she mused.

Not anymore.

Katrina wondered why, after all these years, she'd decided to attend Mass now. Because if her parents' death had made her discard any notion of an omnipotent, beneficial God, Shawn's death had hammered the nails into the coffin of her belief, all but making her an atheist. She couldn't put a finger on the answer, only that there had been something about the sight of the church. It had given her some reassurance, some comfort, which had been what she'd needed most right then.

"And the Lord be with you," the priest was saying.

"And also with you," the congregation answered in unison.

"May the almighty God bless you. In the name of the Father, the Son, and Holy Spirit. Our Mass has ended. Let us go forth in the joy of the Lord."

"Thanks be to God."

The parishioners got to their feet, everyone chatting and

laughing, the solemn hush now lifted. They emptied out of the front doors, leaving only the altar boys behind, who were busy with their duties. Katrina didn't leave. She closed her eyes and rested her forehead on the back of the pew in front of her and tried not to think about much of anything.

Someone spoke to her. She sat back, startled.

It was the priest.

"I'm sorry, my child," he said. He was standing next to her pew. "I didn't mean to give you a scare."

"That's all right, Father. I was just thinking."

"About anything in particular? Perhaps I can help?" He was an elderly man with brown hair that was likely dyed and out-of-proportioned features, namely too-large ears and a small, up-turned nose. His eyes were soft and kind.

"Yes," she said. "I mean, no. I can't talk about it."

"Sometimes it is better to talk if something weighs heavily on your mind."

Katrina shook her head, at the same time thinking it would be a great relief to confide in someone what she'd done—to ask someone, anyone, aside from Jack, what to do.

"Did you enjoy the sermon?" Father O'Donovan asked. "I haven't seen you here before."

"I stopped going to church a long time ago."

"Sadly, that's the trend these days. There seems to be three groups. The faithful who come regularly. Those who stop by for special occasions such as Christmas and Easter. And those who come only when they are troubled and in need of guidance." He paused meaningfully. "If you would like to talk or make a confession, my child, you've only to let me know. I'll be here a little longer."

Katrina watched him cross the nave and enter the confessional.

Then, after a good minute of debate, she joined him.

She took a seat on the wooden bench. A panel in the dividing wall of the booth slid open. All that separated her and the priest was a thin linen curtain. The air in the enclosed space was laced with the organic scent of burned incense.

"Bless me, Father, for I have sinned," she began, making the sign of the cross.

"How long has it been since your last confession, my child?"

"A long time."

"What are your sins, my daughter?"

"I told a lie." She paused, swallowed. She was unable to go on.

"Remember you are not telling God anything He does not already know."

"It was a bad lie," she pressed on. "Well, no, it wasn't. It was a white lie. Nothing big. But it led to some . . . some terrible consequences." Suddenly she found the words pouring out of her mouth as she recounted everything, from the time she'd picked up Zach on the highway to Jack leaving for Zach's house earlier this morning. She didn't reveal Jack's name, referring to him as her "friend." Throughout the tale of deceit and murder, Father O'Donovan didn't once interrupt her. When she'd finally finished, she remained sitting in breathless silence, wondering how she could have confessed so much.

"This is a very serious matter, my daughter," he said softly. "How well do you know this 'friend' of yours?"

"We just met. But I . . . I know him well enough."

"Could you persuade him to go to the police?"

The thought of Jack caving and going to the police at this point was inconceivable. His resolve to see this through to the end undetected was inflexible. "No, he wouldn't."

"Because it seems to me this is much more his doing than your own. Tell me then, my child, would you consider turning him over to the police yourself?"

Katrina thought about all the reasons she had used to talk herself out of such an action. "I can't," she said. "I simply can't."

"I think it would be an option you would do well to ponder."

"Are you going to tell anyone, Father?"

"The confidentiality of all statements during the course of reconciliation is absolute. That is the Seal of the Confessional."

Katrina couldn't bring herself to look up from her hands, which were clasped tightly together in her lap. "Do you despise me?"

"God hates the sin, not the sinner. He is not vengeful or spiteful but merciful and forgiving. Even though you have turned away from Him, He has not turned away from you."

"You can forgive me then?"

"I cannot."

Katrina's heart sank. She was beyond redemption.

"No man, regardless of how devout or learned, has the power to forgive sins," Father O'Donovan added. "That power belongs to God alone. However, He does act through the ministration of men, and through me your connection to God's grace can be restored."

"What would I have to do?"

"Are you truly sorry for having committed these mortal sins?"

"Yes."

"Would you commit them again?"

"No, Father. I would not." That was the truth. She was never more certain of anything in her life.

"Your penance is one hundred Our Fathers and one hundred Hail Marys. Also, you will commit yourself to one hundred hours of community service wherever you see fit over the next year."

"Is that all?" she asked, unable to believe she didn't deserve more. Much more.

"Accepting the penance is the method by which you can express your true sorrow. Spend that time thinking about how you have sinned, praying for those you have wronged, and asking God for guidance in how to proceed. God the Father of mercies, through the death and resurrection of his Son, has reconciled the world to himself and sent the Holy Spirit among us for the forgiveness of sins. Through the ministry of the Church may God give you pardon and peace. I absolve you from your sins in the name of the Father, the Son, and the Holy Spirit."

"Amen."

"Give thanks to the Lord, for He is good."

"Thank you, Father."

"Go in peace my daughter, and may God bless you."

Katrina left the confessional, slid to the center of a nearby pew, and began her repentance. It was far from enough to make up for all her poor decisions. It would not clear her conscience or absolve her from the crimes she'd committed. But at least it would be a start.

Jack was sitting on the front steps of her porch when she returned. Back from visiting Zach. Katrina's pulse quickened. Jack tossed aside the pinecone he had been fiddling with and stood. "Go for a walk?" he asked, and although he said it pleasantly enough, she thought she saw his eyes narrow slightly.

"I needed some space. And Bandit hasn't been walked since early yesterday morning. I left the door unlocked for you." The words were tumbling out of her mouth in her haste. She wanted to find out what he'd learned at Zach's. *Had Zach seen the murder or not?* "So? Tell me. What happened?"

"Do you want the good news or bad news first?"

Katrina groaned inwardly. Bad news? She didn't think she could deal with any more bad news. "Bad," she said, regardless.

"Zach knows."

She experienced a hot flash as she was momentarily flooded with warmth, though it wasn't a good warmth. It left her feeling faint and sick.

"But the good news is this," Jack continued. "He won't tell a soul."

Katrina felt the shadow of déjà vu. "How can you be so sure?"

"You have to trust me on this."

She folded her arms across her chest. "What did you say, Jack?"

"I made him a deal, okay? Let's leave it at that."

"You didn't hurt him, did you?"

"I told you I wouldn't touch him."

"You threatened him?"

"Listen," Jack said, resting his hands on her shoulders and looking her square in the eyes. She felt like they were back out on Highway 2, and he was going to give her the emotion versus reason speech again. But all he said was, "I'm not going into detail. But I am one hundred percent confident he won't say anything to anyone. You have to trust me on that."

She was about to leap on that, tell him she was done with blindly trusting him, but she held her tongue. What did it matter? If Zach was okay—and she would know that for sure tomorrow at school—then what did it matter what Jack had said to him? The details didn't matter at this point. Like doing a head count minutes before the ship went under. So she nodded, feeling very indifferent, and that worried her. It was the feeling of giving up. "So what do we do now?" she asked.

"We relax. Get something to eat? Dinner, maybe?"

"Eat?" she said, surprised. "I couldn't possibly. I'm far too nervous."

Jack's powerful thumbs rubbed her shoulders, making small circles. "What can I do then?" he said. "You name it."

"I think I just need to lie down."

"Hey." He titled her chin upward, so they were looking in each other's eyes again. "You okay?"

"I guess."

"If you need anything, even just to talk, you can call me. We're almost through this."

Katrina nodded, went inside, and closed the door. She heard Jack's Porsche drive away.

Five minutes later the police arrived.

Chapter 27

Crystal Burton was sitting on a bench out front the Kwik Stop, staring at page forty-nine of the dog-eared paperback novel she'd been reading for the second time. She blinked, the words on the page coming back into focus. She backtracked a little and discovered she'd barely read two-and-a-half pages over the past thirty minutes. A page every fifteen minutes? What was she? Brain dead? No, more like heart dead. She'd been thinking about Zach. How he'd told her he liked to read too. The books and movies they'd talked about. His crazy cyborg theory. All the other crazy but neat stuff he'd told her. Kissing him. Doing a lot more than kissing later in the night, though not going all the way. Maybe third base, maybe that's how far she'd gone. She wasn't sure. She was used to getting walked, bypassed, and didn't know the details of the lingo.

What the hell had changed between them? She'd thought he'd liked her as much as she'd liked him. He'd been drunk, yeah, but she had been drunk too, and she wasn't pulling any one eighties this morning. So why was he? Because he was a guy and that's just what guys did? That would suck. Because of the distance between them? He in Leavenworth, she in Seattle? That would still suck, just a little less. Nevertheless, she didn't really believe it. Seattle was only two hours away. It wasn't the Middle East. They could have worked something out. She thought back to their exact conversation. She'd told him she was going to be at Kat's all day, and would he like to come by for lunch, and he'd said, "I better not." That was it.

You walked off because of that? she thought. *Because he didn't want to come by for lunch?*

A part of her knew that wasn't completely true, that she'd seen it was over in his eyes, but she stubbornly blocked that out now. Instead she told herself what she wanted to hear, that perhaps he didn't want to come over because Katrina would be there. They worked together, and maybe he found being with a coworker's younger sister embarrassing, especially given his shady relationship with Kat.

Yes—that was more like it.

The Greyhound bus appeared on Highway 2. It pulled into the vast parking lot and stopped next to the gas pumps. It was hissing and groaning and seemed to sigh with relief as the doors folded open and the passengers began to disembark for a quick smoke or bathroom break. Crystal stood, slung her bag over her shoulder, but she didn't get on the bus. She went to the payphone outside the service station and was happy to find the white pages in the hard plastic case had not yet been replaced by automated directory assistance. She fingered through the thin book. There were only two Marshall Zs in Leavenworth. Thank God for small towns, she thought. She dug a pen and a scrap of paper out of her handbag and scribbled down both addresses. She looked up the number for the taxi service and ordered a cab. One arrived five minutes later, by which time the dark sky had begun to spit rain. She showed the driver both addresses and asked him to take her to whichever was closer.

The first house was on Benton Street across from the Faith Lutheran Church. It was a grand two-story redbrick done in the Federal style, complete with classical Greek columns, a semicircular fanlight over the front door, and symmetrical Palladian windows. Two cast-iron hounds guarded the front porch. Crystal had an inauspicious feeling about this one. Zach might look like a rock star, but he surely didn't live like one. Still, she knocked and was immediately greeted by a real dog's bark, which was quickly accompanied by another high-pitched yelp. A middle-aged woman opened the door, holding a baby. She eyed Crystal through the screen. "Yes?"

"I'm sorry," Crystal began, "I think I may have made a mistake."

"Who are you looking for?"

"Zach?"

The woman frowned. "Can I ask what this is about?"

Zach's mother? Did he live with his parents? "I'd just like to speak with him."

The woman cast Crystal a final, suspicious glance before disappearing inside. A robust man with a shock of salt-and-pepper hair appeared in the doorway. He looked at Crystal curiously. His wife stood close watch behind.

"Uh, hi," Crystal said. "Can I speak with Zach?"

"Go ahead."

"You're Zach?"

"Yes, I believe I am."

"I'm sorry. I have the wrong address."

She hurried down the steps, back to the waiting cab. She told the driver to take her to the second address, on Birch Street. This one turned out to be a wooden thing with a pointed roof and overhanging eaves. The shutters needed a new coat of paint and the lawn needed a mow. This was more like it. She asked the driver to wait once more, then dashed through the rain to the front door. She knocked.

"Who are you?" a bent, ghoulish-looking woman greeted her.

"May I speak with Zach, please?" she asked, though her hopes had been dashed once again.

"Ha! That's a first," the old woman cackled. "A visitor! Side door. Lives in the basement."

Bingo! Crystal returned to the taxi, tipped the driver well for his patience, then went to the side door. She took a deep breath, pushed her wet hair back behind her ears, and knocked. Her heart hummed with nervous excitement. No one answered. She knocked again, louder. A curtain in the door window was pulled back. Zach peered out, like a sentry at a secret fort of bandits. His face disappeared and the door opened. "Hey, Crystal," he said, and for some reason he looked relieved.

"Since you didn't want to come by for lunch," she said, hoping she sounded more casual than she felt, "I figured I'd come by your place." She held her breath.

"Umm—okay, sure." He opened the door farther. "Come in."

Crystal followed Zach down the stairs to a rustic basement, which had wood-paneled walls and oak-colored carpet. An open, half-empty bottle of whiskey stood on the coffee table, next to a metal ashtray filled with cigarette butts.

Her throat was tight. She swallowed. "Crazy night last night, huh?" she said, wondering if he thought she was a fool for showing up unannounced.

"More than you know. Want a drink?"

She never drank so early in the afternoon, but she said yes anyway. The kitchen was spotless, not a single dirty dish in the sink or on the counter. Everything seemed to gleam.

"I thought guys who live alone are supposed to be messy," she said.

"I only keep one plate and one bowl. Forces you to clean up by necessity." He took two bottles of Bud Light from the fridge, twisted off the caps, and handed her one. "Cheers."

They clinked. Sipped.

"So," Zach said, "you mentioned lunch. You wanna make something to eat?"

"Are you hungry?"

He said he was. While he sliced up tomatoes and onions and bell peppers for a spaghetti sauce, she defrosted ground beef in the microwave and formed meatballs. She was beaming the entire time. She couldn't have asked for a better outcome to her impromptu visit. In fact, she couldn't believe she'd been sitting at the Kwik Stop thirty minutes ago, thinking she was never going to see him again. She finished the first beer quickly and asked for another. He opened two more. They ate the spaghetti at the small kitchen table, then went to the living room, sitting down on the soft sofa.

When Zach switched from beer to the whiskey on the coffee

table, Crystal realized for the first time something was off. She'd likely missed it earlier because she was riding the high to be in his house. But now that her nerves had settled down—and she watched him drinking whiskey at a little past noon—she was seeing things differently. Was his edginess because of her? Was he not happy to see her, as she'd initially believed, but disconsolate? Getting drunk to numb the pain of her visit? She blurted, "Do you have a good time? You know, with me?"

"Of course," he replied, looking momentarily surprised. "A great time."

"So how come you don't want to date?"

He hesitated. "You're in Seattle. I'm here."

"Is that the only reason?" she asked hopefully. "Because I was thinking about it, and that's not really a problem. I can take the bus up here on weekends. Or you could come to Seattle. There's a ton of things to do there."

"It's more complicated than that right now."

"What's complicated?" she asked, getting angry. "If I like you, and you like me, what's the big deal? We can work it out."

"Listen, Crystal. I've been giving this a lot of thought as well. And to tell you the truth, I like you. Seriously. I do. But there are some things—"

"It's my sister, isn't it?" She saw him tense. She pounced. "It *is* her. It's Katrina. Well, who cares if you work with her? Or who cares whether you guys get along or not? I don't. I don't care what she says."

"How about this? Let me get some stuff sorted here first. If it works out how I hope it will, then you and me, we can take it from there."

A lightbulb went on. "Do you have a girlfriend?"

"No, it's nothing like that. Honest."

She believed him. The way he was talking and acting, he seemed troubled, maybe even a little afraid. She couldn't imagine about what, but that's how she read it. Still, she was confident he was being sincere. She wanted to press him to explain what this big burden of his was, but she didn't. She was already more than happy with the progress they'd made so far, and she didn't want to jeopardize that. "I guess I can handle waiting a little while," she said, scooting closer to him, trying to make her voice husky. "But as long as I'm here now—"

She kissed him somewhat awkwardly on the cheek and slid a hand up his shirt.

A short time later he led her to the bedroom.

Chapter 28

"Yes?" Katrina said, opening the front door a crack and blocking the space with her leg so Bandit could not bolt outside. Her heartbeat had spiked as soon as she'd looked through the beveled glass and saw the cop on the other side. She tried to appear as normal as she could.

"Apologize for disturbing you, Ms. Burton. I need to ask you a few questions." It was the same police officer who'd come by when she'd reported someone spying on her through her bathroom window. Short and comical-looking, constantly hitching up his belt. He had his peaked cap tucked under his arm once more, playing at being the chivalrous gentleman. That reassured her somewhat: he was just a goofy man in a uniform in a small town. She could handle him.

She managed a smile. "Have you found out something about the peeper?" she asked, hoping that was the reason for his visit.

"Afraid not, ma'am. Different matter entirely. Did you rent a cabin from a Mr. Charles Stanley last night?"

The question cut through her hope like a knife. Conflicting thoughts and emotions ricocheted in her mind, but she couldn't make sense of any of them and had no time to try. "Yes, I did," she said, wondering how much he knew. "Is there a problem?"

"You could say that. Mr. Stanley's dead."

"Oh my God!" she exclaimed. *Enough surprise?* "How?"

"Mind if I come in?"

Katrina stepped back to allow him entrance. Bandit, who loved strangers, especially the postman and children on Halloween night, eagerly sniffed the cop's boots—Officer Murray, she remembered. She led the reluctant boxer to the bedroom, closed the door, then returned to the living room. She thought about offering Murray coffee but decided not to. She didn't want him hanging around any longer than was absolutely necessary. The longer he stayed, the greater the chance he'd have of reading what she was trying desperately to keep from her eyes.

He pulled out his little black notebook, poised his pen above an open page, and asked, "When was the last time you saw Mr. Stanley?"

Katrina's first impulse was to lie and say yesterday morning. But she told herself that was panic taking over. Someone—Charlie's wife, a neighbor—might have known what he'd intended to do. Her second impulse was to look away from Murray as she contemplated the answer. She didn't, recalling that avoiding eye contact was a sure sign of deception. She held the cop's inquisitive gray eyes and said, "He actually stopped by the cabin last night."

"At approximately what time?"

"Oh, I don't know. Nine? Nine thirty?"

Murray's shoulders twitched. He hiked up his belt. "And why was that?"

"According to Charlie," she said, pretending to be amused, "we had the music up too loud."

"A long way for someone to travel to tell you to turn down the music."

She shrugged, knowing if she put her foot in her mouth now, Jack wasn't around to help pry it out. "My cell was off all night. Maybe he tried to call me."

"Any idea why he cared so much about the music being too loud?"

"He said the neighbors called him. I guess they complained."

"Couldn't he have asked them to ask you to turn it down?"

"I'm sure he could have."

"But he didn't."

"No, he didn't." Murray was watching her closely. She added, "When we met him yesterday morning to get the key, he told us some story about renting the cabin out to some college kids last year. They apparently threw a big party and trashed the place. He might have thought we were having a similar sort of party."

A twitch. Hitch. More note taking. "Seems to me if I had one bad experience with a party, I wouldn't be too eager to allow another party to go on there."

"Well, he didn't know we intended to have one."

Officer Murray raised an eyebrow, and Katrina wondered if she'd gone and done it, stuck her foot in her mouth. "What was the reason you gave him for renting the cabin?" he asked.

"Nothing. He never asked," she lied. In fact, she remembered Jack's exact words: *All we have in mind is a little romantic weekend.* "Regardless, it's not as if we were a bunch of college kids. We were all responsible teachers from Cascade High."

"Did the party get out of hand?"

"No."

Those inquisitive eyes on her again. "But the music was loud enough to annoy the neighbors?"

"The place is just like we found it. We brought a stereo down to the dock, yes, so we could hear the music there. That was probably the reason for the noise complaint." She straightened, trying to appear both confused and slightly indignant. "May I ask where all these questions are leading? What does any of this have to do with Charlie's death?"

"Mr. Stanley was in a car accident last night. Apparently he swerved off the road. His pickup truck went up in flames."

"Jesus! How awful." She frowned. "I still fail to see what this has to do with me."

"Just routine questioning, Ms. Burton. You were the last person to see him alive."

Katrina wanted to believe him, but she didn't. "I'm afraid I still don't understand, Officer. If he was in an accident, why is there an investigation at all?"

"There's been no determination yet it was an accident," he said meaningfully.

"What?" She prayed he was reading her shock as puzzlement. "What else could it have been?"

"I can't say much right now, ma'am. I can only tell you the circumstances of his death remain somewhat suspicious." He licked
a finger and flipped a page in his notebook. "Now, if you could
just answer a few more questions, I think I'll be done here."

Katrina felt a rush of cautious optimism. A couple of questions.
That's all. She could do that. And thank God. She didn't know
how much longer she could go before breaking down completely.
Nevertheless, despite seeing the finish line approaching, and
greasing her way out of this one, she knew this wouldn't be the
end, not really. There would always be the guilt. The constant paranoia of discovery. Could she deal with that?

Then tell the truth now and get it over with.

"Am I under suspicion?" she asked, mixing the confusion and
indignation again.

"Why would you be?"

"I shouldn't," she said sharply, perhaps more sharply than
she'd intended. "But you're making me feel like I am."

"Just routine questioning, ma'am."

Katrina kept her cool, though the shot of anger had made her
feel better, more in control. "Go ahead then."

"What exactly did Mr. Stanley tell you when he arrived?"

"I already told you. He said the music was too loud."

"Was he upset?"

"He was irritated, I suppose. He was a very vocal man."

"Vocal?"

"He was foul. Swore a lot."

Murray jotted more notes in his notebook. She wished she
knew what he was writing. *Suspect acting very suspicious. Sweating.
Fidgeting. All the classic signs of guilt.* Her eyes flicked to the words
on the page. She couldn't read upside down. Sensing he was about
to look back up, she tugged her eyes away. "So he told you to turn
down the music? What happened next?"

"We showed him the place."

"Who is we?"

Dammit, she thought. "Just another person at the party."

"Another teacher?"

"Well, no. He's not a teacher. I'm involved with him."

"What's his name?"

Would they run it? Find out about Jack's past? God, she was ruining everything! Right at the end, she was going to blow it all. "Jack Reeves," she told him.

"So you and Mr. Reeves showed Mr. Stanley around. And then what?"

"He was satisfied the place was still in good order. We told him we'd turn down the music. That's it, I believe."

Murray gave his belt a hefty tug. *Tighten that stupid thing!* she wanted to shout.

"Did anyone at the party other than you and Mr. Reeves say anything to Mr. Stanley? Perhaps something that might have provoked him?"

"No. Only Jack and I spoke to him."

"No one else even saw him?"

"No."

"And he left after that. You saw him leave?"

"Yes."

"Did he say where he was going?"

"I imagine he was going home."

"But he didn't tell you?"

"No, I don't believe he did."

"No one followed him?"

She hesitated, frozen inside with sudden fear. *Had the neighbors seen Jack's Porsche follow the pickup? Had someone else?* "Not that I'm aware of."

A thoughtful pause, pen poised. "Earlier today I spoke to his neighbors. They told me they saw two vehicles pass by their place last night. Mr. Stanley's cabin is the last one on the point."

"I don't know who it could have been."

"How many vehicles were at the cabin?"

"Only two. Everyone came in the school bus. Jack and I drove."

"In Mr. Reeves's car?"

"Yes."

"Could you tell me the make and model?"

"You know, Officer, I think I've been rather patient with these questions. But I'm not sure I like the direction you're taking this conversation. Why would you need to know a description of Jack's car?"

"Process of elimination, ma'am. I assure you, it is nothing more than that."

"It's a Porsche. Black. I wouldn't know the model. I'm not familiar with cars."

Murray wrote that down. "Is it possible, Ms. Burton, that Mr. Reeves may have left without your knowledge?"

Process of elimination, my ass. "To follow Charlie? Why in heaven's name would he do that?" She shook her head. "I'm sorry, Officer Murray, but this is absurd. I think I'm done here."

"Did Mr. Stanley and Mr. Reeves have an argument?"

"Absolutely not."

He nodded. The notebook went back in his belt. Katrina thought she might faint with relief. "That's all I need for now then. Again, I'm sorry to have bothered you, Ms. Burton. I'm just tying up some unanswered questions. Probably turn out Mr. Stanley fell asleep at the wheel."

"I can't imagine what else it could be."

"If I have any more questions, I'll be in touch." He turned to leave. "By the way," he said, as if in afterthought, "Mr. Reeves isn't from Leavenworth, is he?"

"No. How did you know that?"

"I don't recognize the name. I know most people around these parts. Is he staying in town, do you know?"

"I . . . I don't know. I've only known him a few days."

"I see. Thank you again, Ms. Burton. Have a good day."

He left. Katrina watched as he jogged through the rain to the cruiser. She closed the door and went immediately to the bathroom, where she thought she might be sick. She wasn't. Still, the strength seemed to have left her body, and she had to hold onto the sink for support. She glanced in the mirror and was relieved to find she appeared calmer than she felt. Then she realized she had to call Jack. Because if Officer Murray discovered where he was staying, which wouldn't be too difficult, she needed to explain everything to Jack first, so they would be on the same page with their stories.

She went to the bedroom, grabbed her phone that was next to the futon, and punched in Jack's number. It rang and rang.

Jack didn't pick up.

Chapter 29

Jack was in his room at the Blackbird Lodge, dressed in black track pants and a black T-shirt, absorbed in his daily martial-arts training. His heart was beating steadily, his breathing deep and even. He had entered a familiar state in which his mind had become a blank slate, detached from the clutter of everyday life. "Don't think about the kick or the punch, Jack-san," his karate teacher had instructed him years ago. "Thought leads only to contemplation, hesitation, and ultimately error. Instead feel what is right, act and react, tap into instinct." After one particular class, while an eight-year-old Jack had been waiting outside the dojo for his old man, who'd been late to pick him up as usual, his sensei had gone into much more detail on this philosophy, telling him when early man developed the faculty of reason, this rendered all but the most basic of instincts obsolete. It lent man the ability to self-consciously change beliefs and attitudes, leading to the capacity for freedom and self-determination, to form complex social structures and civilizations, and to dominate the world. But this same faculty also made men and women individually weak, transforming them into the most inefficient, accident-prone species on the planet. To demonstrate this point, he asked Jack if he'd ever seen a monkey fall from a tree, or a tiger sprain an ankle while in pursuit of a gazelle, a crocodile drown, or a spider slip off the wall. It was a lesson that had stuck with Jack over the years, defining him, and from that day forth he knew if he ever wanted to be the best and strongest at what he did, he would have to become that tiger, that crocodile—ruthless, an unthinking machine.

Someone, Jack realized abruptly, was knocking at the room's

door. He took the buds from his ears halfway through a Johannes Brahms piano concerto and stuck them in the waistband of his pants, next to where the tiny MP3 player was clipped. He went to the door and peered through the peephole. A cop, small and odd-looking. He frowned but nevertheless opened up.

"Mr. Reeves?" the cop said, looking up, apparently startled to see such a large man towering over him.

Jack smiled. "Yes, sir."

"Officer Murray. May I have a minute of your time?"

"Come on in." He stepped back to let the cop enter. "So what brings you here?" he asked, closing the door again.

"There's been an accident. I'm doing the legwork."

"Accident? Hope no one was hurt?"

"Afraid so. A Mr. Charles Stanley. He was killed last night."

"Charles—" Jack pondered for an appropriate amount of time. He widened his eyes. "You mean old Charlie?"

"I believe you were at his cabin last night?"

"Nice little place. What the hell happened?"

"He was in a car accident. He went off the road. Hit a tree. Whole truck went up in flames."

"Poor soul. Christ. He was a character, all right."

Jack's cell phone began ringing. He frowned to himself. Not many people had his number. Those few who did rarely, if ever, called him.

Katrina?

He did the math, making connections. The cop must have spoken with her first. That was the only way he could have found out about Jack's involvement last night. And if that was the case, he needed to find out what she'd told the cop.

"Excuse me," he said. "Be right back."

At the desk he picked up his phone. His invisible frown deepened when he saw seven missed calls on the display.

What the hell had gone wrong?

"Hello?" he said, turning his back to the cop and walking to the far corner of the room.

"Jack!" Katrina exclaimed. "God, Jack. Where have you been?"

"Exercising."

"A policeman just came by my place about thirty minutes ago," she said, speaking fast. "I think he wants to talk to you. I said you weren't from around here, so he'll probably be checking all the motels and hotels. We have to get our stories straight."

"Yes, that would be good."

"Jack? Is something wrong?"

"No, that's fine."

"What? He's there, isn't he?"

"Yes."

"I told him Charlie came by," she said, lowering her voice. "He knew anyway. I said Charlie came because he wanted us to turn down the music. I didn't say anything about him wanting to shut down the party. I said we showed him the place and he was satisfied. But the cop talked to the neighbors and learned two cars left. He thinks someone followed Charlie. I told him I didn't know who it was, but then he asked how many cars were there, and I told him only the bus and yours, so he thinks you followed him. God! I'm so sorry. I didn't know what else to say. Maybe you can tell him you were just going to the store to get some more liquor or—"

"That's fine. I'll take care of everything for you."

"I'm sorry, Jack."

"Is there anything else?"

"No, that's all, I think."

"Thanks for calling. I'll get back to you later." He hung up.

Officer Murray was waiting patiently where Jack had left him, turning away from the window when Jack approached, as if he'd been doing nothing more than watching the rain, which was bullshit. He'd been listening to every word.

"Sorry about that," Jack said, not offering to explain who it was on the phone. He'd performed numerous interrogations over the years and knew only guilty people thought they needed to give excuses. "Where were we?"

"I have a few questions for you, Mr. Reeves."

"Just Jack," he said, sticking out a hand.

"Er—Michael," the cop said, shaking awkwardly.

"Fire away then, Mike."

He took a notebook and pen from his belt. "You were with Ms. Katrina Burton when she spoke with Mr. Stanley?"

"I was."

"What did Mr. Stanley say?"

"Said he wanted us to turn down the music. Can you believe that? Crazy bastard drives all the way from Skykomish just to tell us to turn down the music."

"Actually, he didn't come from his home in Skykomish."

Jack shook his head. "I don't understand."

The cop studied Jack for a moment, seeming to size him up, the way you do when considering whether to tell someone something important or not. "Here it is," he said finally, apparently swayed by Jack's easygoing nature. "I get a call from Lucky late last night—he's the sheriff in Skykomish. Says there was a suspicious accident on the road."

"Suspicious?"

"Well, yes and no. Automobile fires are pretty common. About thirty every hour on the highways across the country. But those that happen when there's no one around to see them, well, they're more likely to be under suspicion for arson."

"I don't think Charlie's looking to collect on the insurance, Mike."

Officer Murray laughed and stuffed his notebook and pen away. He hadn't written a thing. "No one thought twice about foul play until Lucky got ahold of Mr. Stanley's wife. She's in Wenatchee Hospital. Bad hip or something. Mr. Stanley was there with her when his neighbor called and complained about the noise. He told his wife—Luella, her name is—he tells her he needs to go to the cabin to shut down some wild party and he'd be back soon. Only he never comes back. Instead he's found way over by Skykomish, his truck on fire. Didn't really add up, you know what I mean?"

Jack's blood boiled. He could never have known.

"So they investigated the fire further," Murray added.

"And?"

"It looks like the crash caused an oil leak that combusted."

"Is that unusual?" Jack asked ingenuously.

"No, it happens."

"Case closed then."

"Should be," Murray said, nodding, though the nod didn't mean he agreed. "But Lucky was an old friend of Charlie's. Grew up here in these parts with him. He wants to know exactly what happened. Wants to know why Mr. Stanley was going back to Skykomish when his wife was waiting for him at the hospital. Says it's not like Mr. Stanley to do something like that. He wasn't a spur-of-the-moment fella."

"Maybe he had to pick up something? It could be any number of reasons."

Officer Murray hitched up his belt and shrugged.

Jack said, "Let's cut to the chase then, shall we? What can I do to help you that Katrina couldn't?"

Murray eyed him. "I don't believe I mentioned I had spoken with Ms. Burton."

"So you didn't speak with her?"

"No, I did. But how did you know that? Was that her on the phone—"

"Last I spoke to Katrina was early this morning."

"Then how—"

"How else would you have known I was staying here? Katrina is the only person who knows. I'm just connecting the dots here, Mike."

Murray took that notebook out again, flipped through the pages until he found what he was looking for. "No," he said, tapping the page with a bony finger, "Ms. Burton told me she didn't know where you were staying."

"How did you find me then?"

"There are only a few hotels in Leavenworth. I called up each one."

"Maybe I'm mistaken then. Maybe I didn't mention to her where I was staying." Jack shrugged dismissively, but he was more wary now. The funny-looking cop was sharper than he appeared. "Anyway, we're getting sidetracked here. What do you want from me?"

"Did Charlie mention to you where he was going?"

"No, I'm pretty sure he didn't."

"But you left right after him, isn't that correct?"

"Yes, I did."

"Did you see which way he went?"

"Now that you've mentioned it, you're right. He did turn west. Toward Skykomish."

"Did you go west also?"

"No, I headed east, back to Leavenworth."

"Do you mind me asking why?"

"Sure." Jack could not, as Katrina had suggested, tell Officer Murray he'd gone to a convenience store to pick up booze. That could be easily checked out. Nor, for the same reason, could he tell Murray what he'd told everyone else at the party, that a friend had stopped by. It unnerved Jack to know there would be two stories going around, but hopefully, if he played it right, the investigation would end here and now. "You keep this between you and me, okay, Mike?"

"That depends."

"I needed protection."

"Sorry?"

"I'm banging that broad, Katrina," he said, slanting the cop a buddy-buddy smile. "I forgot the condoms, and she's a bit of a prude. Won't go bareback."

"So you went to where?" he asked, pen poised once more.

"Right back here. I have a stash in the suitcase. Just in case, right?"

"I see." The pen and notebook disappeared in the belt, for good this time. "Thank you for your help in clearing that up, Mr. Reeves."

"Jack."

"Right."

Jack walked Officer Murray to the door. Murray paused in the hallway, looked back, and said, "You take care of yourself. Those are some nasty bruises on your face."

Jack raised a hand to his face self-consciously. His right cheekbone was sore to the touch, his nose swollen. Some of Katrina's coworkers had commented on the bruises this morning. That was the last time he paid them any attention. "Yeah," he said. "Goddamn booze. Walked right into a tree while out taking a piss."

"Good thing you didn't poke an eye out. You'd be explaining that story to everyone from now until your grave."

"Take it easy, Mike," Jack said, waving him off.

Katrina was having a horrible nightmare. She was trapped in a small dark room, surrounded by wraithlike people who had formed a ring to prevent her from escaping. They tightened the circle, shuffling zombie-like toward her. All of a sudden she could make out their faces. They were people she knew: school friends, relatives, old teachers she'd had, colleagues she'd worked with, even Diane Schnell, the VP, right in among them, sharp and bony. She was the one who began the chant of "Liar!" her tight features contorted in hatred. Soon everyone had taken up the chant, saying it louder and louder. Katrina searched the blur of faces for some sign of sympathy. There was none. Each person looked as though they wanted to gut her right there and then, and maybe eat those guts as well. She clamped her hands over her ears, squeezed her eyes shut, and sank to her knees. Someone grabbed her. She screamed, but nothing came out of her mouth. Her throat had shrunken to the size of a straw. The hand gripping her hair shook her violently. She tried to smack it away, the way you smack at a buzzing fly, wild, without coordination. It wouldn't let go. She began clawing at it, desperate. To her horror, the hand was soft and mushy. She pulled away big clumps of wet, rotten flesh.

Shawn. God, it's Shawn, come back from the grave.

When she finally broke free and spun around, she didn't find Shawn behind her but Charlie, his hair and eyebrows burned away, his skin red and blistered, missing in places, white maggots crawling over the exposed sinew and coagulated veins. Behind him the throng of people came ever closer until they were right on top of her, cold hands pulling at her clothes, clawing and scraping her. Soon all Katrina could see were squirming limbs and putrid, grinning faces. She pulled herself into a fetal position and screamed her silent scream until she thought she must be dead.

Something changed. She'd jumped scenes, she realized, the way you do in dreams. She knew that without looking around. She opened her eyes and discovered she was in another room. This time she was bound by heavy, rusted chains to a dirty stone-and-mortar wall. Directly across the room from her was a man, manacles spreading his arms six feet high off the ground. He hung there, his head slumped forward, like a forgotten scarecrow.

No! she thought, instantly recognizing where she was.

As if on cue, the faceless butcher appeared. He was dressed in long black robes and a cowl, like the Devil of Death. Instead of a scythe he had an alien-looking blade in his hand. He began going to work on Shawn. Carving, slicing, skinning, snipping. Katrina yelled and yelled at him to stop, her voice finally found, but he didn't stop. He kept on doing what he was doing. When there was little of Shawn left, he turned around, something he'd never done before, and pulled back the hood that had always hid his identity.

It was Jack.

Katrina woke with a start. Her heart was thumping, and she was completely disorientated. She had laid down when it was still light out, but now her bedroom was completely dark. Rain was falling outside, tapping against the window like the bony fingers of an evil presence who wanted to get in. Something was beside her. She almost jerked away from it before she determined it was only Bandit, snoring softly. She heard what sounded like a game show coming from the other room. Had she turned on the TV earlier? No, she had not.

Had Jack? Was he here?

That possibility frightened her. Badly. She told herself it was the aftereffects of the dream. But the part of her that separated truth from bullshit was having none of it. The longer she sat on the futon, listening to the monotonous, disembodied voice of the host—Pat Sajak—the more nervous she became.

Her fear of Jack, she realized abruptly, was very real.

It seemed incomprehensible, but at the same time indisputable.

Had she always known this—at least, since the revelation he'd killed Charlie? Had she somehow sensed it at the time but had shelved it because she didn't want to consider it?

Maybe. She didn't know. What she did know was this: now that the possibility had been raised, she had no problem dredging up a series of disturbing incidents which, taken separately over the last twenty-four hours, had been overlookable, but taken together and examined with an adrenaline shot of fear and fresh eyes drew a much more sinister picture. How Jack had manhandled Zach and Charlie, for instance. His refusal to involve the police. His unintentional admission he'd kicked in Charlie's head. The bloodlust she'd seen in his eyes when he'd gone after the Good Samaritan.

Yes—that was the game changer, wasn't it? Up until then she'd been on his side. She'd still cared for him. Still was doing everything she was doing for him. But after he'd chased the red-haired man into the woods—that's when she'd begun to see him in a different light. That's when some of his shining armor began to fall off, and she began to glimpse what lay beneath the gloss and polish. His emotionless efficiency in disguising a murder. His apparent lack of remorse over what they'd done. The ease at which he could lie.

Katrina shook her head, dumbfounded. It was a terrifying, baffling revelation, made more so by the fact she had truly cared for him.

Jesus! How had she not seen the truth?

The answer, of course, was obvious. His charm and charisma had so completely won her over she'd been unable, or unwilling, to recognize his true nature.

She'd been blinded by love, to use the old cliché.

Okay, Kat, now that we're thinking straight, being honest with ourselves, let's turn to the Good Samaritan again, shall we? So, what do you think? Is he sitting at home with his family, watching a Disney movie? Playing Monopoly? Or is he lying in the woods somewhere, stiff and dead and rotting? Because Jack didn't threaten him, did he? Didn't tell him to walk home so he could think about that threat. Why would Jack do something like that? Leave a loose end untied like that? Why would he do that when it would be so much easier to simply kill him? Because Jack doesn't mind killing people. Doesn't feel it. Some people are like that. They don't feel. And it's always those people who don't feel on the inside that shine on the outside, isn't that right? The attractive, amiable Ted Bundy next door.

Katrina pushed herself off the futon and stood. Her chest was tight, her mouth sand-dry. She worked it to get some saliva moving. She crossed the bedroom quietly, and inched open the door. She peered through the crack, down the hallway. She didn't see Jack, but she saw his legs, which were crossed at the ankles. He would be sitting in the armchair. She had a wild urge to bolt out the back door. But she couldn't do that. Couldn't run. Not yet. She might not be looking out for Jack anymore, but she was still looking out for herself, still unsure about what her next course of action would be. Until she figured that out, she had to keep on the path she was on. Had to find out what happened with the policeman. And the fact Jack was here, and not in custody, was a good sign.

She took a deep breath, pulled herself together, and went to the living room. On the TV a female contestant on *Wheel of Fortune* was shouting "Come on! Big money!"

Jack turned to face her when she appeared. "You're alive!" he said, standing.

"What happened with the policeman?" she asked immediately.

Jack explained everything to her.

"He bought it?"

"Hook, line, and sinker. He was just following up for the sheriff in Skykomish. He has nothing."

"Will he be by to see me again?"

"Can't see why. I had him eating out of my hand."

Katrina had thought she would feel ecstatic. Liberated. Because they had done it. They had beaten the system. Gotten away with murder. But the truth was she didn't feel much of anything.

Except fear—fear of the man standing before her.

Jack ran a hand through her hair, pulled her close, and kissed her on the lips. She flinched. He pulled back. His eyes probed hers. She had no idea what conclusions he was drawing, whether he could see past her act. All she knew was she felt extremely vulnerable under his stare.

"Something wrong?" he said, and there was a hardness in his voice that wasn't there before.

"I'm still—you know—all this."

"It's finished."

"I know," she said, holding his eyes. "I know."

Chapter 30

Zach climbed out of bed as quietly as he could and gathered his discarded clothes from the floor. It was dark outside. The only light in the room came from an Asian rice-paper lantern he'd picked up at a gift shop when he'd been in Wenatchee for the day. Before closing the bedroom door, he glanced back at Crystal. She was curled up in a half moon, a small lump under the forest-green sheets, her hair fanned out around her head. Seeing her there, in his bed, gave him a virile feeling. Especially since he no longer had any reservations about pursuing things with her. His realization that Jack had likely threatened Katrina to help him get rid of the body of the old man, just as he'd threatened Zach to keep quiet about what he'd witnessed, had changed that. It had lessened, if not nullified, her culpability, and put her firmly on his side. If he went to the police now, he would not be destroying her. He would be helping her. Crystal would understand that. And far from being outraged with him, as he'd originally feared, she would be grateful.

But first, of course, he had to confirm all this. Which meant paying Katrina a visit.

Zach crept up the stairs and left the basement. It was still raining, the sky low and dark. He pulled the hood of his sweatshirt over his head and went east on Birch Street, past Orchard and Cascade. He turned onto Ski Hill Drive and continued along until he reached Wheeler. As he walked down the street, he thought back to the night he came here to see what Katrina's place looked like, spying on her through the window, coming back the next night.

He shivered. What had he been thinking? But that was exactly it. He hadn't been thinking. He'd been caught up in something ugly and petty, and he really hadn't been thinking.

It was four minutes past nine when he reached Katrina's property. He stopped dead in his tracks.

Jack's black Porsche 911 was in the driveway.

Zach's mind reeled, trying to figure out what this meant. Had he been wrong about Katrina? Was she, in fact, in league with Jack? Not a prisoner of fear, but a willing accomplice? Were they inside celebrating their victory?

Only one way to find out.

He dashed down the driveway, then cut across the lawn so he was next to the trunk of the massive ponderosa pine, safely concealed in thick shadows the boughs created.

Nobody was in the front bay window. Not yet, anyhow. He watched and waited.

He never noticed the man in the unmarked sedan parked across the street.

Chapter 31

"Jack," Katrina said, "there's something we need to discuss. It's about us."

Jack flicked off the TV and gave her his full attention.

"If this is finished, as you say, well, we have to decide what we're going to do from here. What are your plans?"

He shrugged. "Like I told you before, I was heading east. But to be honest, Leavenworth is growing on me."

Katrina tried not to let her disappointment show. This was going to be just as hard as she'd imagined. "I didn't think you were a small-town type of guy."

"I'm not. But change is good, right? Keeps you young."

It was then Katrina realized she didn't know Jack's age. She'd always imagined him to be in his mid-thirties. The fact she was only guessing struck a chord within her. It hit home how little she really knew about him. "So what are you thinking? A few more days? A week? Months?"

"If you're worried I'm going to leave you, don't be. I'll stick around however long you want. We'll see how things go from there."

"That's sort of what I'm getting at." She paused. Swallowed. Pressed on. "I think the best thing we could do now would be to lay low. Separately."

Jack didn't react, or she didn't think he did at first. Then she saw something fleeting and dark in his eyes, the only indication he'd understood what she was saying and wasn't happy about it. "Would you care to elaborate?" he said.

"Jack, I've been through a lot. We both have. But I'm not made like you. I don't have your strength. I need time to rest. To recover. To sort things out in my head. It's going to take a while."

He pulled his ponytail over his shoulder and began stroking it. Katrina had never seen him do that before. It was oddly disturbing.

"Can you understand?" she pressed.

"Oh, I understand perfectly." The darkness was back in his eyes, no longer a misty apparition but a black fire. "You need space, am I right?"

"Yes."

"And if I decide to stay in Leavenworth for a while, because I think it's such a nice place and everything?"

"That would be your prerogative."

"You would simply ignore me?"

"No, of course not," she said, knowing full well that's exactly what she would do.

Jack studied her, long and hard and intense. She almost buckled under his stare and looked away, but she didn't. Then he shrugged. "You're worried. Stressed. Get a good night's sleep and you'll feel differently about things in the morning."

His words carried a finality that made them seem more like a threat than sound advice. But before she had time to let them sink in, let alone respond, someone outside shouted.

"Hey, you!"

Zach whirled around and squinted through the rain. He was so surprised to see a small man in a yellow windbreaker pointing a pistol at him that he cried out in alarm. His muscles bunched, as if his body was getting ready to run. But you couldn't outrun a bullet.

"Police! Put your hands where I can see them."

Zach mutely obeyed the order, all the while wondering what the hell was happening. The cop grabbed his wrists and shoved them behind his back. He was about to clasp a pair of handcuffs on them when the front door to the bungalow opened and Jack marched out, followed by Katrina, her face drawn and pale. That damn dog of hers—what had she called it? Baxter?—began barking wildly. She shooed him back inside and closed the door again.

"What the hell's going on here?" Jack demanded. His face registered surprise. "Zach? *Mike?*"

Jack knows the cop?

"Evening, Mr. Reeves," the cop replied, tipping him a nod. "Looks like I caught your Peeping Tom, Ms. Burton."

Katrina looked bewildered. "Zach?" she gasped.

"What Peeping Tom?" Jack said. "What's going on here?"

The cop shoved Zach up the porch steps and out of the rain and explained what happened last week, and Zach realized Katrina must have called the police after he'd fled.

"You never told me about this," Jack said to Katrina.

"It wasn't something I felt comfortable about."

Zach couldn't believe the irony of what was happening. Jack was looking at him with an expression of disgust. Zach had an urge to shout, "Yeah, well at least I didn't kill anyone, you son of a bitch, so don't look at me like that."

"You mean it was you, Zach?" Katrina said. "You were the one spying on me?"

There was more sorrow in her eyes than accusation. How could this have happened? He was here to help her. Now she would never listen to him. He opened his mouth to say something but closed it again. He had nothing to say.

"I don't understand," Katrina said to the cop. "How did you know he would be back tonight?"

The small man twitched. "Well, I didn't."

"Why are you here then?"

"To be truthful, Ms. Burton, I was keeping an eye on you."

Katrina blinked in surprise. She and Jack exchanged looks.

Did the cop already suspect them? Zach wondered. *But how? Who told?*

"Because of Charlie's accident?" Jack asked, incredulous.

"Yes, sir. That's right."

"Goddammit, Mike," Jack snapped. "He had an accident. Can't you understand that?"

"I'm just doing my job, Mr. Reeves."

"This isn't cops and robbers. It might seem like a bit of fun for you. Trying to catch make-believe criminals. But you're beginning to become a nuisance."

"I understand perfectly, Mr. Reeves, that this is a very serious matter."

Katrina said, "So you were both spying on me?"

Zach wanted to tell her he hadn't been spying, but it was too late for that. The first flash of lightning lit up the black sky, followed by a peal of thunder.

"Would you mind telling us all what you thought you might accomplish coming out here, Mike?" Jack said, clearly struggling to keep his cool. "What you thought you might witness in this very serious investigation of yours?"

The cop twitched again. "Oh, it's probably nothing."

"If you don't stop with these games and give me a straight answer, Mike, I'm going to call up your chief and slap you with a harassment charge."

"Officer Murray," Katrina said, more politely, "it's late and I'm tired. If you could please explain what exactly you think is going on to warrant putting me under surveillance, I'd appreciate it."

The cop tugged up his khaki pants as he considered her request. "How about I just say there were certain statements in both of your stories that left me a little perplexed."

"That's not good enough, Mike," Jack said.

"Let's start with Mr. Stanley driving all the way to his cabin from the hospital in Wenatchee, leaving his sick wife by herself, just to tell you folks to turn down the music."

"I told you—"

"I know what you told me, Mr. Reeves. But I started thinking, if I was angry enough to drive the thirty clicks for something like that, would I just leave? When I told this to Lucky over in Skykomish, he told me Charlie would never do something like that. More likely he would have had a fit and tossed you all out. Also," the cop went on, gaining momentum, "I didn't quite swallow that bit of yours, Mr. Reeves, about why you had to return to the Blackbird Lodge. That's not to mention the mystery of why

Charlie was heading home, instead of back to the hospital after he left the cabin. Or those bruises on your face, for that matter."

Seeing Jack under fire, knowing he was teetering on the edge of being found out, Zach felt a surge of hope. Maybe this was all going to work out after all. Maybe Jack's murder of the old man was going to come to light without any intervention on Zach's part. That would be perfect, he thought. But what about Katrina? Well, she didn't really do anything, did she? Jack forced her to help dispose of the body. Zach would vouch for her. Tell the police she, like him, had been threatened and made to do what she'd done out of sheer terror of the crazy Indian.

"This is absurd," Jack said, sounding suitably outraged.

"Quite possibly," the cop replied. "And if that's the case, then you have nothing to worry about, do you? In the meantime this fellow is coming along with me." He made to handcuff Zach once more.

"Wait," Jack said, something brewing in his eyes. Zach could see that much. "I didn't tell you everything earlier, Mike." The porch went quiet as a tomb. Nothing but the rapid patter of rain falling on the roof. "It's a long story. Why don't you come inside, out of the storm, and I'll explain it all as best I can?"

The cop hesitated.

"It will clear everything up for you," Jack insisted.

A lengthy pause. Then he nodded. He shoved Zach forward.

Jack gave them both a reassuring smile as they shuffled past him, but for Zach it was anything but reassuring, and suddenly the last place he wanted to be was inside Katrina's house.

Chapter 32

"Can I speak with you for a moment, Jack?" Katrina said when they were all inside the living room.

"Not right now," he answered. "Mike deserves an explanation, and I'm going to give him one."

Katrina was freaking out. The fact that Officer Murray was putting together all the pieces was bad enough, but that paled in comparison to the fear she felt at what she thought Jack had planned. Because now that she was seeing Jack with fresh eyes, she would not be deceived again. She would not allow herself to be deceived again. She knew his true character, knew he had murder in him. Cold, calculated murder, not accidental murder. And she knew he'd brought Murray inside to kill him and maybe Zach as well. The question was: what was she going to do about it that wouldn't get herself killed in the process?

"Jack," she tried again, "I really need to talk to you."

Officer Murray was looking at her oddly.

"I said, not now."

"Yes, Jack. *Now.*"

Perhaps he saw the steel in her resolve because he shrugged, excused himself, then went to the bedroom. She followed on his heels and closed the door. He whirled on her, his eyes blazing. "What the hell do you think you're doing?" he hissed.

"What are you doing, Jack? You can't talk your way out of this one. Not anymore. Do you understand that? It's over. You have to accept that. We have to turn ourselves in."

He looked appalled. "Are you mad? We're doing no such thing."

"Listen to me, Jack," she said, her face inches from his. "If you touch that police officer, I don't care what you tell me afterward, I will not go along with anything you say. I caved before because Charlie was already dead and nothing could be done for him. But I will not—will not—stand by and let you harm another person. If you do, I'll go to the police right away and confess everything." Her hands were trembling so badly she had to ball them into fists.

"Jesus Christ, Katrina! I'm not a common thug. You think I get off on this? What happened yesterday happened because there were no other alternatives. You know how suspicious this looks, dragging me in here? Give me some credit and let me take care of this for both of us. I have a plan. It will work. No one will get hurt. Okay?"

"Promise me you won't touch him."

Jack didn't promise. He didn't say anything. Just opened the door and returned to the living room. Katrina had no choice but to follow.

"Sorry about that," Jack said. "Anybody like a drink?"

Zach said, "I would."

Jack ignored him. "Mike?"

"No, thank you."

"All right, then," Jack said as he wandered to the window to look out at the now driving rain. With his back to them, his hands clamped behind him, he looked like a man admiring a Monet in a museum. "I wasn't completely honest with you, Mike. What can I say? You got me. So I'm going to come clean, something I should have done from the beginning." He turned around, and if Katrina didn't know better, she would have said he looked genuinely contrite. "You want to know what happened when Charlie came by? I was telling the truth when I told you he said the music was too loud. I told him I'd turn it down. But you were right, Mike. He had driven a long way and he had come with a purpose. To kick us all out."

"Ms. Burton," Officer Murray said. "Would you have a pen and paper? I'd like to get all the facts straight."

Katrina went to the kitchen and retrieved a pen and a notepad from the counter. Then, with an abrupt burst of daring, she scribbled "Be Careful" on the first page of the yellow paper. She didn't know what she hoped to accomplish, but she didn't have time to think about it.

All she knew was she didn't trust Jack.

She returned to the living room and handed Murray the notebook and pen. She watched him closely as he opened it to the first page. He seemed to freeze for a beat before glancing up at her. She didn't think anyone else saw the quick exchange.

"So Mr. Stanley told you to leave," Murray said as if nothing had changed, though Katrina was sure everything had. "Then what?"

"I said we weren't going anywhere. We'd paid him for the night and had given him a one-hundred-dollar deposit. I told him the only way we would leave would be if he gave us a full refund, considering we had only been there a couple hours. We argued for a bit—"

"Did it get physical?" Murray was eyeing the bruises on Jack's face.

"Come on, Mike. He was an old man."

"Was anyone there to witness this dispute?"

"No. It was just Charlie and me. Katrina was inside the cabin. Everyone else was down at the dock. So we argued for a bit, and when I realized we were getting nowhere, I finally told him he can keep the rent but I wanted the deposit."

"One hundred dollars?"

"That's right. He decided that was reasonable, but he said the money was back at his home in Skykomish, and if I wanted it, I'd have to come and get it."

Katrina was studying Officer Murray, to see if he was buying any of this. Because even though she knew he'd read her message, Jack was putting on an impressive performance.

"So you followed him in your car?" Murray said.

"That's right."

"Why not ride together?"

"He never mentioned his wife, so I never knew he'd be coming back east to get to the hospital in Wenatchee. Besides, I didn't really care for the man much. Now, this is where it gets, well, murky, for lack of a better word. We were almost to Skykomish when Charlie's truck crossed the middle line. There were no oncoming cars, thankfully. But he didn't pull back and I figured he must have fallen asleep. I blasted the horn. I'm not sure if it woke him up or not—maybe it did and he just reacted too slowly. Hell, he might have had a heart attack, for all I know. The bottom line is he went straight off the road, right into a big cottonwood. By the time I got to the truck, smoke was already pouring from the engine. I was about to pull Charlie out, but I realized he was already dead."

"How did you know that?"

"He wasn't wearing his seat belt. Was thrown forward into the windshield. His face was a bloody mess. Of course I also checked his pulse." Jack paused, as if contemplating something. "I really can't tell you why I didn't pull him out regardless. It was a gut reaction at the time. I've thought about it a lot since, and I think I knew if I pulled him out and waited around for you guys, the cops, I'd have a lot of questions to answer. On the other hand, if I just left—it sounds bad, I realize that—but if I just left I'd be free of the situation. After all, he was already dead, right?"

"So you left him to burn in his truck?"

"Hell no! If I knew the truck was going to go up in flames, I would have pulled him out. At the time there was only smoke. I never thought it would progress to a full-fledged fire."

Katrina was absolutely speechless. Jack was incredible. He'd just given an Oscar-worthy performance. She half expected him to start thanking members of the academy—half expected him to give her a smile and a wink that said, "Stick with me, kid. I'll show you the world." Suddenly she found herself regretting tipping off Officer Murray. Had she just screwed everything up?

"I have to tell you, Mr. Reeves," Murray began slowly, "if you had reported the accident in the first place, you would have been in a much better situation than you're in right now. It's always better to tell the truth, no matter how difficult that may be. If you try to cover it up, especially something this serious, it's going to come back to bite you in the ass, like it did here."

After the last twenty-four hours, Katrina would say that was very fine advice indeed.

"Believe me," Jack said, "if I could do it all again differently, I would."

Murray tore a couple pages from the notebook, tucked them away in his pocket, then handed the notebook and pen back to Katrina. "Well, that certainly answers a lot of questions," he said, hiking up his pants. "Thank you for coming clean with me, Mr. Reeves. But I have to warn you that what you did, even though you confessed, was a criminal act. You're going to have to come into the station tomorrow morning and give me a detailed statement. And since the incident happened within the township of Skykomish, it'll be up to Lucky to decide what to do from here. He might let you off light, he might not." Murray looked at Katrina. "Ms. Burton, may I have a quick word with you in private?"

"Of course," she said, wondering how she was going to explain herself.

Murray turned to Zach. "Wait here—"

"He did it," Zach said woodenly, staring at Jack. "He murdered the old man. I saw him."

Chapter 33

Zach had been watching the unfolding drama with incredulity and dread. Jack was going to get away with it. He was going to get away with murder. He was too smooth; the cop, too gullible. All the voices in his head screamed at him to remain quiet, to let this thing play out on its own, but he knew he couldn't listen to them. If he didn't do something now, he never would. He didn't think he could live with that on his conscience.

"He did it," Zach said, looking at Jack. "He murdered the old man. I saw him."

The expression on Jack's face twisted from cool satisfaction to stunned disbelief to a hatred so intense Zach wanted to run for his life.

But then Jack grinned, his face once more a mask of calm. "He's crazy," he said, waving his hand dismissively.

"A pickup truck came to the cabin," Zach explained. "The old guy you're talking about, he started arguing with Jack. When Jack bent into his Porsche to get something, the guy whacked him on the head with his cane. Then he hit him again. That's how Jack got those marks on his face. The old guy started down to the dock, to tell everyone to leave. But Jack got up, snuck up behind him, and beat the living shit out of him. Then he dragged the body into the bushes and went inside, like nothing happened."

"That's complete garbage," Jack said. "I told you what happened, Mike. Why don't you ask Zach here what he was doing off in the bushes anyway? Spying again? Who the hell hangs out in the bushes?"

"I wasn't in the bushes. I was on the dock one lot over with Katrina's sister. When I saw the truck go by, I went to see who it was."

"Tell us why you went to the other dock in the first place, why don't you?" Jack said.

Zach shrugged. "The party was lame."

Jack held up a hand to cut him off. "A couple things need to be explained here, Mike. First and foremost, Zach apparently has some unhealthy crush on Katrina. When he saw me at the party, and he realized she was with me, he made a drunken scene—something he evidently does often. He was going on about how much he hated me. Everybody there heard him. I had to remove him from the cabin with force, which probably didn't raise his opinion of me any. This . . . this absurd accusation is simply his attempt to get back at me. Either that, or now that his perverted little secret is out, he's trying to bring someone down with him."

The cop's shoulders jerked. He studied Zach. "You have anything you want to say to that?"

"Yeah," Zach said. "Jack's full of shit. He came over to my house today and threatened me. Said he was going to kill my mom if I didn't keep quiet about what I saw."

Zach noticed Katrina's eyes widen, which confirmed she wasn't in total cahoots with Jack. That relieved Zach more than he would have thought possible.

"Theoretically speaking, then," Jack said, "you've just risked your mother's life. You're either one hell of a shallow person, or you haven't thought your story through very well."

The truth was Zach didn't believe Jack's threat. Maybe he had at first, but the longer he'd thought about it, the more he came to the conclusion it was all too convenient and artificial. "If you go to prison, you can't kill her," he said, willing Jack to slip up and say there was a second man, thus proving he had knowledge of the plan. The look in Jack's eyes said it all: "Good try, chump, but I'm not stupid."

Zach turned to Katrina for help. She appeared torn, unable to decide what to do.

"Do you have any proof to back up these allegations?" Mike said.

"I saw it happen."

"Did anyone else see any of this besides yourself?"

"No."

"Did you tell anyone else?"

"No."

"So someone commits murder, but you keep it to yourself?"

"Who was I supposed to tell?"

"The police."

"That's what I'm doing now!"

The cop shook his head, as if he was embarrassed to have considered Zach's story. "Sorry to have bothered you with all the questions, Mr. Reeves, Ms. Burton."

"Katrina," Zach said desperately.

Katrina was so pale she had turned white. Her eyes were haunted.

The cop noticed as well. "Ms. Burton?" he said, frowning. "Wasn't there something you wanted to tell me earlier?"

She nodded. "It's true," she said in a voice so soft Zach wasn't sure he'd heard her correctly.

"What's true?"

"Jack. He killed Charlie. And I helped him make it look like an accident."

"She's traumatized," Jack snapped. "Doesn't know what she's talking about."

"Mr. Reeves," the cop said in a none-too-confident voice while puffing up his chest. "You're under arrest."

"Get out of here," Jack snarled. "And take that lying piece of shit pervert with you."

"Turn around, Mr. Reeves. Put your hands on your head."

Jack stepped forward, dwarfing the cop. Zach was roughly Jack's height, but he nonetheless felt as if he was standing in the path of an approaching tsunami.

"Don't be difficult, Mr. Reeves," the cop said, his hand going to the gun in the holster beneath his windbreaker.

"I said get the hell out of the house."

"Jack," Katrina said, coming up beside him, "it's over."

He shoved her roughly to one side. She fell to the floor, crying out in surprise. The cop whipped out his pistol and aimed it straight at Jack. Everybody froze. Zach no longer felt shamed at having been caught or triumphant at seeing Jack lose it. Now he was plain scared.

"Turn around," the cop told Jack again.

"You're going to shoot me?" Jack said. "An innocent man?"

"If I have to, yes."

Seething with rage, Jack turned around and raised his hands to his head. The cop snapped one cuff around his left wrist. Before he could lock the second in place, Jack spun, surprising everyone. What followed happened very quickly. A gunshot fired, loud as a cannon in the small room. Jack jerked sideways, as if hit by a sledgehammer. Somehow he managed to drag the cop down with him, batting the pistol free. It skittered across the hardwood floor.

Zach dove for the weapon. Jack lunged also. They reached it at the same time, both grappling for control. Jack drove an elbow into Zach's face. When he shook the stars clear, he saw Jack clutching his wounded shoulder, grimacing in pain, but holding the pistol.

Regaining his wits, the cop charged into the melee. Jack whirled in time to fire off two quick shots. Both hit the small police officer square in the chest. He dropped to the floor, motionless, blood staining the Polo shirt beneath his windbreaker as if he had been wearing a big red bull's-eye.

Katrina screamed.

And in that moment Zach knew he was going to be next. Fueled by desperation, he ducked his head, raised his arms, and leapt through the large bay window. Glass exploded all around him. He hit the ground on all fours and screamed in pain. A shard of glass had gone through his left hand like a skewer. Nevertheless, he didn't sit there worrying about it. He scrambled along the front of the house until he reached Katrina's Honda Civic. He crouched behind it, alert and hyperkinetic, as if he'd just been given a shot of adrenaline straight to the heart. Rain poured down on him as he buzzed through his options. Flee up the long driveway? No way.

Jack would pick him off before he reached the street. Remain where he was? Double no way. Jack would be outside any moment to hunt him down. That left one option. Keeping low to the ground, on the far side of the Honda, he made a mad dash toward the east wall of the house.

A gunshot rang out but missed. Then Zach was racing safely along the side of the bungalow. The forest that bordered the back of Katrina's property loomed before him, tall and sinister. He ran for his life.

Chapter 34

"You bastard!" Katrina shouted. "You killed him!"

Jack was leaning out of the broken window that, incredibly, Zach had leapt through. Bandit had escaped from the bedroom and was running in circles, barking crazily, likely confused as to who was the good guy or bad guy in all this.

"I had to," Jack said, not looking at her. "He was attacking me."

"You *shot* him! You said you wouldn't! You *promised*!"

"Circumstances changed."

"He was half your size."

"It was unavoidable."

Jack faced her. His shoulder was a big red mess. The gunshot had torn a wad of shirt and flesh free. The blood from the wound had soaked his white button-down a bright crimson all the way to the elbow. Nevertheless, he seemed to be doing a superhuman job of ignoring the pain. He pushed past her, went to the dead cop, searched his pockets, and found a second magazine for the pistol. He started toward the back door.

"Let Zach go," Katrina said, hurrying to catch up. "You're in trouble enough as it is." But those were just words. They wouldn't change anything. Jack was beyond reasoning with now. So she grabbed his arm, twisting him around, and hit him as hard as she could in his injured shoulder. He roared with pain, thrusting her aside. She landed a few feet away, in a sprawled heap. Bandit immediately took up position in front of her, growling fiercely, his body so stiff it was trembling. Winded and unable to summon a strong voice, she said quietly but with deadly intensity, "Do not kill

Zach, Jack. If you do, I swear to God I will make sure you spend the rest of your life behind bars."

He seemed momentarily conflicted, as if he wanted nothing more than to scoop her up and carry her away from all this. But the vulnerability passed as quickly as it had come, and a look she could only describe as a killer instinct replaced it.

"Stay here," he told her. "It's still okay. We're still okay."

He threw open the back door and charged into the night.

Wheezing, she climbed to her feet and followed.

Chapter 35

Zach risked a glance behind him and wished he hadn't. Backlit by the light of the open door, Jack was a raging silhouette, stampeding across the lawn and closer than Zach would have thought possible, given his head start. He reached the edge of the forest but didn't slow. He hurdled over fallen trees and wet shrubs and was soon swallowed by the vegetation, which was good. If he couldn't see where he was going, Jack couldn't either. He only wished he could muffle the noise he was making. With each step he was raising an alarm of snapping twigs and flapping branches, all of which were dead giveaways to his position. Distinct from the racket he was making, he could hear Jack behind him, hopefully having an equally difficult time navigating the thicket blindly. In the distance Katrina was yelling for Jack to stop, to come back. Her dog was barking loudly, almost howling.

Zach caught his foot on a root and slammed into the muddy ground. Dazed, he lay where he had fallen. He listened. Aside from his labored breathing and trip-hammering heart, which seemed to be beating directly behind his ears, there was no sound of pursuit. Just the hard drone of rain.

Something was wrong. Something felt wrong.

Then he understood.

No one was crashing through the woods in pursuit. Jack, Zach knew with morbid certainty, must be waiting not far back, motionless, a predator listening for its prey to give itself away.

Zach didn't dare move.

The seconds ticked by.

Five. Ten. Fifteen.

Katrina called out.

More barking.

Twenty seconds. Twenty-five.

The waiting became unbearable. Particularly since Zach was becoming more and more convinced Jack knew exactly where he was and would pounce any moment.

A crackling noise, like a stick breaking under a foot. Fifteen feet to his right.

"Zach?" Jack said softly. "I know you're listening."

Crickets. Rain.

"Why didn't you just keep your stupid mouth shut?"

A few more steps, parallel to his hiding spot.

"You fucked me up, Zach."

To Zach's horror, he realized Jack had turned in his direction and was coming directly toward him.

Katrina called out again.

"You ruined what I had with her. And I'm going to make you pay for that."

Twigs snapping.

"I'm going to find you," Jack went on in his homicidal whisper. "Then I'm going to kill you. I swear to you, I'm going to rip your fucking head off and impale it on a stick."

Less than ten feet.

Zach knew if Jack didn't spot him, he was likely going to step on him. He had to do something. But what? Fleeing was no longer an option. Jack was too close. Fighting? Yeah, right. Even shot, Jack would make quick work of him. He was a machine. He was tracking Zach down with a bullet in his shoulder. Not to mention he had the cop's gun.

As silently as he could, Zach maneuvered his good hand into his back pocket and withdrew his wallet. He rolled onto his side, praying nothing was going to crack under his weight and reveal his presence. Nothing did. He lobbed the wallet into the trees.

It made the thinnest of sounds as it whistled through the vegetation—but it was enough to send Jack steamrolling in that direction.

Zach used the barrage of noise as cover. He pushed himself to his knees and felt about on the ground for something else to throw. A stick? Too long. Something flat and rough? Bark? Whatever it was would have to do.

Off to his right there was a commotion of thrashing sounds, likely Jack kicking aside undergrowth, searching for Zach. Zach gripped the bark like a Frisbee and sent it off with a good flick of his wrist. It sounded as if it had gone much farther than his wallet. Made more noise as well. But to Zach's confusion he did not hear Jack take off after it. In fact, the night had once again become as still as it was black. That lasted only a moment before he heard Jack prowling stealthily through the trees and bushes. Coming back in Zach's direction.

Zach began to despair. He was trapped. He was going to die. The only variable was how. Would Jack shoot him in the head? Snap his neck? Beat him to death, like he had the old man?

No, Zach, you're forgetting. He's already told you how he's going to do it. Something about ripping off your head and a sharp stick?

Zach groped blindly in the darkness until he was touching a tree next to him. He got to his feet and pressed himself against it, keeping the trunk between himself and Jack. The bark was rough against his cheek, which was still sore from when he'd gone down straight on his face. The scent of sap and pine needles filled his nostrils.

Jack kept coming in his direction. He stopped on the other side of the tree.

They were only a few feet apart. Zach held his breath. Balled his hands into fists. Fire consumed his injured hand as the glass skewer jigged deeper in the wound. It was a miracle he didn't cry out—

He had an idea.

Wincing, he pinched the glass between his fingers and pulled. The broken sliver wouldn't budge. He ground his teeth tight against the pain and continued wiggling the glass in a sawing motion until slowly, excruciatingly, it began to loosen.

Then it was over.

Dizziness assaulted him. For a moment he thought he might faint. But it passed and he held the makeshift three-inch dagger in front of him. It didn't feel as reassuring as he would have liked.

"I know you're nearby, Zach," Jack said, his disembodied voice terrifyingly close. "I can smell your fear."

Zach was alarmed to discover he could smell Jack too, the same musky cologne he'd been wearing when he came to Zach's house to threaten him and steal a photo of his mother.

Jack moved. Undergrowth whished. He appeared suddenly, an arm's length away, a dark wraith against an even darker background.

If he glanced to his left, he'd spot Zach.

He didn't. He took several steps forward, and then he was past, his broad back exposed. Close enough. Zach rammed the glass down between Jack's shoulder blades with all the strength he could muster.

Jack bellowed in pain and surprise. So did Zach as the glass weapon, upon impact, sliced a fresh wound in his hand.

Zach stumbled backward, one lame hand clutching the other, which was already gushing blood. He turned and ran, heedless of what might lay in front of him.

A gunshot fired. Missed.

Another shot. Another miss.

He heard Jack giving chase once more.

Chapter 36

Jack reached over his shoulder to disengage the dagger sticking out of his back. But where there should have been a handle were only razor-sharp edges, causing him to slice his hand open. Swearing, he left the dagger or whatever it was in place and spun in the direction Zach was now fleeing. He aimed the cop's SIG-Sauer P226 and squeezed off two quick rounds. In the aftermath, when the report of the shots stopped echoing in his ears, he was furious to hear Zach still moving through the forest, farther away.

Jack made chase. With each step, however, he could feel his strength leaving him. The wound in his back was a mere annoyance in comparison to the ferocious, thumping hole in his shoulder, which continued to bleed profusely. He knew he had to dispose of Zach very quickly. It was the only way to salvage this catastrophe. He already had a plan to explain the carnage. He would arrange the bodies so it would appear that when Mike busted Zach spying on Katrina, Zach somehow got the pistol and shot him to death. When Jack and Katrina came outside and confronted him, Zach threatened them, and Jack killed him in self-defense. The only hitch would be getting Katrina to go along with it.

Up until this evening she had held together remarkably well. Even when she told him she wanted some space, he knew that was her anxiety talking, and once she had a few days to let everything settle, she'd be ringing him up for company. But when he'd shot the cop—which she'd inevitably caused by blowing the whistle on them—well, that had taken everything to an entirely new level. Jack could operate on that level. But could she? He wasn't sure. All this death was a lot to deal with. What was the body count now?

Four? Yes, when Zach was taken care of. Three she would know about. Could she deal with that? Three deaths on her conscience? A cop as one of them for good measure? He wasn't sure. The difference between them was he understood the destruction as a necessary means to avoid prison, whereas she only saw it as cold-blooded murder. She was too pure, too innocent—too naïve—to accept good and evil were one, interchangeable, neither existing without the counterpart, and sometimes one had to be used to achieve the other.

This was a fact of life and something he hoped he could get her to see after he explained his plan to her. And if she didn't take to it?

He couldn't leave behind any loose ends.

Invisible branches continued to slap at his face and rip his skin. He charged ahead, never slowing, until he smashed into a tree trunk with his bad shoulder. The trumpeting pain, combined with the impenetrable darkness, distorted his perception so he no longer knew in which direction he'd been running. Only willpower prevented him from passing out. If he let that happen, he would die.

Suddenly he heard splashing. Someone crashing through water.

Jack forced his legs to carry him in the direction of that sound. A few short steps later he burst through the trees into an open glade that housed a large pond dimpled with the machine-gun patter of the rain. A crack of lightning flared overhead, Jack could see Zach forty feet out, swimming frantically toward the far shore. He planted his feet, aimed, fired. Zach cried out.

Jack ran a few feet into the water and fired again. Click. He ejected the empty magazine and seated the spare one he took from the cop with the heel of his palm. He rolled his hand over the top of the slide, pulling it back toward his chest, and returned his attention to the pond.

Zach was no longer in sight. He'd disappeared below the surface.

Jack remained where he was and waited. When the weasely fuck resurfaced, dead or alive, he'd put a hole in the back of his ratty little head.

Chapter 37

Katrina was beginning to lose hope she would catch up to Jack and Zach. She couldn't hear them anymore. It was as if they'd both vanished—or died. Still, she pressed forward, putting one foot in front of the other. To turn back would be to give up. And she would not do that, no matter if it meant she had to walk all night and morning.

Bandit barked and looked back at her, urging her on. Apparently he still had their scent.

Good.

A thousand thoughts were swarming through her head. First and foremost were those of Zach. She couldn't let Jack get him, couldn't let Jack kill him. She was still struggling to adjust to how quickly her entire perception of Jack had changed in such a short period of time. Only yesterday she had thought, well, yes, admit it, she had thought she'd fallen in love with him. He had swooped into her broken life and had seemed like the man who would make everything better. But just as quickly as that romanticized image had formed, it had been tainted. Hell, it had been vaporized.

If only I'd been more alert—

A gunshot bafflingly close. She reflexively ducked her head. A burst of sound from somewhere ahead of her. Bandit took off in that direction.

She charged after him, praying it wasn't too late.

Chapter 38

The shot whistled past Zach's head, splashing into the water ahead of him. Knowing the next, or the one after that, was going to connect with the back of his skull, blowing bits of brain all over the water, he took a deep breath and dived.

Suspended in blackness, he aligned himself so his belly was parallel to the bottom and swam in what he hoped was the direction opposite Jack. He was already out of breath from the run through the forest, and his lungs began to burn badly. He knew he would have to go up for air soon. He also knew if he did so, and he wasn't far enough away from Jack, he would be an easy target. He kicked and kicked harder. Maybe it was desperation, maybe mind over matter, but somehow he managed to get a second wind and keep going for another twenty feet or so before his lungs felt ready to explode once more. Abruptly he touched slimy weeds, which became denser and denser, brushing his face, entangling his limbs. This encouraged him. It meant he had gone the right way. There had been no weeds where he'd entered the pond.

He stuck his head above the surface of the water and took a huge breath. The air was like poison to his overworked lungs, causing him to heave and cough. Serendipitously, a clap of thunder resounded overhead at the same time, swallowing the noise he made. He turned in a circle, relieved to find he was concealed by a nest of weeds and lily pads. He made out a lone shape on the edge of the far bank, which had to be Jack. Zach couldn't remain there, treading water. Jack would start scouting the perimeter of the pond soon. Nor could he swim anywhere, no matter how quietly. Once he left the cover of the weeds, Jack would spot him. His only option, it seemed, was to crawl up the shore and make a break for the forest again.

He peddled through the water until he felt the muddy bottom beneath his feet, then he slithered out on all fours like a lizard. Dirt and slime were surely infecting the cut in his hand, but he couldn't think about that.

The blast of a gunshot sent him flat to his stomach.

Chapter 39

Katrina stumbled into a clearing. Although there was no longer a canopy of branches overhead, the storm clouds had rubbed out the stars, leaving the night smudged in blacks and grays. The rain was falling harder than ever, pelting her exposed skin and face, blurring her vision. She held a hand to her eyes and scanned the tall grass, the large pond, the perimeter of crowding trees. She didn't see Jack or Zach anywhere.

A gunshot made her jump. She cried out, covering her head and dropping to her knees. Another gunshot. She heard the bullet ricochet off the tree to her right.

"Jack, stop!" she shouted. "It's me!" She raised her head and saw a shadowy figure circling the pond toward her.

"Katrina?" Jack said when he had closed to within ten yards of her. He was hunched over, almost limping. The closer he came, the louder Bandit growled.

"Shhh, boy," she said. "It's okay. Just wait."

Jack stopped before her. He looked terrible. His shoulder injury looked bad, but it was his face that shocked her. Lines etched the skin around his eyes, brow, and mouth, making him appear twenty years older. Even in the poor light, she could see he was as pale as a ghost.

Lightning flashed, slicing angular wounds in the sky. Thunder boomed.

"You should have stayed in the house," he told her. "I almost shot you."

"God, Jack," she said. "Look at yourself. You need to get back to the house." That was her last best hope, she knew: get him to focus on his own health, thereby giving Zach the time he needed to get good and far away.

"What don't you understand?" he said harshly. "If Zach gets away, we're finished."

"We're already finished, Jack."

"You're giving up? Just like that?"

"I'm not giving up. I don't want to get away with it anymore."

"I don't believe that."

"I wouldn't be able to live a day in peace."

"You'd get over it."

"Two people are dead, Jack. No, I wouldn't get over that. I never will."

"You'd still have to live with your conscience in prison."

"At least I would have accepted my guilt. There would be closure."

The look on his face became one of disgust, like he didn't know her anymore. "You have no idea what you're talking about with all this holier-than-thou bullshit. After a week in the slammer, after the things that would be done to you, someone as pretty as you, you'd do anything to be free again."

"I won't let you kill Zach."

"I have a plan."

She glanced at the gun in his hand and wondered if she could wrestle it free. Not a chance. Should she sic Bandit on him?

"Listen," he went on, and the anger that had been in his voice had been replaced with feverish excitement. "Zach was spying on you, right? The cop busts him. He somehow gets the gun and shoots the cop. We hear the shot, come outside, confront him. He resists. I kill him in self-defense."

"No, Jack."

"Yes."

"It won't work," she said, simply to buy Zach some final seconds.

"It will."

"Nothing has so far."

"We're right at the end. Just see it through."

"The first question people will ask is why Officer Murray was watching my place."

"Because you reported a Peeping Tom a few days ago."

"He died in my house. If he busted Zach outside, he would have died there as well."

"So we move the body."

"They can tell things like that."

"Not these yokels."

"It's finished, Jack. It's time you accepted that."

"I will not accept that."

"Then you're on your own." She felt satisfied Zach was long gone by now. Her mission was accomplished. "Goodbye, Jack."

He raised the gun. "Afraid it's not that simple."

"What are you doing?" she demanded.

"You think I'm going to let you just walk away from me?"

That's exactly what she'd thought. It was over. Zach had escaped. Jack had lost. Very soon the police would be swarming her house. Jack, who urgently needed medical attention, would be taken to a hospital and arrested for murder. There was no way he could talk his way out of it this time.

"Jack, there's nothing to gain from shooting me."

"If you're not with me," he said, his eyes flashing, "you're against me."

"Jack—"

He aimed the gun at her forehead.

Chapter 40

When Zach realized that Jack wasn't shooting at him, he scrambled toward the forest. Bits and pieces of Jack and Katrina's conversation floated to him. He could only make out a few words above the roar of the rain, but from the forceful tone, he knew they were arguing.

Zach reached the tree line. He was home free. All he had to do was keep going, find his way to a road or a cottage, and get to a police station.

But he didn't flee.

Katrina was likely in trouble. After all, she'd just betrayed Jack to the dead cop. What would he do to her? Zach didn't know, but he did know she had risked herself coming out here to save him, and he couldn't in all good conscience leave her on her own.

He picked up a stick about the length and width of his arm. He didn't ruminate on what he was about to do. If he did, he would chicken out. He zeroed in on Katrina and Jack's voices and spotted them in the dark, two lumpy shapes standing next to a tree. He started toward them, slowly, quietly, stopping when he was less than twenty feet away. He could see them better now. Jack's back was to him.

One chance.

He gripped the stick more tightly, brought it back like he was up to bat, and closed the remaining distance between them with long, careful steps.

"Jack," Katrina said, and there was breathless terror in her voice.

Jack raised the gun. He was going to shoot her.

Zach abandoned stealth and made a final dash. Jack spun around at the last moment. Too late. Zach cracked the stick across the side of his face. Something that could only be blood splattered everywhere. Jack collapsed to the ground with a grunt. Zach was still pumped up on fear and adrenaline and craziness and he kept swinging the stick, bashing Jack's head in as hard as he could, over and over. Katrina appeared beside him, shouting something, pulling him away. Panting, he stepped back. He felt spaced out. He blinked and looked at Katrina.

"You okay?" he asked, and his voice seemed like a stranger's voice, like when you listen to yourself on the answering machine.

She hugged him fiercely. "He was going to kill me," she blurted, the words muffled by his sweater.

Zach looked over her head at Jack. The boxer was sniffing around the limp body. "He's not going to hurt you now," he said.

"Is he dead?"

"I don't know." He stepped apart and felt for a pulse. "No, he's alive."

"What do we do with him?"

"Leave him."

"What if he comes around?"

"There's no way we can carry him back to the house." Zach shrugged, trying to read Katrina's face in the dark. "Should I . . . I don't know—finish it?"

"Kill him?" She sounded appalled.

"If he comes around, he's going to come after us again."

"Then we don't have any time to waste," she said decisively. "We have to get back to my place, call the police, get them out here."

"I don't like leaving him."

"There's no other option." She retrieved the pistol from where Jack had dropped it in the mud. "And we'll have this, just in case."

Chapter 41

Katrina's living room resembled the scene of a drug bust gone wrong. Officer Murray's body was sprawled dead center. An arm was bent awkwardly behind his back. Glassy eyes stared at the ceiling. His yellow windbreaker and Polo shirt were stained red, with more syrupy blood pooled around him. Most of the glass in the front bay window was on the lawn. What remained in the frame resembled jagged teeth. A stack of boxes had been knocked over, spilling the few things she'd left in them across the floor. *A drug bust gone wrong?* she thought. *Hell, this was all because of a lie gone wrong.*

"Lock the doors and windows," Katrina told Zach. "I'll be right back."

She went to the bedroom, shadowed by Bandit, peeled the sheet off the futon, and returned to the living room, where she used it to carefully cover the poor cop's body. She grabbed her cell phone and called the police. She spoke to the dispatcher for a few minutes, explaining what had happened, answering some questions, then hung up.

Zach had returned from his task of securing the house. He said, "What do you want me to tell them? The police? I'll tell them whatever you want me to."

"I want you to tell the truth, Zach."

"But you don't have to be involved. I'll say I saw Jack kill the old man, then drive the body away, all by himself."

"The truth," she repeated. "That's it."

"Are you sure?"

"I've never been more sure of anything in my life."

There was only one chair, so they both settled down on the floor to wait for the police to arrive. Katrina wondered what was going to happen to her. She could not, as Zach had suggested, put all the blame on Jack. Even if it worked, and she emerged from the circus that would surely follow this night blame free, she would not be able to live with herself. She'd made a mistake, one with unthinkable consequences, and she had to pay for that, even if it meant she would grow old, childless, behind bars.

"Did you hear that?" Zach whispered suddenly.

Katrina was immediately alert. "What?"

"The back door. It sounded like someone was trying to get in."

Jack! she thought. He'd followed them back here!

"Are you sure?" she demanded. All she could hear was the drone of rain on the roof.

"I . . . I don't know. I think so."

Katrina got to her feet. "You locked everything, right?"

"Except that." He nodded at the front window.

"It's at least five feet off the ground. Jack would have to hoist himself up and through. No way. Not with his shoulder and all that glass."

"He's pretty strong," Zach said doubtfully, fear permeating his voice.

"It doesn't matter. The police will be here any minute. We just need to stay put."

"Can you use that?" Zach asked, indicating the gun.

She nodded. "If I have to."

Jack stared at the back door, wondering what to do. The bitch had locked it. No matter. He would find a way in. He had to find a way in. Because that little shit Zach was with her.

The prick had surprised him, just as old Charlie had. But it didn't matter. It had worked to Jack's advantage. Now he knew where Zach was. If he acted quickly enough, he could still have everything turn out his way.

No witnesses.

Jack would have kicked down the door, but he wasn't sure he

had the strength. Aside from the fact his head felt like someone had just played polo with it, the entire left side of his body was numb, the right side not much better. Besides, noise was not good. He could only assume Katrina had the SIG, since he hadn't been able to find it when he came around.

He stumbled along the side of the house, trying the windows, finding them all locked. A wave of dizziness washed through him.

Think. Don't lose focus. Think.

He crouched down and pried the screen off a basement window. The window slid open without protest. *Yes.* He lowered himself in, his shoulder screaming in protest as he contorted his body to fit through the small space.

Then his feet touched the floor and he was inside.

"Maybe it was nothing after all," Zach said. He was pacing back and forth.

"But maybe it was," Katrina told him over her shoulder. She was peering out the window. "Where are the damn police?"

"You don't happen to have another gun around somewhere, do you?"

She turned. "How about a knife?"

"Yeah, anything. A knife would be good."

Katrina started down the hallway to the kitchen. Just as she was passing the basement door, it exploded open. One of Jack's massive arms wrapped around her, tugging her forcefully against him. His other hand smothered the gun, aiming it upward, toward the ceiling. She screamed in surprise. Kicked and struggled. But she couldn't free herself from his viselike hold. He shoved her forward, back to the living room. They crashed through the door. Zach, who had obviously heard her scream, had backed up to the bay window, like maybe he was thinking about jumping through it again. Bandit leapt at Jack. Jack swung his foot, catching the dog under the jaw. Bandit dropped to the floor, motionless.

"So you wanted to leave me for dead, huh?" he hissed into her ear. It sounded as if his throat was full of razor blades.

"We could have killed you," she said. "But we didn't."

"Should I thank you for that?" He directed her arm so she was now pointing the gun at Zach. "Should I thank this cowardly piece of shit for hitting me when I wasn't looking?"

"Zach, jump!" she shouted.

"If you move a muscle," Jack growled, "I'll snap her neck."

Zach glanced at the window but didn't move.

"What do you want?" she said.

"Exactly what I'd planned. To leave a lot of bodies and let the cops sort it all out. Only now you're going to be part of the death toll."

"They'll figure it out."

"I'll take my chances. Now pull the trigger."

"No!"

"Do it!"

"You're going to kill me afterward."

In the distance came the howl of approaching sirens.

"No fucking time for this," Jack snapped, adjusting his hand so it cupped hers, his finger on top of her trigger finger. "Say goodnight, Zach."

At the last moment Katrina cocked her arm back, trying to aim the gun at Jack's face. She squeezed the trigger. The slug plowed harmlessly into the ceiling. But the noise of the blast an inch from Jack's ear blew his head back, causing him to loosen his grip on her.

She dropped to the floor, unable to hear anything except a maddening ringing.

Seizing the opportunity, Zach rushed forward, bowling into Jack, knocking him backward. For a moment they struggled like drunken dancers, each trying to keep to their feet. Zach was out of control, throwing wild haymakers, trying to hit Jack's bad shoulder. Then, with a grunt that seemed to indicate he'd had enough, Jack pulled some martial-arts combo, punching Zach in the gut, elbowing him in the jaw hard enough to loosen teeth, and finishing up with a skull-crushing head butt. Zach would have collapsed had Jack not grabbed him by the hair and yanked him back up so he had him tight against his body.

The world was swimming. Through bleary eyes, Zach saw Katrina scuttling away, the pistol aimed at them. He suddenly understood that Jack was using him as a human shield.

Outside cars screeched to a halt. Red-and-blue lights flashed through the window, momentarily eclipsed by a shock of sky-wide lightning. The sirens went silent. A burst of thunder shook the house.

"It's too late," Katrina said. "Let him go, Jack."

"Looks like we're all dying here tonight."

Zach felt Jack's arm tighten over his throat.

"Wait!" Katrina raised the pistol in a nonthreatening manner. "I'll set this aside if you let him go."

"No!" Zach said. "He'll shoot you!"

Jack gave his hair a snappy tug, which shut him up.

"Okay," he said. "Set the pistol down."

She did.

"Now kick it toward me."

"Let him go."

"The gun first."

She hesitated but kicked the weapon forward. Jack shoved Zach aside and snatched it up. Armed, he started toward the hallway, apparently believing he still had time to make an escape out the back, when someone on a bullhorn outside said: "How the hell are ya, Jack? It's been a long time. But what d'ya say? Have a few minutes to chat with your old buddy from Virginia?"

Chapter 42

Katrina watched Jack freeze midstep. He slowly turned around. His face was impassive, but she thought she saw something in his dark eyes she'd never seen before: fear. He went to the front of the room and flicked off the lights. Pressed his back against the wall, next to the shattered window Zach had jumped through. He shouted above the storm, "Is that you, Russ?"

"I'm glad you haven't forgotten the voice of a good friend."

"You're no friend of mine. Not anymore."

"Ah, Jack. But you're too hard on me. I'm not the one who's a wanted fugitive. That's you."

"What are you doing here, Russ?"

"What do you think? I've come to haul your ass in."

"How did you find me?"

"News travels fast these days, Jack. When we got word of a Jack Reeves involved in a possible homicide up in the beautiful state of Washington, we called the locals for a description. I was whisked up here just as quick as can be on one of the Agency's private jets."

Katrina had been listening to the exchange with rapt attention. Agency? As in, CIA? What was going on? Why would the CIA be after Jack? Surely not for accidentally killing someone in an underground fighting match?

Jack said, "You should have known you'd never bring me in alive."

"Then I'll bring you in dead."

"I have hostages."

At this Katrina stiffened. The whites of Zach's eyes grew wider. She glanced around the room. Their only chance of escape would be down the hallway to the kitchen and out the back. But the door to the hallway was closed. There was no way she or Zach could get it open and flee through it before Jack picked them off with a bullet in their backs.

Silence reigned for what felt like an eternity. Then the man on the bullhorn said, "I'm coming in to talk to you, Jack. I'm unarmed."

"I know how this works, Russ," Jack said, stroking his ponytail. "I know you can't cut a deal."

"What options do you have? The place is surrounded."

"Maybe I'll just clean house now. Get it over with."

Katrina took Zach's hand and squeezed it; he squeezed back. Her eyes fell on the limp form of Bandit, and she looked away.

"I just want to talk, Jack. Where's the harm in that?"

Jack seemed to consider this for a moment. Then he went cautiously to the door and inched it open a crack. "Come on in, Russ. But I'm not going to promise I'm not going to shoot you."

Jack turned to Katrina and Zach and waved the gun. "Get over to that wall, both of you."

"Jack—"

"Now!" he shouted.

They went to the far wall and hunkered down. Jack crouched behind them. Katrina thought his motivation was to get them all out of any possible line of fire through the front window. The seconds ticked by. Katrina could hear both her and Zach's breathing, quick and shallow. Jack, however, remained perfectly quiet, despite his injuries.

Finally, the door pushed farther open. A wedge of light, nothing more than a shade of gray fainter than that in the room, spilled across the hardwood floor. The outline of a man appeared, silhouetted against the storming night.

"Close the door behind you, Russ," Jack said.

The man obeyed. There was a sharp sound as the metallic tongue clicked home in the strike plate. Despite the shadows, Katrina could see the man named Russ was roughly Jack's size, thick in the chest and shoulders, with hard features and a bald head.

He was dressed in navy slacks and a crisp white shirt, no blazer, revealing an empty gun holster.

Jack aimed the pistol at him. "How many outside?"

"Twelve."

"Don't bullshit me, Russ. This town's got a three-man police department. One's lying over there on the floor, dead. That leaves possibly two outside, the chief and some part-time senior citizen who's twice retired. You expect me to believe you brought a ten-man team with you?"

"The Agency's been itching to get you. At any cost."

Katrina couldn't stand the not knowing any longer. "Are you CIA?" she asked the man.

He looked at Jack, who shrugged.

"Yes, ma'am," he said. "Special Agent Russell Nowicki. I used to work with Jack Stone here."

"Jack Stone?" She looked at Jack. "You said your name was Reeves."

Jack smiled humorlessly. "Guess I haven't been completely honest with you, sweetheart."

"And you worked for the CIA as well?" She shook her head, trying to come to terms with everything. "Who are you?"

"Jack was one of our top agents, ma'am," Nowicki said. "He began with a brief stint in the CIA's domestic station in New York. This was right after nine-eleven. His supervisors saw his potential as a rising star and sent him to serve in Egypt, Afghanistan, then as a station chief in Iraq, to oversee the oh-three invasion."

"Go on," Katrina said, riveted by these revelations.

"Two years ago Jack was charged with destroying eighty-seven CIA videotapes showing the waterboarding of Al Qaeda terror suspects. Unfortunately for him, the Justice Department put together a solid case for his prosecution. Nearly eleven months later a federal judge sentenced him to time behind bars. Jack escaped custody while being escorted from the courthouse. He went underground and has been in hiding ever since."

"I was serving my country," Jack snarled, and there was a ferocity in his voice Katrina had not heard before. "Doing what I

thought was best for the Agency. Dozens of agents and contrac-
tors had cycled in and out of Iraq to assist with the questioning. If
those videos ever surfaced, the identity of those people would have
been compromised. Lives would have been put in danger. And
what's the thanks I get? Treated like I'm the enemy?"

"You went against standing orders from the White House."

"Don't make this political."

"Jesus, Jack. It is political. Your cowboy shenanigans caused a
real shit storm. Because of the investigation you instigated, we had
to turn over sensitive documents, including classified cables from
around the world, which are now floating around on WikiLeaks.
The bloody director was summoned before a grand jury. Not to
mention that *Washington Post* story about the existence of secret
CIA prisons overseas, which got the president in hot water. So tell
me, Jack, how is it not political? What was the Agency supposed to
do? Someone had to take the fall."

"They should have given me a medal," he said simply.

"Killing two cops wasn't the answer, Jack."

"What?" Katrina blurted. She was still trying to come to terms
with what she was hearing. It was too much, too bizarre. "What do
you mean, two cops?"

"That's how he escaped custody," Nowicki told her. "Took out
the cops escorting him from the courthouse. With his bare hands.
Snapped one of their necks. Strangled the other with the handcuffs on his wrists. Took their car, drove off. Went completely off
our radar—until this afternoon."

Katrina had gone numb all over. She had cared for Jack. She
had slept with him.

A serial murderer. Maybe even a genuine sociopath.

"You lied to me," she said. "About your past. About everything."

"No, not everything," Jack told her. "Not about my past. Not
about my training in martial arts. Just about my job. And that
wasn't really lying since I signed an oath not to tell anyone who I
was except on a 'need to know' basis. And I'm sorry to say, sweetheart, but you didn't classify as need to know." He stood, yanking
Katrina to her feet as well, holding her against him. "Now that's

enough talk. I want you to go back out there, Russ, and clear the street except for one car. Leave the keys in the ignition and the engine running. She's coming with me. I see anyone out there, I shoot her. I see anyone following us, I shoot her. Get it?"

"All right, Jack, if that's what you want. No problem. I'll clear the street. Just don't do anything rash."

A squeak sounded from behind them.

Before Katrina knew what was happening, Jack squeezed off two rounds, dropping Special Agent Nowicki to the floor. Then he spun and released a firestorm of bullets through the hallway door, all in one fluid motion. The door swung open and two men dressed in black combat gear tumbled head over heels into the living room.

Just as Katrina was gaining her wits, Jack was jerked backward. He was still holding her, and she went down with him, landing on top of him. He dropped the pistol. She sprang off him and picked it up. She whirled around, holding it before her in both hands, backing up.

To her amazement, Zach had Jack in some kind of full nelson, and she realized Zach must have been the one who'd tugged Jack backward off his feet. Very quickly Jack grabbed Zach by the scruff of the neck and flung him off him like a rag doll.

"Don't move, Jack!" she yelled.

He stared at her, his eyes burning with rage.

"What are you going to do, Kat? Shoot me?"

"Yes," she said.

"Your hands are shaking so badly you couldn't hit the blind side of a barn."

"I swear I'll do it."

"No, I don't think you will." He pushed himself to his feet. "You know why I don't think you will?"

"Shoot him!" Zach said. He'd also regained his feet and came to stand beside her.

Jack's gaze flicked to him. "I'm starting to really regret not ending you in that shitty little basement of yours when I had the chance."

"Zach," Katrina said, never taking her eyes off Jack, "go outside and get some help."

"Who?"

"Anybody!"

"I'm not leaving you alone in here with him."

"Will wonders never cease," Jack mocked, taking a step toward one of the commandos lying on the floor—toward his weapon. "The peeper actually has a backbone."

"I said don't move, Jack!"

"You're too good to shoot me, Kat. You don't have murder in you. I've witnessed that firsthand." He crouched down and picked up one of the two assault rifles on the floor. "Isn't that right?"

Fast as a snake, Jack swung the barrel toward her. She was faster. She squeezed off three shots. The first missed but the second plowed into his chest and the third nicked his shoulder, spinning him about. He stumbled sideways, groping the wall for balance, then sliding down it, leaving a red streak on the beige paint. He coughed, spitting blood everywhere.

"Guess I was wrong," he mumbled, more blood bubbling from his mouth, and she knew she must have hit a lung. "You're more like me than I thought."

He made a final guttural sound, then went quiet.

And still.

"Is he dead?" Zach asked, breaking her trance.

Time sped up. Sounds returned.

"He has to be," she said. "Has to be."

She looped her arms around Zach's neck and held on tightly just as the front door banged open and more men in combat gear spilled into the room, aiming their guns, shouting orders.

"You didn't have a choice," Zach said into her hair seconds before he was tugged away.

"Yes, I did," she replied softly. "You always have a choice."

Epilogue

January 3. Four months later.

Katrina was walking with Zach through the snow- and slush-covered sidewalk along Front Street, enjoying the scenery. If possible, Leavenworth was even more beautiful when painted white and done up in Christmas lights and decorations.

They passed King Ludwig's, the restaurant Jack had taken her to on their first date, and she thought back to the night she'd been forced to shoot him. After arranging for Bandit to be taken to the town's vet, the police chief, a man by the name of William Darcy, had escorted them back to the station, which had gradually filled up with FBI and CIA agents, all of whom had drilled her with question after question about Jack and everything that had led to the deadly climax at her bungalow. When she was finally allowed to meet with an attorney, she entered a guilty plea to a single-count indictment charging her with being an accessory to murder. She hadn't wanted to go through with a trial. She knew what she did, knew it was wrong, and took full responsibility for it. At the sentencing, however, the deputy district attorney prosecuting the case recommended to the judge the minimum sentence in light of the circumstances of Jack Reeves's—or Jack Stone's—character and her own lack of a criminal record. The judge agreed, placing her on probation for one year.

Katrina did not celebrate. She knew she'd gotten off far easier than she should have. She immediately began her personal penance, dividing her free time among several charities, which required her to travel to a number of towns throughout Chelan County. She found this a rich and rewarding experience, and she knew helping others would be a central component of her routine for a long time to come. Meanwhile, life in Leavenworth had continued with much more normalcy than she would have thought possible. Almost everyone she spoke to was sympathetic to her plight. To her great relief, when she returned to school, no one mentioned the party or Jack again. Small towns might be fertile grounds for gossip, she'd learned, but like any tight-knit family, they could also be understanding and supportive to one of their own, even one as relatively new as herself.

As for Zach, she'd become good friends with him over the past several months, compounded by the fact he and Crystal were now in a serious relationship. In fact, the three of them tried to get together at least once a week, usually a Friday or Saturday evening for dinner and cards.

"So where's this place you wanted to go?" Katrina asked Zach.

"Right there," he said, pointing across the street to a pub.

"Ducks & Drakes?" she said, frowning. "I've been here. In fact, you were here with me for that school thing when I first got here."

"Ah, right," he said. "I must've forgotten."

She gave him a curious look but followed him to the door. She went in first—to a completely dark room. Before she could say anything, the lights flicked on and a chorus erupted in: "*Surprise!*" Katrina was amazed to see all her coworkers and friends huddled together in the center of the room, holding drinks. Crystal stepped away from the crowd, restraining a grinning Bandit by the leash. She kissed Zach on the cheek, then gave Katrina a big hug.

"Happy birthday!" she said.

"My God." Katrina felt herself glow. "Wow, Chris. This is . . . wonderful."

"Thank Zach. He organized everything."

"Thank you, Zach," she said. "This means a lot to me."

He nodded, color touching his cheeks.

"Come on, Kat," Crystal said, "let's get a drink."

Katrina started toward the bar but stopped when she noticed Zach staying behind. "You're not coming, Zach?"

"I've quit drinking." He shrugged. "New Year's resolution."

"Congratulations! I'm so proud of you."

His color deepened. "Thanks. How about you? Anything?"

"I didn't make one."

"No time like the present."

She thought about it for a moment. "To run a background check on all potential boyfriends."

"Good one," Zach said, and although what she'd said was meant to be a lighthearted comment, a haunted look passed briefly behind his eyes. Like her, he wasn't over what had happened yet, and he probably wouldn't be for a long time to come. "By the way," he added, "I've been meaning to ask you. Have you made up your mind on whether to stick around Leavenworth for a little longer? There's been talk that you might leave at the end of the year."

"To be honest, I've been thinking about it."

"And?"

She glanced around the cozy pub, seeing the many people who had become her close friends. "Let's just say I'm not going anywhere quite yet."

Zach nodded. "Fair enough."

"Hey!" Crystal called from the bar. "You guys coming or what?"

"You take care of her," Katrina told him. "She's all I got left."

"I will, Katrina. Of course I will."

"Good." She smiled. "And Zach?"

"Yeah?"

"I think it's about time you started calling me Kat."